W9-AEB-435

Praise for Erin McGraw

For *The Seamstress of Hollywood Boulevard*:

"Vivid, lively, and quite, quite wonderful, McGraw's story is a meticulous evocation of a time, a place, and an absolutely unforgettable woman. I loved every word." —Karen Joy Fowler, author of *The Jane Austen Book Club*

"At the heart of this beautifully written, brilliantly plotted novel is McGraw's heroine—the talented, spirited, adventurous Nell. From the opening sentence I would have followed her anywhere. *The Seamstress of Hollywood Boulevard* is an irresistible and deeply compelling portrait of a young woman sewing her way to a new life." —Margot Livesey, author of *The Missing World*

For *The Good Life*:

"Erin McGraw has a consistently winning stance in her wide-ranging stories—she is insightful, funny, deeply humane. I love the way her mind works." —Amy Hempel

"I love these stories about nice normal people trying—and failing—to cling to their fondest delusions. Erin McGraw brings her wonderful characters from dark into light with deftness, humor, and incredible kindness." —Molly Giles

For *The Baby Tree*:

"I have long been a fan of Erin McGraw's fine fiction, and her splendid new novel has only deepened my devotion. With seemingly effortless skill, *The Baby Tree* brings together complex issues of faith and morality in a plot that is by turns funny and serious, romantic and menacing, but always suspenseful. I only wish that her feisty heroine, Pastor Kate, lived next door." —Margot Livesey

Also by Erin McGraw:

The Seamstress of Hollywood Boulevard
The Good Life
The Baby Tree
Lies of the Saints
Bodies at Sea

BETTER FOOD *for a* BETTER WORLD

BETTER FOOD *for a* BETTER WORLD

A novel

Erin McGraw

SLANT

BETTER FOOD FOR A BETTER WORLD

Slant
An Imprint of Wipf and Stock Publishers
199 W. 8th Ave., Suite 3
Eugene, OR 97401

www.wipfandstock.com

ISBN 13: 978-1-62032-668-8

Cataloging-in-Publication data:

McGraw, Erin (1957–)

Better food for a better world : a novel / Erin McGraw.

x + 232 p. ; 23 cm.

ISBN 13: 978-1-62032-668-8

1. Restaurants — California — Fiction. 2. Self-actualization (Psychology) — Fiction. I. Title.

PS3563.C3674 B4 2013

Manufactured in the USA.

To Andrew

Acknowledgements

SPECIAL THANKS ARE DUE to Phil Stephens and Sheila McKenna, for teaching me about music and performance, and to Leslie Cooksy, for teaching me about agriculture.

Heartfelt thanks also to Greg Wolfe, who forgives me over and over and who has the energy of five normal people. To Julie Mullins, my great gratitude for her sharp eye and exquisite taste.

First and last thanks always to Andrew. Always.

Marriages to marriages
are joined, husband and wife
are plighted to all
husbands and wives,
any life has all lives
for its delight.

—WENDELL BERRY

ONE

Vivy

WHAT WAS THE SADDEST thing in the world? Listening to Hank Shank—"Take it to the bank"—play "We Shall Overcome" on the banjo. Standing at the back of the superheated room, Vivy Jilet studied a wrinkle on the banjo's grubby face and wondered whether Hank had made the instrument himself. Its stumpy neck looked like a finger cut off at the joint, and the string ends bristled up aggressively from the tuning pegs.

"We are not afrai-ai-aid," Hank Shank quavered, plunking dull, bottom-heavy notes that had only a nodding acquaintance with the ones coming out of his mouth. To listen was painful, and Vivy guessed there was plenty more to come. Hank Shank was singing verses she had never heard, and wore the folk singer's dolefully sincere expression, the one that promised listeners they would be spared none of the travails of the people.

She resettled herself, leaning back against the hot wall. The situation would not improve when he stopped singing. Since taking the stage half an hour ago, Hank Shank had filled the spaces between songs with stern lectures about the evils of consumerism, urging members of the dwindling audience not to let themselves be co-opted. "To resist society's consumerist pressure is a revolutionary action," he said.

Suppressing a yawn, Vivy wondered whether Hank Shank had updated his rhetoric since 1968. Then she wondered whether he realized he was on a stage in an ice cream store, and that his act was being

3

punctuated, not by cries of "Stick it to the man!" but by the chirping of a cash register.

If the cash register had been chirping more often, Vivy wouldn't have cared about Hank. He was performing here at Natural High Ice Cream—Better Food for a Better World, the sign promised—because Nancy Califfe, one of the store's six owners, had decided it needed a gala to celebrate its third birthday. "Something special," she had said, "to draw people in. I know the perfect person."

Vivy should have known right then. If Nancy could be counted on for anything, it was her flawless reliability when it came to issues of marketing: always, always wrong. Vivy and the other partners spent most of their time blocking Nancy's tone-deaf ideas—the raffle whose first prize was twenty-five cubic feet of mulch, the community pitch-in day to help the partners clean out the storeroom.

"What are you going to give people for helping us?" Vivy had asked.

"What do you mean, 'give people'?" Nancy said.

The store had begun as a lighthearted kind of business, three couples pooling their money and time to run an ice cream shop. The good-natured enterprise let them pretend they were back in college—they came to work wearing cutoffs and T-shirts, and they laughed their way through planning meetings, where they came up with ice cream names like Shade Grown Coffee Crunch and Che Guevara Guava. When Nancy said the store needed a new slogan, Vivy and Sam, Vivy's husband, proposed "Natural High Ice Cream: Street Legal." Nancy actually let that one through, a rare bit of flexibility on her part, now that Vivy looked back.

Nancy had always had a bit of sand to her; store ownership had hardened it to cement. But all of them, Vivy supposed, were becoming more themselves: Nancy's husband Paul was perpetually angry, David and Cecilia Moore were earnest, and Sam was lazily goofy, drawing cartoons of Nancy with flames coming out of her mouth as she proposed another awful idea at the weekly meetings she insisted on. She drew precise financial charts and Venn diagrams, and Sam made cartoons of them too.

Nancy talked at length about community corporate management. She contacted a printing company and had high-minded slogans printed on Natural High napkins made of recycled paper. "Small is beautiful," she reminded them. "Harmony is sustainability." While Nancy talked, Vivy rubbed her neck, trying to ease the sense of a tight collar closing. She'd joined a company, not a religion. Sam called Nancy the Right Reverend Nancypants, a title that gave Vivy lasting pleasure.

"We are not alo-o-one," moaned Hank Shank, a line Vivy thought debatable. He was singing to Vivy, Sam, and a dwindling clientele, including the lazy bunch of teenagers who were sprawled in the corner and hadn't bought anything for half an hour. So far the gala had netted Natural High fewer customers than a slower-than-normal Saturday, and if the store didn't see a good late-afternoon surge, receipts would be way down for the day.

In fairness, the low turnout wasn't completely Hank Shank's fault. That morning, when they'd pulled in a good crowd, the store's air-conditioning had gone on the fritz, and by the time Vivy and Sam got there, the place was pretty much a riot, if any room so thickly hot could house a riot. Sweaty, shrieking, over-revved kids rocketed between tables or jiggled on their mothers' laps, and mothers dipped napkins in cups of ice water, first to wipe their children's sticky mouths, then to cool their own foreheads. Piles of damp napkins clumped in wads across the floor while dry ones, folded into rough fans, lay abandoned on tables. The flimsy recycled paper wilted in the sodden air.

People had started to leave the store before Hank Shank ever showed up, and who could blame them? Paul, who imagined himself mechanically minded, was out back with the compressor, beating on it with a wrench, to judge from the noise. Nancy was on the phone with the service company, explaining the company's responsibilities to its clients. Vivy wanted to walk into one of the big freezers and stay there for a while, but she was in Nancy's line of sight. If Vivy had been smart, she would have stood next to Sam behind the counter looking busy, just to make sure Nancy had no grounds to unspool her pet lecture about fiscal responsibility and the bottom line. Vivy had made the acquaintance of the bottom line long before Nancy ever dreamed up the charts demonstrating its glowering existence.

Just out of college—actually, for Vivy, a few months shy of her bachelor's degree in theater, which she never did bother to finish—Vivy and Sam had gotten married and started Stage Left, a theatrical agency for offbeat acts. Like most things those days, the business had started after a marijuana-stoked conversation with friends who shared their interest in, as Sam said on a breathy exhale, guerilla art. A guy they knew from an econ class had put together a whole stand-up comedy routine about insider trading, and wanted to hitch out to New York so he could deliver it from the floor of the stock exchange. There was the woman who had trained her four parrots to perform a ragged cancan, and the tightrope walker who had managed to run a rope between the top floors of two dormitories and was halfway across before the campus police showed up. "He wore a bowler hat," Sam had pointed out, which Vivy agreed was the genius part. They were also huge fans of the Strikes and Spares, dancers who dressed like tenpins and performed in bowling alleys, leaping between lanes. Talent like that needed exposure, they said, nodding, agreeing with themselves. Talent like that deserved an audience, and lacked only the framework of management to gain one.

The next morning, when Sam and Vivy were sober, the idea still looked good. Sam had taken some management classes to appease his parents on the way to his BA in art; he could put together enough of a business plan for the parrot lady to somberly show it to her birds and ask their opinion. Mr. Insider, the comedian, took the plan, folded it, and tucked it into his underwear. Remembering those moments now, Vivy felt longing for her old friends seize her like a cramp.

For nearly ten years she and Sam had kept Stage Left going. Twice they had gone to Europe, where crowds accustomed to Cirque de Soleil and buskers at every corner had an amiable appreciation for a troupe of unicycle riders armed with Etch A Sketch pads. There had never been a year that could be called financially secure—not one year, as Sam pointed out sadly, that they'd had a profit to declare to the IRS—but they had all pulled together, and Vivy had never been bored. Not once.

When she became pregnant with Laszlo, she and Sam saw no reason to stop the company. It could only be good for a child to see new places and know many kinds of people. Only three months old, he had whooped with joy every time he saw Marteeny tuck her feet up into her armpits, and Louise let him sleep, sometimes, with her waltzing poodles. By the time Laszlo started school, he had already been taught to read by a juggler and how to add by a stockbroker. He had the best tutors in the world.

But when she got pregnant a second time, Sam took things harder. While carrying one child to performances was charming, carrying two, he said, was a chore. The delight of playing with a baby had already been used up. Now, when Vivy appeared backstage with tiny Annie in her arms, the acts kept rehearsing instead of hurrying over to lift the baby away from her. "We can't do this," Sam said.

"Do what?" said Vivy, but she knew she had lost. It was all too much: the taller and taller pile of unpaid debts, the performers' needs, and the performers themselves, who were not so charming after twelve weeks of close companionship in the bus Sam spent half his time repairing. When Vivy answered the phone and heard Nancy's voice, she knew without hearing the particulars that her life was over.

She hadn't been so melodramatic at the time. Both she and Sam loved El Campo, a dot on the east edge of the Sacramento Valley. Towns there were still cheerfully grubby, stocked with as many Grateful Dead fans and macramé makers as dot-com hotshots. To move into a little house with a porch and glider was a new adventure, as was getting Laszlo enrolled in school and then teaching him he really did have to stay there all day, with his socks on. Vivy had stayed interested as long as she could.

Sam seemed content. He worked part-time for a halfway house in Auburn. When he first took the job, he and Vivy joked he would wind up seeing all their old acts again, but if any of them had tried to check themselves in, he wasn't telling her about it. He worked there thirty hours a week and at the store another fifteen, and proclaimed himself happy and solvent. Vivy knew he liked being able to bring the kids with him to either job, now that they were big enough, and he told her he was showing them the world. True, she supposed, but not much of it.

Since they had come to El Campo, she had sold rollerblades and tamales, canvassed for two political campaigns, and worked at the cannery—seasonal work, her favorite. At night, often, she dreamed of Stage Left, and when she woke up she needed several minutes to remember her new life, her real one, and then the disappointment was hot.

The old acts had been ingenious and playful. They had also been skilled, which Hank Shank emphatically was not. By this point—what was it, the seventh chorus?—he wasn't even trying to hit the high note on "I do believe," trudging through the song as if it were the Bataan Death March. As he droned along, Vivy kept an eye on the drooping Natural High birthday banner, calculating a quarter inch of sag for every degree the temperature rose. The air bloomed with heat—outrageous weather for northern California in April, ninety-five degrees as they approached two o'clock. Every citizen of El Campo should have wanted ice cream in weather like this—cones and sundaes and cool coffee drinks mortared with whipped cream. Hank Shank was driving people away. Not an inconsiderable achievement, Vivy thought.

Now that she was thinking, her thoughts carried her well past Hank Shank, stooped on his stool on the little oak stage. The Etch A Sketch Drill Team! Teeny Marteeny the contortionist! Unchecked, her angry memory was running through Stage Left's entire old corps of acts. Any of them would have had the store full to bursting, selling ice cream hand over fist. In the corner, teenagers rolled up their T-shirts, rubbed ice cubes over one another's bellies and moaned. "Oooh, baby. That's so *good*." Then, bored, they pulled balloons down from the ceiling and mangled them. They ignored Hank Shank, finally on his feet and bowing for the few people applauding—Nancy, basically.

Vivy stooped to pick up a napkin at her feet, noting its slogan: "Know Your Vision. Embrace Your Vision. Make Your Vision." Without hesitation, she envisioned a stack of hundred-dollar bills, enough to buy a few weeks' vacation. Then she glanced out the door and envisioned Fredd the Juggler.

She found Fredd ten years before on the boardwalk at Sausalito, where Vivy and Sam had gone because Vivy was hungry for mussels and Sausalito still had some cheap restaurants then. Fredd was enormous, his shoulders like hams and his thighs like bigger hams. He spilled out of his tank top like fruit spilling out of a bag, and his grin was unexpectedly sweet, wide-spaced teeth set into his gums like individual pieces of corn. His size alone would have made Vivy stop, but then he wrenched the concrete top off of a trash can that had Sausalito Clean! stenciled on it. Sam was watching too, and whistled. "Gotta be at least seventy pounds."

Tossing the rough green top lightly from hand to hand, Fredd grinned. "What do you think?" he called to the growing crowd.

"Awesome!" said a kid.

"Scary," said a girl who didn't sound scared.

"Not bad," Sam said, "but one is easy. Let's see you do it again."

Fredd beamed his corn-kernel smile back at Sam as if he'd hoped for just this invitation. The next trash can was about fifty feet away, and by the time Fredd got there, he was balancing the first top on his thick forearm. Wrenching up the second one took even less time. Maybe another strong man had been there earlier and loosened it up for Fredd.

"Now juggle," Sam said.

Even Vivy murmured, "No," but Fredd looked delighted. With a soft grunt he heaved the first trash can top into the air, then the second. His catch, as the first one plummeted, was delicate to the point of daintiness, and he relaunched it well before the second one fell into his big, waiting hand. Vivy had seen a lot of juggling. She didn't much care for it, all that circus shtick. But watching Fredd juggle those heavy, rough concrete wheels, with grace, was watching something impossible happen. After about a minute, Fredd started to giggle, as if he couldn't contain himself. Naturally, the crowd burst into applause, and so he caught both tops and bowed, but she could see his disappointment. He wanted to juggle more. By the time they left Sausalito that day, Vivy and Sam had a contract with Fredd, written and signed on a series of bar napkins.

No Stage Left act had been as popular as Fredd. Once, at an outdoor festival with the Etch A Sketch Drill Team, she watched him juggle two unicycles, the ungainly machines glittering as Fredd heaved them six feet over his head. She still shivered when she remembered it. Nancy would have had a cow. That thought was all it took for her to fish her phone out of her pocket. She still had Fredd's number. He answered on the first ring for Vivy, his old friend and biggest fan. No, he wasn't far. He didn't often leave the area anymore, what with the kids.

"Kids?"

"Jesus, Vivy. Don't you ever open your Christmas cards?"

Sometimes she did, though sometimes not until March. He would come on over. It would be fun. "Will I get paid?"

"You will be paid," she said. He would. Somehow.

"I'm on my way."

She hung up as another trio of teenagers sauntered to the door, and she put a hand on the girl, a twig of a human being with magenta hair. "You should stay. There's a juggler coming who's amazing. You've never seen anything like him."

"And as long as we're in here, you'll want us to order more ice cream. No thanks." The girl pulled her wrist away.

"I don't care if you sit there and play five-card stud," Vivy said. "But you should really see this guy."

"You work here, right?"

"I'm just trying to tell you. It's not something you'll want to miss."

"You know, if you really want to please your audience, can the juggler and bring in somebody to fix your air-conditioning." The girl flipped her pink hair over her shoulder and sidled past Vivy, the two boys in knee-length cutoffs and eyebrow rings attending her. All of them practically fleshless, nothing but sinews and joints. Fredd would be able to juggle them, if Vivy could keep them here. Over at the counter Nancy and Sam stood rinsing scoops. Nancy's lush, showgirl body commanded the narrow space; beside her Sam appeared practically elfin, although he was not a small man. Later Vivy would tease him about spending the day at eye level with Nancy's breasts.

Twenty minutes passed before Fredd pulled up in the rusting, belching VW van he had been driving since 1988. Ignoring Nancy's pointed look, Vivy hurried out and let Fredd wrap her in his burly arms, his orange and purple shirt smelling like old cheese, his shaggy mustache scrubbing her cheek. "Still a lady-killer," she said as he beamed at her.

"Still a flirt."

"Me? I'm a business gal. I've sold out."

"Don't try to fool me. You've still got it." He looked at the sign in front of the store. "Really?"

"Don't get all choicey now. I'm about to put you back onstage."

He glanced at the store, its small platform and low ceiling. "If you want to call it that." He trotted to the back of the van and unloaded clubs, knives—he held up a torch and looked at Vivy questioningly.

"Are you nuts?"

Shrugging, he pulled out a box of ping-pong balls. If there wasn't much wind, he could juggle six of them. If there was no wind, he could juggle a dozen.

He paused and considered every bit of paraphernalia until Vivy grabbed his massive arm and pulled him into the store. She was a tugboat with a wayward tanker. Fredd kept trying to shake hands with everybody he could reach, including a stubble-headed teenage girl with two rings connected by a tiny chain in her nose, who looked up from her pocket-sized video game and said, "Jesus. Finally."

"You won't be sorry you waited," Vivy said to the whole store, yanking at Fredd's elbow. "This is an act worth waiting for. The Man of a Million Moves: Fredd the Juggler!"

She pushed him onto the platform, half afraid to let go even then, but nobody liked a stage better than Fredd. A moment after she freed his wrist he was flipping knives into the air, slinging the bright blades so close to the light fixtures and few remaining balloons that Vivy cringed. Parents pulled their children back while the teenagers started to inch forward. Behind the counter, Nancy looked like thunder, but Sam grinned. Vivy relaxed. This was going to be fine.

"Sorry I was late. I'll make it up to you by giving an extra good show," Fredd said, working his toe underneath the knives at his feet and flicking them up; he was juggling five, then six, then seven—big blades, real chef's knives. Vivy wondered whether she could get him to give her one. She could use a good knife.

In a nice segue, he switched from knives to clubs, tossing and catching the big wooden bats behind his back with an easy grace that she'd always found sexy. Sam chafed her from time to time about the hungry way she watched Fredd, and his lengthy, smelly, muscle-bound hugs.

"Okay, we're moving into the audience participation part of today's show," Fredd said, the clubs circling around his head like a menacing halo. "What do you want to see me juggle? I'll take anything you give me." A kid threw a napkin that Fredd used to dab at his neck before he tossed it up. The paper's slight weight sailed slowly, out of sync with the bright red and blue clubs. Another kid lobbed one of the store's beige coffee mugs at him, and a woman, looking daring and embarrassed, ducked up to the stage and handed Fredd her wristwatch. Vivy couldn't imagine how he kept all the oddly weighted objects in rotation, much less how he could do so while he showboated, catching the wristwatch under his leg, strolling around the stage, whistling. Spontaneous bursts of applause bubbled up, and Vivy glanced back at Nancy, who was transfixed like everybody else.

He finished by setting the clubs upright, one at a time, in a circle around his feet, and throwing the other items back out to the audience members who'd given them to him, even the napkin. People were laughing, a few kids over by the window whistled, and Vivy looked at Sam, who mimed wiping sweat from his forehead in relief. Vivy mimed the same gesture back at him, wiping off real sweat. Despite the fans whirring away from every side, the room was a slow-bake convection oven.

"Okay, now let's try a real challenge," Fredd was saying. "Hey Vivy—do you think I could have some ice cream cones?"

"Depends." She grinned. She liked being part of the act. "Depends on what you want. Carob is heavier than vanilla, you know. We weigh."

"Let me have two of each in the little squat cones. Press the ice cream down hard." Nancy slowly reached for a scoop. She lacked Vivy's pleasure in the unexpected, but she was the one who brought the cones up to the stage, the ice cream already starting to glisten. Kids were pounding on the tables.

The pounding turned rhythmic as Fredd carefully got the cones moving in a tall arc, circling with a preposterous dignity. For once, Fredd looked as if he were actually concentrating, which made the image even sillier—this gorilla of a man in his loud shirt and baggy pants frowning, chewing on his lip, gravely keeping four ice cream cones in midair. Kindergartners jumped on their chairs and screamed with joy, and Fredd finished wonderfully by giving each cone to one of the kids in the front row. Their parents led the applause.

Noise ricocheted around the uncarpeted store and pulled folks in from the street; every chair was taken. Parents with children wedged themselves next to the windows. Teenagers jostled and elbowed until the front row was pushed forward, right under Fredd's feet. Vivy did a quick head count: sixty-eight. Eighteen more than Nancy had projected in the planning meeting.

Fredd waited until the latest wave settled in, then shot a foxy look at Vivy. "My finale is a very special act, a little gesture to my old friends. Could I have some water?" Looking solemn, Sam filled a pitcher and handed it over the counter to be passed up. By now the crowd was too tight for him to make a path. Fredd, meanwhile, turned his back and pulled some items out of his satchel. Vivy heard the light clink of glass. When the pitcher made it to the stage he poured the water into what seemed to be a series of glass tubes, and not until he turned around, the tubes already circling between his hands, did she realize he was juggling bongs, three of them: purple, blue, and green.

The bark of laughter was out of her mouth before she could stop it, but that seemed all right; the kids were cheering. Fredd could have juggled twenty flaming torches and not have delighted them so. Vivy held her thumbs up high so he could see them, and he wiggled his eyebrows back at her and started singing something in his reedy little voice—maybe "Take It Easy," but the words were hard to make out over the din.

This was the kind of joke Sam loved more than anything, and Vivy glanced back at the counter to catch his expression. Instead she caught Nancy's, unhappy and determined, as she tried to force her way from behind the counter. But the crowd kept her penned. She managed only to push aside one boy, who looked back at her and said something Vivy wished she could hear. It was enough to get Nancy talking, and from the set of her back Vivy guessed the topic was the importance of community over the individual, a beloved riff. More kids turned around. One of them made an irritated shushing motion. They weren't creating much of a commotion in all the room's uproar, but they created enough. Fredd, glancing over to see what was going on, slipped a little, and water splashed on the kids sitting directly in front of him. "Hey!" a girl bellowed. "Hey! This vest is *suede,* you asshole!"

Fredd bellowed back, "It's two million degrees in here. You should thank me for cooling you off."

"I should thank you for third-rate juggling?"

The bongs sailed right to the ceiling. "This is not third rate," Fredd said.

"You're right." The girl looked bitterly at her vest and pointed to the water stain. "It's tenth rate."

That did it. Fredd's arrogant, strong-man smile turned sullen, and his hands turned into blocks. One of the bongs flew a little to the left, and he grabbed for it, then for the other two as they sailed the other way. He managed to recover them, but the bongs tipped, throwing water in every direction, splashing customers within five rows. For a moment, the air sparkled with water, and the teenagers whooped and dived into one another—trying to get into the spraying water? Away from it? Impossible to tell.

Fredd himself jumped back, a dainty, skipping motion, and a tardy one. His pants and shirt were soaked. But then, so were the teenagers around him, who rose to their feet and cheered, lifting their wet arms to catch more breeze. Fredd looked at them sourly and then bowed, holding the dripping bongs. Everyone in the room except Nancy and the girl with the suede vest was standing and applauding, arms pumping despite the heat. Smile, Vivy muttered urgently at Fredd. They loved you. But he wouldn't look at her, or at the people pressing toward the stage. He frowned at the floor like an immense, sulky child. Smile! she mouthed fruitlessly, stretching her mouth.

In a moment his crowd, which she had worked so hard to maintain, would start to break apart. She watched three couples hurry out onto the sidewalk. Two kids whipped out cell phones. The bright tension that had rippled through the audience gave out between one breath and the next, leaving disappointment, headaches, too many people in a hot, messy room.

Vivy could already hear the lecture gathering in the back of her brain, the one from creditors and her parents that she carried around, pointing out how she and Sam had gone bankrupt on acts like Fredd. The lecture never acknowledged the incandescent reviews their acts had gotten, how the waltzing dogs had appeared on television in St. Louis and Mobile. Instead, and frequently, the hectoring voice reminded Vivy that by the time their old college friend Nancy proposed a partnership in an ice cream company, Sam and Vivy didn't have the money for stamps to mail out their bills.

Vivy was moving down the track of her old disappointment now, stopping at every station while she automatically bent down to pick up two napkins, then straighten a chair. Just seeing Fredd made her long for the raucous, hell-raising energy of her old friends. She and Sam could have dug themselves out. They could have saved the acts and emerged with the lives they'd meant to have. Nancy had caught them at a weak moment, promising security. But after five years Vivy and Sam still owed the bank close to $80,000 for their partnership, money they borrowed upon convincing the loan officer of Natural High's excellent long-term prospects. Vivy couldn't put her hand on a nickel that hadn't been spoken for first by Natural High. "I guess he's done," said a customer at the door.

Vivy snapped her head up and marched onto the stage. She grabbed

Fredd by the arm, which felt like grabbing a pillar. "Hey there, hand-some," she said above the customers' chatter and the scrape of chairs. "How's about you teach me to juggle?"

"You've got some timing," Fredd said.

"Famous for it," Vivy announced. For the moment, at least, people had paused to watch. "Come on. I don't know the first thing about juggling. How do you begin?"

"Most people don't learn in front of an audience."

"We'll start a new trend. Don't you have a beanbag in that satchel?"

After a moment, his body stiff, Fredd stooped to rummage through his bag, and Vivy faced the roomful of mildly curious faces. They were tidying themselves, pulling up purses and wallets. She leaned out to them. "I've always wanted to juggle. Now, I'm not all that good with my hands, so I'm counting on you all to stay and lend me moral sup-port. After I learn, Fredd'll teach some of you, and whoever juggles the best will win a free cone. In the meantime, though, you should go ahead and order. It isn't getting any cooler in here."

How many years had passed since she'd huckstered? She'd been good at it, coaxing people into auditoriums to hear the Peruvian flute player or see King Cool pour molten tin in his mouth and spit out little metal pebbles, amazingly regular. Now she was scrabbling for words, repeating herself just to keep sound coming out. But she had stopped the migration for the door. One couple, already standing, perched on the edge of their table to see what would come next.

Like a wrathful ghost, Fredd materialized before Vivy holding a handful of tangerines. "Do this," he said, zipping the fruit back and forth, a blur of orange between his hands.

"Well gosh, what's the big deal? Anybody could do that," she said, and customers laughed. "Come on, Fredd. Show me at a speed a mere mortal can imitate."

"I'm not a teacher," he said.

"No kidding," she said, and got another laugh. He handed her the tangerines, and she made deliberately bloopy, impossible tosses. When one of the tangerines rolled off the stage a young father nudged his son to fetch it. "Thank you," Vivy said, and added, "I'll bet your daddy would buy you an ice cream cone if you asked him." The man saluted her and headed for the counter. Vivy made her next toss a little sharper, her next catch a little more deft. As a matter of fact, she was a decent juggler. She'd taught herself during long nights backstage, but she didn't think Fredd remembered that.

Slowly she improved her tosses and catches, and slowly Fredd nosed back out of his sulk, smiling as he tossed more tangerines at her and adding some fancy catches of his own. Vivy glanced at the counter where Sam and Nancy were scooping Strawberry Swirl and Triple Vanilla and Mocha Crunch for a father with two small boys, a pod of middle school kids, and one dreamy teenage girl with acne. "This is easy!" she accused Fredd. "You never told me it was easy."

He shrugged and wiggled his eyebrows. "Here," he said, and fired a tangerine at her so hard that she ducked and scattered her fruit all over the stage. One of the tangerines split, its sharp-sweet smell tingling in the air like a shock. The kids yipped with laughter, and Fredd turned to face them. "Who's next?" he said, and three girls jumped up.

Vivy retired to a corner and rubbed her hands, stinging with tangerine oil, on her shorts. At the counter, Nancy was busy with an uneasy-looking middle-aged couple. They stood a careful twelve inches apart, the space between them snapping with tension. First date, Vivy guessed. Nancy would be dredging up some weightless small talk to help them out, and Vivy's heart went out to the man and woman. However hard she tried to keep it light, Nancy's small talk weighed pounds.

"There you go!" Fredd said when the giggling girl with blue eyeliner managed a single pretty catch. Under the weight of his approval, she dropped the next three tosses and stood pointing her finger at her head like a gun. From the floor, people called up encouragements, and the two who had perched on their table slid back into their chairs. The store felt like a big living room. "'A Community Business Serving Its Community,'" Vivy said, one of the napkin slogans she found particularly obnoxious.

After the girl fled the stage, Fredd picked out a college couple wearing matching running shorts. In five minutes he had them tossing Indian clubs at each other, precise as a metronome. Watching them reminded Vivy that real jugglers didn't strive for unhesitating ease, which was boring. Real jugglers took pleasure in the unbalanced, the nearly missed, the little accidents that brought life to an act. Only the amateurs wanted perfection.

While the couple perfected their feed, Fredd strolled to the other side of the stage and hoisted a little girl in a pink T-shirt onto the stage. The girl craned and pulled away from him, her eyes wary and her mouth loose, and Vivy, watching, dug her fingernails into her damp palms. But Fredd sat down on the stage, glanced at her parents for their okay before settling her on his lap, and very gently started to juggle ping-pong balls he pulled, one at a time, from his pocket. The balls bobbed an inch in front of the girl's nose, light as butterflies, and she dimpled as Fredd added a fourth ball, and a fifth, and a sixth. When he started to bounce them off the top of her head she pealed with laughter, and when Fredd handed her back to her beaming mother, the woman promptly bought ice cream for her whole table.

Fredd looked over at Vivy, who nodded. Calculating fast, she guessed the store had done break-even business for the day, and there was still the afternoon walk-in business, the late night rush. Fredd stood to take a final bow, but as he straightened, protests broke out from the tables closest to the stage. "I wanted to be next," groused a skinny boy whose Led Zeppelin T-shirt draped over him like a curtain. "I wanted to juggle the bongs. When are you coming back?"

Fredd shrugged and looked over at Vivy. "When am I coming back?"

"You're our favorite juggler. How's next week?" she said, a rash offer, and just what the audience wanted to hear.

"Good to go. Next week," he grinned at the boy in the T-shirt. "We'll do my Jimmy Page special. I'll juggle seven lead balls while I play 'Stairway to Heaven' on the harmonica." Vivy grinned while the boy pumped his fist and cried, "Yes!" She felt as proud of Fredd as if he'd been her son, especially as he paused on his way to the back of the store to autograph ping-pong balls for the kids who shouted and tugged at his baggy pant legs.

It took another fifteen minutes to give him his check, to jaw a while, and finally to watch him drive off. By then the kids around the store had quieted; several of them had fallen asleep under the tables where their mothers chuckled and sipped iced tea. A dense stillness spread over the store—thick, succulent as mud. The air wrapping around her like a pelt, Vivy slipped behind the counter and into the back room, where Sam was setting out a fresh tray of nuts from the freezer. "Shh," she whispered. She wrapped her hands around the icy metal tray, then ran her cool fingers under his shirt, pressing the spots where sweat had soaked the cotton through.

"Nice," Sam said.

"A little break provided for the management."

"Nancy's going to walk in," he whispered, leaning back against her hands. "Then won't we be embarrassed."

"I'll tell her I was driven wild by desire for you."

"What's the real story?"

"I was driven wild by desire for you." She pressed her hands flat against his hips. "'Know Your Vision. Embrace Your Vision. Make Your Vision.'"

"With a store full of customers?"

"Call this a promise for later."

"Vivy?" Nancy called from the counter. "Can you help me here?"

After pressing her cool fingers one last time against the small of Sam's back, Vivy edged back out front, where a line of kids giggled and cut their eyes at one another. They propped themselves against the counter and ordered stupendous amounts of ice cream—triple dips with mix-ins, four-fruit smoothies. The boy who won a free cone ate that, then returned to the counter to buy a second. From his bloodshot eyes Vivy had a pretty good idea what he'd spent the last hour doing. She gave him an extra half scoop.

While Vivy took an order for Brown Sugar Butterscotch over

Vanilla Crunch from a kid with blonde, halfhearted-looking dread-locks, Nancy said, "Things got bad for a while there with Fredd. Good thing you were able to set everything straight."

"It was fun. Reminded me of the old days."

"That girl in the vest will probably send us her dry-cleaning bill."

"The rest of the audience loved Fredd. They were standing up and cheering. When is the air-conditioning guy supposed to get here?" Vivy said. Even in the freezer case, the Roasted Almond Carob was as loose as pudding. "Anyway, that girl was a pill. And I kept people here. I hustled."

"You did," Nancy said. "You also promised Fredd a berth for next week. The company may not be able to afford it."

Vivy studied Nancy's thick auburn ponytail, her long, vanilla-white forearms. She wore a beige and brown Natural High T-shirt, as always—Nancy and Paul had one for every day of the week. Presently, Nancy's was sweat-glued to her high, round breasts. "We'll be fine," Vivy said. "Customers will come back to see Fredd again. They want to hear him play that harmonica."

"If they remember," Nancy said.

"If you provide first-line talent, people remember." Vivy took her time, watching Nancy's flushed profile. "As a matter of fact, I think we should start hiring more acts. Real ones, not flunked-out banjo players."

"Hank didn't get any customers wet. And he was good value."

Vivy picked a walnut from the tray of mix-ins. Then she picked out two more. Lunch. "I know tap dancers. I know comedians. I know a woman who makes blown-glass fruit and then eats it."

"That's horrible."

"I'm just telling you that I could bring in acts other than jugglers. I've still got connections. I'm an underused commodity."

"That's one way of looking at things." Nancy turned to look down at her. Sam's very first name for Nancy was The Seven Foot Tall Humorless Woman. "I don't want to point out the obvious here, but we're trying to be an example of effective partnership, not a venue for sideshow acts."

"Maybe we should expand our vision," Vivy said, holding out against the anger that licked at her, even though she felt as if Nancy had just attacked her children. She spread her feet for balance and picked her words. "I think it's time."

"We have a partnership," Nancy said. "Better get your hand out of the nuts. The health inspector warned us about that."

"I haven't forgotten about the partnership. I'm very big on the partnership," Vivy said. "All I'm suggesting is that you let me contribute a little more to the common good."

Nancy turned away, but not before Vivy saw the tight fold to her lips, the hard lines on either side of her mouth. "I'll meditate on it," she said. "I'll spend some time thinking."

"And you'll tell the others to think, too? We could bring this up at the next meeting."

"There's nothing for them to think about yet," Nancy said. "If you're looking for something to do, you could scrub out the far bin. It's got leftover water in it. The health inspector warned us about that, too."

Vivy smiled. Taking great care to use only her fingertips, she plucked one more walnut from the tray. Then she turned to the plump boy goggling at the Cherry-Berry Swirl and asked him whether he would like two scoops or three, adding that Cherry-Berry was on sale, a sale she had just made up, all by herself.

TWO

Cecilia

IN THE FRONT CORNER of David and Cecilia's living room, Sandy Mc-Gee, the most diligent of Cecilia's violin students, sawed at a G major étude. Cecilia tapped out the time on her thigh and shaped her mouth into an encouraging smile. Talent didn't always show at once; sometimes it needed time to be lured, to reveal itself like a slow miracle. Cecilia often found herself thinking about miracles when she was with Sandy, who shot her bow like a pool cue and whose red, bitten fingers displayed an embedded instinct for the wrong note.

After their first month of classes Cecilia had given the girl sheet music for easy fiddle tunes, "Old Joe Clark" and "Bile Them Cabbage Down," songs that would make the most of her good ear and sense of rhythm. But when Sandy looked at the illustration of a man sitting on a stump beside a happy pig, tears came to her eyes. "You don't think I can play real music, do you?"

"This is real. People study for years to play this. It's more popular than Mozart." Cecilia had picked up her own violin and played a few bars of "Old Joe Clark." Usually kids liked the bouncy melody, but Sandy bit her lip. When Cecilia put her violin down, the girl started again with her honking rendition of "Twinkle, Twinkle, Little Star."

In the two months since then she had barely improved. Her vertiginous notes wobbled around the tiny apartment—every week Cecilia imagined paint peeling, light bulbs rattling. Now she pressed her hands

22

together, trying to catch her last flake of patience before Sandy's playing scoured it away.

"Lightly," she said, pointing to the bow the girl clutched as if it were a steak knife. "Easy. *Listen* to the sound you're making."

Sandy drew the bow across the strings, losing control partway through so that the bow rode right up on top of the bridge and produced a yowl. She scrubbed a furious hand across her eyes. "I practice. I know it doesn't sound like it. Every day. My mom makes me go out to the garage."

"Think of your bow as a feather on the strings," Cecilia said.

"I try. It doesn't help."

"And relax your shoulder. Move your arm from your elbow."

Chewing her ragged lower lip, Sandy confronted the sheet music, its single line of fat quarter notes stairstepping up the staff, and re-settled her face against the chin pad. When she finally brushed at the strings, the bow landed so lightly she hardly made a noise. "Better," Cecilia said.

She listened, she nodded, she discreetly rubbed her arm. Very Blue-Berry ice cream, on special this week and selling like nobody's business, always left her arm sore. David theorized the high sugar content in Very BlueBerry made it more difficult to scoop. He'd once actually talked to a chemistry TA at the university about temperatures and bonding properties of sugar molecules. The next day he insisted on coming to work during her shift, taking her place behind the counter and chipping at the rock-hard ice cream while she was left sponging tables that were already perfectly clean. Since then she'd been loading up on Advil, doing her own scooping, and assuring him she felt fine, never better.

"'Fine?'" he'd said last night after dinner. "I don't think 'fine' is good enough. I want you to feel magnificent."

"Fine is good, David. Most people wish they felt fine. Fine is—fine." She nodded at him brightly. His broad face wore an eager expression, right at the brink of enjoyment.

"I want you to feel perfect," he said.

"I don't think I could take the pressure."

He had pulled her onto his lap, and she leaned against his heavy arms, even though the embrace was sticky in the room's heat. "Well, 'fine' still isn't good enough," he said, shaking her long hair out of its braid. "We're going to have to do something about that."

What he wanted her to feel was pregnant. He had brought up the subject two months before, pointing out that they had been married five years, and he was coming into some money from his father, and they had savings. Why wait? Cecilia couldn't think of any reason, and she was happy to throw away the condoms and tubes of Conceptrol that slid around in their bedside drawer. But she hadn't been prepared for David's enthusiasm. Not only did he initiate sex every night, until Cecilia heard herself sighing as soon as the dinner dishes were done, but he turned nosy, asking when exactly her latest period had started and marking the kitchen calendar with a black dot that she could see from across the room. He talked about cervical mucus. Sharply, and more than once, she warned him that he'd better calm down. He brushed his hands across her breasts and said he hadn't been so excited since she'd let him court her, a pretty piece of talking that made her blush and relent.

David, she reminded herself, was a good-hearted man, as uncomplicated as water. His round, soft body cushioned her knobby joints, his beard scrubbed genially at her face, and his gentle nature soothed her daily onslaught of worries, her sense that she had never quite done enough. Cecilia knew she had fallen in love with him in large part for his ability to ease her fretful soul. "Everything will be all right. Shh, now," he said night after night. Although she never believed him, she knew he believed himself, which sometimes was enough to make her relax.

But lately his easy faith only made her nervous. She felt like a high-strung dog, alert to every sound or shift in the wind, while cheerful, oblivious David strode beside her. When he talked about fitting a crib into the bedroom with them or thought up baby names—"Wolfgang," he suggested, trying to please her, "Wolfgang Ludwig Johann Sebastian"—she answered by not answering, chattering about the store, asking him about his tomato plants, complaining, like everybody, about the heat. He looked at her with a puzzled disappointment that made her heart hurt. Now of all times they should be sharing a dreamy, sweet dialogue. But she couldn't control her edgy spirit. She wanted a baby well enough; she just didn't want it as much as he did. She had never wanted anything as much as he, so very suddenly, wanted this baby.

Sandy finished her étude—half whisper, half hee-haw. "Again," Cecilia said.

"I bet you don't really want to listen to this."

"Keep playing the notes. It's always hard at first to find the music."

"This"—Sandy held the violin by the neck and wagged it in front of her—"isn't music. When is it going to get better?"

"Sandy, I don't know. There's no timetable. You do your best and keep trying. Or else just quit and go watch TV."

"You're not very encouraging."

"You're not the first one to tell me," Cecilia said, surprised when she got a grin out of the girl. It was Sandy's bad luck to catch Cecilia when she was worrying about her husband, a man who would have cheerfully told Sandy to play what she was good at, not what she loved. Trained as a botanist, he believed in practical goals: If corn didn't thrive, plant beans. If tobacco failed, try berries. So Cecilia studied her husband and tried to figure out what harvest he had missed, that he was so ready to plant a baby in its place.

She had come up with no answer yet. She should, she knew, bring the issue up at Life Ties, but every time the thought occurred she let it slide away again. She wasn't ready for the glare of interest, the advice on everything from baby-raising methods to her and David's sexual positions, the frank stares that would fix, week after week, on her meager belly. The group's basic rule was members *could* bring their problems to meetings, not that they had to. Cecilia clung to the distinction.

Normally, so long as she stayed safely out of the fray, Cecilia liked Life Ties. The group was loosely allied with a Unitarian church that half of El Campo more or less attended for its good youth group and monthly wine-and-soup suppers. One of the church's many outreach organizations, Life Ties was a support group for married couples, meeting weekly in the church's fellowship hall and using the church's Xerox machine for its mailings. Dimly based on AA, the group had rules and goals and slogans, but mostly the meetings were just talk: disappointments, surprises, betrayals, the occasional triumph. People talked, and then the others gave feedback. Somehow, amazingly, the talking helped. Husbands and wives discussed and revised and recommitted themselves to their marriages. They explored their difficulties. They found new solutions. "Cheaper than divorce," somebody always said. "The weekly news," somebody else would add.

The group met on Sunday nights, sometimes twenty people or more, sometimes only six. All the Natural High partners came at least sometimes. Vivy and Sam often slid in late. Other couples showed up with a rough regularity, new members appearing when old ones decided they'd had enough.

The couples Cecilia liked best had been long married. They told stories of domestic savagery both ornate and inventive. By their standards Cecilia and David's five years of marriage, so considerate, so mannerly, hardly constituted a marriage at all. In five years Cecilia had never had an affair, never squirreled away money from the checking account or hit David, never—to take a recent example from a doctor's wife—spread resonant rumors about his personal hygiene until patients refused to shake his hand.

Other people stole, they whispered, they destroyed. Their lives struck Cecilia as remarkably full of options. Sometimes, after hearing about slashed upholstery and mangled hard drives, Cecilia felt abashed at the puniness of her own actions. Then David would speak up with reassuring clarity about sharing, communication, and the importance of a united effort, and Cecilia would sit up straight again. The meetings renewed her pride in him, an emotion she suspected would slip away if she didn't have Life Ties to remind her of it.

Lately, he had been listening to the happy couples, the joyful ones who sailed together through tribulations. At home he quoted them, his face alight with glaring hope. Cecilia couldn't help herself—the more David talked about uplift, the harder she listened to the squabbling couples, the ones going over and over some worn-out patch of discord. She liked the peculiar self-possession of people who could quarrel weekly and with heat about who deserved the good parking space beside the house. The night a couple married twenty years came into the meeting already growling, Cecilia made sure to sit close, so she could hear.

"You want that boat," said the man. "Don't say you don't."

"I want a life," snapped the woman. "I want to come home at six o'clock and take off my shoes."

"You have to sacrifice a little to get the life you want."

But do you have to sacrifice bare feet? Cecilia wondered. And who gets to decide?

"You get paid for overtime. I don't," the man said. "And you like to fish. You like it more than I do. You have to look ahead."

"Do I? Thank you for telling me. What else, if you don't mind saying so, do I have to do?"

"You'd cut off your own arm to spite me, wouldn't you?"

The woman paused. "No," she finally said. "I like my arm."

When the laughter—nervous, short-lived—sputtered out, that week's group leader stepped forward to make the speech about conflict's deep roots, and asked the man and woman to come back next week with new plans for their future. "Who else?" he asked, and Cecilia kept her eyes on the soft blue linoleum until a pair of newcomers, married not quite a year, came to their feet, the man pulling the woman up beside him. "He," the woman said, jerking her chin at her scowling, straw-haired husband, "he thinks coming here is a good idea."

"What ideas do you have?" the husband asked. "Buy some cocaine, go out to a club, buy some more cocaine?"

"He thinks I'm his problem. He's his own problem. A big one."

"You don't want a husband. You want a playmate. Somebody to sit in the sandbox with you."

The woman—short, broad, her forehead high under a helmet of

shiny black hair—laughed, a sound like tearing cloth. "You're right. I'd like a playmate. But instead I've got the goddamn nursery school teacher checking to make sure I pooped on time."

Even Nancy, two seats down from Cecilia, looked uneasy, although she usually welcomed confrontation and stout talk. David was the one who said, "Come on, you two. The fact that you're here together means you're willing to find some common ground."

The man said, "The fact that we're here together means I forced her into the car."

"He shoved me into the front seat," the woman said. "I could get him for assault."

"You can start this if you want," the man said, his voice winched tight. "There are lots of crimes we can talk about."

"He loves to threaten me," the woman said. "He loves to tell people that I'm a whore and a jailbird. Like he's the angel Gabriel. Where do you think I met him?"

"Where?" Nancy asked.

"In detox." When the woman smoothed back her ridge of glossy hair, Cecilia could see the fan of acne over her temple. "But I don't tell people that."

"Why not?" the group leader asked.

"Look at him. Isn't he better than God? Nobody would ever believe he was hopping around a room, clawing at his T-shirt."

"I believe you," David said. So did Cecilia. The man's face, which had been bright with anger, had gone chalky, his lips gray. Cecilia thought he might claw at his T-shirt any second.

"He doesn't like me to tell people," the woman said. In the room's hush she sat quietly, then rested her hand on her husband's arm. He looked at her hand until she moved it away again.

David said, "The important thing is to finish what you start. Once you make a decision, stay with it. Even if you find out it isn't turning out the way you expected. Keep going anyway."

Cecilia nodded. The next day she would realize David's words weren't quite in line with the Life Ties philosophy, but for now the man and the woman nodded too, and the group leader proposed they all take a break. Vivy headed for the parking lot, Sam stayed for tea, and David hastened to the new couple to give them his phone number.

Sandy McGee squealed up three more notes, then lifted her bow from the strings. Cecilia glanced at her watch: ten minutes left.

"Can I play my second piece now?" Sandy asked.

"Good idea." Cecilia cranked her smile back into place. "Think for a second before you begin. Remember: you want to sound like trickling water."

The girl obediently paused, then dragged her bow across the strings, smearing the opening four notes.

"*Lightly.*"

After two more attempts, Cecilia stood and said, "I think that's enough for today," taking the sheet music from the stand. Sandy looked up with her brackish green eyes, then took her time unlatching the violin case and nestling her violin back into its velvet.

While she was still loosening the strings of the bow, a knock came at the door, and Cecilia sighed. A part of her was always waiting for some neighbor, perhaps the woman two apartments down, so edematous that her ankles looked like quivering bags of fluid, to complain about the noise. Feeling Sandy's interested gaze, Cecilia went to the door, searching for words of appeasement that dissolved when she found Sam, with his shaggy, exuberant curls, grinning at her.

"Hey," he said. "How's that design coming? I'm on my way downtown. If you want, I'll take them right now and swing by the copy shop. Save you a trip."

"Oh Sam—I forgot all about it Darn it. I'm in the doghouse now." She'd meant to design the new ad last night, something Paul could post to the website and they could use for new flyers. But Cecilia had spent last night brooding about David, and the design was nothing but a stack of rough sketches on the kitchen table. "I'll get them in by this afternoon."

"We can do them right now, if you want," he said, shrugging. "Take a half hour. I can still drop them off for you."

"You're a lifesaver," she said, then stepped back to let him into the apartment and put her arm around Sandy. "This is my new Paganini," she said.

"I heard her," Sam said, and turned to the girl. "Do you like playing the violin?"

"Not exactly," Sandy said, wiggling with embarrassment. "Do you like listening?"

"Not exactly," Sam said, and Sandy let out a bray of laughter.

Cecilia gave the girl's shoulders a squeeze and turned toward the kitchen. "What kind of ice cream today?"

"Mocha Crunch." Sandy looked back at Sam as they followed Cecilia. "This is the best part of the lesson," she said.

"I believe it."

"Hard work deserves a reward," Cecilia said, scooping out a generous cone for the girl. "Now, remember: move your arm from the elbow. You want a touch that's light, but firm."

"A feather on the strings." Sandy's smile was ironic, older than her years, already defeated.

Cecilia matched her smile. "That's right." A tan dot of melted Mocha Crunch shone on Sandy's violin case as she threaded her way back to the front door and left it half open behind her.

"Am I wrong, or is that girl's heart breaking?" Sam asked.

"Every day a little more. It's killing me. Want some Mocha Crunch?"

"I'd think you got enough of this at the store," Sam said, nodding at the freezer stocked with brown and beige Natural High cartons.

"This is how I keep violin students: bribery. Believe me, Sandy McGee doesn't leave here feeling uplifted."

"I listened for a few minutes. You have amazing tolerance," Sam said.

Cecilia winced. "Was it too awful? The poor girl tries, but I think she's working off sins from some other life."

"I did wonder what the song was supposed to sound like."

Cecilia walked into the living room and fetched her violin from the top of the piano, where it had lain untouched for days. "Something like this," she said, returning to the kitchen and swinging the violin onto her shoulder. She skimmed her bow over the easy notes, the baby tune. Sam clapped in time, so she played another chorus, nudging the sequence, speeding up the tempo, turning and working the melody a little. The lighthearted music chimed in the space between her and Sam. Attentive now, Sam really clapped, and Cecilia showed off, adding the first six measures of a Bach partita before putting down the violin. "It starts that way, anyway."

"Speaking of Paganini."

"BA in music." She made a mocking face.

Sam shook his head, setting his curls bouncing. "You should be giving concerts, not lessons."

"And who's going to come hear me, my mother? I haven't noticed a big call in El Campo for violin concerts."

Sam leaned back and stretched out his hairy legs. They reached halfway across the kitchen. "Take it from an old promoter: people don't know what they want until you give it to them. 'Imagination Is the Mother of Desire,' or whatever the hell it is we say on the napkin."

"'Right Imagination Is the Parent of Right Desire,'" Cecilia said, laughing. Sam had a knack for making things easier; he found ways to soften corners. With his sloping grin and his ambly-shambly grace he reminded her of a clown. David said that even in college Sam had been the jester, the one who could break up tension in a room. Cecilia could well see why Vivy, that coiled spring, had married him. What she had never been able to see was why Sam had married Vivy. Now she said, "You've got to keep your eye on the details."

"There's your slogan for the new design: 'Natural High Ice Cream: Keeping Our Eyes On the Details.'"

"'Keeping Our Eyes On You,'" Cecilia said, grinning to match his sloping, goofy grin.

"'We Know What's Good For You: Natural High.'"

"Hey, I can use that one." Cecilia sat down across from Sam and picked up a fresh piece of paper and a pencil. Sketching fast, she drew a cartoon man with a bulb of a nose and a toothy smile. He wore an

old-fashioned body builder's leotard and stood with his biceps flexed.
The muscles popped up round as scoops of ice cream. In each hand Cecilia put a sundae. Then, casting a quick look at Sam, she drew springy
curls all over his head and printed "You Know What's Good For You:
Natural High" under the figure's floppy feet. "There," she said.

"My feet aren't that big," Sam said.

"Artistic liberty."

"I didn't know you were an artist. On top of playing the violin."

"I doodle, that's all," she said, reaching for another piece of paper
and a ruler. Suddenly she felt self-conscious, as if she should point out
how bad she was at math and tennis. His gaze rippled over her like a
breeze. "Why don't you watch some TV or something? You'll make me
nervous if you sit there."

"Actually, I wouldn't mind having some ice cream. I skipped
breakfast."

"Help yourself. Don't eat the Triple Vanilla—it's old."

She marked off four straight lines to make a frame, and then started
to draw in her cartoon weight lifter, but the easy confidence had gone
out of her hand. She kept lifting the pencil, making pointless little
lines; she could see already that the new figure lacked the charm of her
first sketch. Several times she glanced up to check on Sam, who had
heaped a bowl with Almond Carob and now strolled around the small
kitchen, spooning ice cream into his mouth and humming. She said,
"This is coming out all nervous."

"Why not just use the one you already drew? It's perfect," Sam said.

"It has a smudge. You don't know the first thing about being a
perfectionist."

"I try not to." He sucked another lump of Almond Carob from the
spoon.

"Easy to see you were never a musician," she grumbled, glancing at
him sideways but pressing down the corners of her mouth. "You front
office people never care about the nuances."

"So I'm the cigar-chomping front man? Thank you very much."

"And I'm the grubby little fiddler down in the pit with the nervous twitch. Little Miss Pure Art." She was prattling, she knew. But it was a relief to chatter with Sam Jilet and watch his suntanned toes idly work his flip-flops on and off.

"I can be pure," Sam said.

"No, you can't. Only performers are crazy enough to be pure. You, you'll always have one foot on solid earth."

"I can be Ivory soap. Ninety-nine and forty-four hundredths per-cent pure."

A fat drop of ice cream had fallen onto Sam's shirt, and a brown ring like a minstrel's outlined his mouth. "Here," Cecilia said, handing him a store napkin from the stack she and David kept on the table. This one read, "Responsible Action Is the Gate to Freedom." She also handed him "The Boat of Commitment Can Sail Over the Waters of Uncertainty" and "The Marriage of Intention and Action Bears the Offspring of Clarity and Joy." The last one was David's contribution after a night of brainstorming, and Cecilia thought it was pretty good, even if it did sound like it came from a fortune cookie.

Scrubbing at his shirt, Sam leaned across the table to read the next one: "'Our Goal Is Not Gold, but Wholeness.' That had to be Nancy's. Everybody else's goal is gold. So is David pure? He's not a performer."

"He's Ivory soap. Like you." Embarrassed, rushing, she added, "He's very supportive of my music. It was his idea to have me give lessons."

"Not exactly performing."

Cecilia shrugged. "It's something. And we really do need the money. Not that it's much."

"David says you guys are ready to start a family."

"Did David? I didn't know we were going public with that piece of information." Looking back down at her drawing, Cecilia added a tuft of grass under the weight lifter's feet, then regretted it. Fussy. "David's full of plans, but they all hinge on me getting pregnant. Which I'm not."

"Relax. The baby will come, and after the first few sleepless nights you'll wonder why you wanted it so much."

"Listen, you don't need to tell anybody about this," she said without looking up. "I feel a little vulnerable. I had a dream that Life Tie-ers were hanging over my bed, and Nancy was giving me advice."

"Vivy's had that dream too. Then she dreams of bringing an AK-47 to bed with her," Sam said. "If anybody had told me back in college that Nancy Califfe would turn into the thought police, I would have fallen out of bed laughing."

"What was she, a flower child?"

"Baby, we were all flower children." He clattered his bowl into the sink and sat across from Cecilia again, leaning back in his chair, his hands locked loosely behind his head. He was all lines—tendons, bones, as ropy as a boy. "She was strictly long dresses and Birkenstocks. She looked like a cross between a Quaker and Grace Slick."

"*Nancy?*"

"She had a German shepherd named Garcia with a bandanna around his neck."

"You're making this up."

"Swear to God," he said, holding up his hand. "She used to come by everybody's apartments with loaves of whole wheat bread she'd made. You could build a wall with that bread. And she was slow. We used to tell her movies started an hour earlier than they really did so we could get to the theater on time."

"I can't even begin to imagine this," Cecilia said. "What happened to that person?"

"Beats me. She and Paul got caught up in some guns-and-sombreros group that was ready to bring on the revolution. By the time she gave up on Che Guevara, she had turned into the Nancy you know and love."

"This is amazing. David hasn't told me any of this stuff."

"He may have forgotten. He's changed too."

"If you tell me that he used to wear tie-dyed T-shirts I'll know you're lying." Even to her own ears her voice seemed round with suppressed laughter.

"Naw. David's always been a white T-shirt guy. But he was the Plant Man. He liked plants better than food. He liked plants better than girls. None of us ever figured him to work behind a counter."

"Ice cream wasn't exactly a career choice, you know. He got his PhD in botany, but by the time he came back home every job was agribusiness. If he'd had an MBA people might have been interested. When Paul and Nancy offered him partnership, it looked pretty good."

"And now you get to live a life filled with Natural High napkins," Sam said.

Cecilia plucked "Our Goal Is Not Gold" from the pile, stared at it a second, then folded it into a small square. "You want to know the worst? We liked the napkins. We were all set to live lives full of intention and action."

"'Were.'"

Cecilia unfolded the napkin, then folded it again, lining up the edges more precisely. "I'm just a little sick of it all, you know? Most times I can think of something better to do on a Sunday night than go to Life Ties. Last week K-Camp broadcasted Joshua Bell and the Berlin Philharmonic. There are days when I look at my life and I don't recognize one thing about it."

"What do you want to do?" Sam asked. "Would you rather be playing in an orchestra?"

"Let's not talk about heaven," Cecilia said, making herself meet his gaze and smile. "Sorry to get so worked up. I'm just frustrated. I won't mean half of this tomorrow."

"And half of it you will."

"Pretty self-indulgent, huh?"

"Are you kidding?" He leaned forward and looked at her steadily until she began to tremble, and looked down. He said, "I wish I had anything I wanted to do as much as you want to play your violin."

"Don't even say it." She reached for another napkin to fold. "Don't—talk."

Sam didn't. Instead he watched her fold, and the silence between them thinned like high-altitude air.

When Cecilia spoke her voice was very tight. "You know what David likes? Leaf texture, quality of the soil, humidity. The little balcony outside our bedroom is so jammed with tomato plants we can't even walk out there. Every year he goes out to the community plots and helps people with their peppers."

"Would he leave Natural High for a plant job?"

"He would have at first." She studied the napkin, compressed into a square the size of her thumbnail. "Now he's settled in. I think he'd rather not know." Instantly, Cecilia felt like a traitor, although she hadn't said a word that wasn't true.

"Maybe I'm going to be out of line here," Sam said. His voice sounded strange too, or maybe Cecilia's alarmed brain was distorting things. "Maybe this is information you don't want. But there's a walnut orchard over toward Mineville that's looking for a part-time guy. Half farmer, half overseer. New people bought the property as a tax shelter, but now that they've laid eyes on the place they're hot to get production up. It would mean a chunk of time out of town every week, but I thought about David as soon as I heard."

"How would he square it with Natural High?"

"Long-term investment. We have to buy our walnuts someplace, and we like to support local growers. Besides, there's no actual rule against outside work, even though Nancy acts like there is. Head, heart, and soul to Natural High."

Cecilia was shaking her head, although she was already envisioning David striding among his trees, his fingers stained from the walnut juice, his voice lifted in song. Giving in, she imagined herself joining him, strolling under the canopy of branches while he pointed out new grafting techniques. And then—why stop now?—she imagined them at home together with their milk-faced children, smiling, hand in hand, any flutter of unease pushed aside by David's hearty farmer's joy.

She said, "Don't say anything to him; let me think about it."

"I don't know how long the job will be open. It's not like David's the only underutilized gardener in El Campo."

"Let me *think*." She stood and moved to the kitchen window, away from Sam. The job would fulfill David's deepest self, remind him of his truest desires. It would give him an outlet for all his hope and good cheer. It would take his eyes off of the kitchen calendar and direct them back to the sky and horizon, where they belonged. Therefore, her job, the job any Life Ties member would declare her obligation, was to make him take it, whether he wanted to or not.

Entr'acte (1)

When outsiders ask what we do every week, we say, "Look after one another." Anybody who likes the sound of that wants to hear more. Anybody who looks uncomfortable isn't Life Ties material.

Like the members of any club, we have a common interest, and more than for the members of most clubs, that interest is personal. When a couple walks in the door we know which partner does the laundry and how often, and who pays which bills. Everything comes with a bill, Vivy would say. Half of marriage is keeping your account books straight.

Vivy and Sam, Cecilia and David, and Nancy and Paul take a lot of the limelight. They show us all the things marriage can be: Nancy and Paul fight, Cecilia and David talk, Vivy and Sam laugh. Fighting and talking are safe. A little laughter is good, but too much laughing hides problems. We have spent many hours discussing the heartache behind Vivy and Sam's joking. There are several theories. We keep a close eye.

The newcomers listen, but they keep their opinions quiet, which is sensible. Newcomers already have their hands full. They're usually here because one of them—sometimes both of them—just had an affair, and they come in shivering with guilt or fury. As soon as one of them starts talking, they go off like firecrackers. More than once we've had to pull them off each other, and when we get them separated they're crying, they're kicking, they're trying to kiss each other. They give off a kind of light. They may be miserable, but they've never been so alive.

At meetings the new members talk for twenty minutes at a shot. They turn into Clarence Darrows. Somebody eventually has to cut them off, or we'd be sitting here all night. After the group leader asks the new people how they'd like to atone and rebuild their marriages, the ones who have good long-term Life Ties potential propose massive jobs—digging up wide banks of yews, reshingling the whole house. We have to talk them into something reasonable, but secretly we're all thinking they were right in the first place. People who want to repair their marriages have to put their backs into the effort.

After four, six, maybe even eight months, the new ones start to calm down. They don't talk so long, and we can tell by their soft, wandering hands that they're having sex again. We stop hearing about every time someone didn't get all the grit out of the lettuce. Sometimes we can see them looking around, looking out the window. Sometimes we can see them falling asleep.

The drop-off is pretty quick—only a few weeks before they're gone. When we see them on the streets they nod and smile but then look away, embarrassed at all we know and hoping we don't remember their stories.

Of course we do remember the stories, at least the good ones. We cherish them. Those stories are the very things that bring meaning to the Life Ties Statement of Beliefs recited at the start of meetings:

- We believe that we are put on this earth to improve it. Through our marriages, we become models.

- We believe that marriage is a total union. We share our thoughts, fears, emotions, and intentions with our partners. Marriage creates a single unit, without boundaries or divisions.

- We believe that our marriages are the center of our lives. Every choice we make must consider our marriages first, last, and foremost.

- Every decision made alone is a betrayal. Every decision made in community helps us build. Through new marriages we build a new community. Through a new community we build a new world.

- Marriage is our first strength, our full humanity, our unique creation. We gather each week to reaffirm our unions, to celebrate our strength, to admit our failings, and to vow to improve.

When David and Cecilia read the Statement, they linger over the words as if they were prayer. Nancy and Paul frown, looking for some point of order. But Vivy and Sam barely pay attention. Sam stretches out and closes his eyes while Vivy fiddles with a button. One night she hemmed a pair of pants. Offended, the newcomers tell us that the Jilets look like a couple of teenagers kept for detention. The newcomers are surprised Vivy and Sam come back at all. The newcomers look at us for an explanation, so we tell them all there is to say: Vivy and Sam are there like weather. You never know what it will be, but you know there will be some. One reason to come back is to watch them. Another is to see how long they can last.

THREE

Vivy

AFTER A FEW WEEKS working from home, Vivy had already lined up a dozen acts for the store, including the Hula King (twenty Hula-Hoops in motion at once), the Two Toms (political impersonations), and Extraordinary Laurel LaRue (feminist jokes while reassembling a carburetor). On a tip from Laurel, Vivy had also penciled in a parrot choir, although birds weren't her favorite kind of animal act. She was still trying to track down the waltzing dogs. Sam was certain they had retired their dancing slippers—even poodles, he said, couldn't waltz forever. But Vivy kept sleuthing anyway, calling agencies and old friends, straining to remember the name of the dogs' trainer. A man who had been able to get six teacup poodles to balance on their front legs and spin in unison wouldn't just stop.

Phone call led to phone call, and Vivy set up office in the kitchen, spreading her calendar and computer and calculator across the table. The old acts had moved to Nevada, New Hampshire, San Diego, to towns and trailer parks where they could live with family and find work driving school buses. "Oh jeez!" shrieked Teeny Marteeny, the four-foot-ten contortionist, when Vivy finally tracked her down in a tiny town in California so far north it might as well have been in Oregon. "Oh jeez Louise! You can't hire me—I've gotten fat!"

"I'll bet you can still do handstands. Anyway, this is an ice cream store, not Winterland. Why don't you come down and give us a try?"

"I'm huge. I look like a beach ball." She started to cry, and Vivy patiently held on to her end of the line. She'd been hearing a lot of tears. Many of the old acts hadn't seen a stage since Vivy and Sam had folded the company, and Vivy's calls reminded them of the lives and hopes they'd used to have.

She heard the story over and over: when no other promoter had shown any love for peculiar talents or countercultural agendas, the performers had tried to represent themselves. They printed up business cards and contacted civic centers. They were willing to entertain at grade schools. They accepted $100, $50, $30, fees Vivy would have hung up on.

"I wanted to perform," the Hula King told her. "I figured that if I got enough low-rent gigs, I'd eventually break big."

"It doesn't work that way," Vivy said. "If you sell low, you stay low."

"I shagged my butt," the Hula King said. He paused between words to gather himself. "I was going to show everybody some hustle. Make the rubber meet the road. But once you and Sam were gone, you know what I learned? Personally, all by myself, I didn't see any reason people would want to see a guy standing up on a stage with twenty Hula-Hoops. I mean, I wouldn't pay to see me. Without you there to talk me up, all I could think was people would be better off going to a movie. All those years I thought I was paying you to get me gigs, but I was really paying you to tell me I was worth something."

Vivy scheduled him three months out, to give him time to get his old moves back.

Now, while Marteeny stammered and hiccupped, Vivy calmly wrote her in for the second Saturday in June. "You can stay with us. Laszlo will love to see you."

"Laszlo. He must be almost a grown-up now."

"He's ten," Vivy said.

"I'll tell people I'm going to visit old friends. A family. They'll understand that." She cleared her throat. "There's a man here who wants me to marry him. People here don't know what I used to do."

"That's for sure," Vivy said, laughing. In the old days Marteeny had been at least as famous for her ardent kisses, distributed equally among males and females, as she had been for her yielding, pliant joints. "Do you want to marry him?"

"I don't know. He has very strong opinions. It doesn't seem right to say yes, and it doesn't seem right to say no." Marteeny sighed. "You and Sam—you guys were cut out of the same piece of cloth. You guys are obvious. This man and I aren't obvious."

"I called just in time. You need to talk to some friends," Vivy said.

Sam strolled into the kitchen and started rummaging in the cupboard. Vivy nodded when he held up a can of refried beans. The kids liked tostadas, which Annie treated as an opportunity to mound nothing but cheese and olives on her plate. "We can't wait to see you," she said gently into the phone. "Sam sends his love."

"Who do I love?" Sam said when she hung up.

"Teeny Marteeny. Hold onto your hat: she's gotten fat, and she's going to get married."

"Jump back. To a man?"

"A cattle rancher. He doesn't know about her dark past. You want some help with dinner?"

"You could round up the kids. This rancher's going to be surprised when she presents him with triple-jointed babies."

"He wants a wife, and she's ready to try out for the role. She told me she couldn't keep doing the split forever." Vivy waited for Sam's quick laugh before she trolled into the backyard, where Annie was dressing paper dolls in geranium petals, and then into the living room, where Laszlo was prone in front of a cartoon.

"Just till the commercial," he mumbled. A girl with a triangular head was explaining to a wizard that his potion hadn't worked. Now the world was in bigger trouble than ever.

"If Annie gets the table set before you come in, you're going to have to do all the cleanup after dinner."

"I'm safe."

Vivy shrugged and headed back for the kitchen, where Annie was sitting on the unset table. Vivy lifted her off and put a stack of plates in her hands. "See if you can get it all set before your brother comes in.

Surprise him," Vivy whispered.

"Surprise," Annie stage-whispered, and started enthusiastically clattering the plates into place. Vivy handed her the forks and said to Sam, "I told Marteeny she could stay with us for a few days. I didn't think you'd mind."

"Who's Marteeny?" said Annie.

"She's our old friend. You'll like her," Vivy said.

"Does she have a little girl?"

Sam said, "She's pretty little herself. And she can pick up her leg and put it right behind her head."

"No way," said Annie.

"Can so," said Laszlo, sauntering in from the living room just in time to grab the plastic cups from Annie and toss one down at each plate. "I remember her. She could turn her arm all the way around just to scratch her back. How cool is that?"

"She's one of the stranger strangers we've taken in," Sam said.

"Marteeny's not a stranger," said Vivy. "She's long lost family, and it's time for us to get reacquainted. And not just with Marteeny."

"Vivy—" Sam began.

She handed him the cheese grater. "I'm not doing anything wrong. The store isn't going to lose money. These people are coming so cheap it hurts. I had to force the Hula King to accept more than fifty bucks."

"Well, see now, right there—"

"These are talented performers. They are professionals."

"Okay," Sam said. "Uncle."

"Are they all going to stay here?" Annie said eagerly.

"No, baby. Just Marteeny." Vivy glanced at Sam, wondering if he remembered the mornings spent looking for performers who had slipped out of motel rooms to score drugs or find sex or take walks in breathtakingly dangerous parts of town. Perhaps he did; he was grating enough cheese to feed all of the Strikes and Spares.

"Have you booked any musicians?" he said. "Audiences always turn out for music."

"The flute players all seem to have gone back to Peru. I can't track down Sweet Baby John or Buck the Yodeler. Fredd said he could get me some leads on a drum orchestra, but he hasn't called me back yet. Napkins under the forks, Annie."

"Get Marsha Marsha!" Annie said.

Laszlo plucked the bunched-up napkins that Annie held like a bouquet. "Marsha Marsha's a cartoon, dummy. She can't give a concert."

"Laszlo," said Sam and Vivy on the same breath.

"Sorry-I-said-dummy. But she's still a cartoon."

"Okay. No Marsha Marsha," Vivy said. "Who wants juice?"

"If you want to book a musician, you're overlooking one," Sam said.

"Who?"

"Cecilia Moore."

Handing the carton of apple juice to Laszlo, Vivy studied her husband's face. Suddenly it looked overly innocent, the smile too cheerful, the eyes too scrubbed of guile.

"I stopped by her apartment the other day to pick up handbills for the store, and she played her violin for me. She's a real violinist. I mean, she's an artist."

"She played her violin for you," Vivy said. "Golly."

"I hate violins," Laszlo announced.

"Me too," said Annie.

"You would have liked this," Sam said.

Vivy was having trouble tamping down a smile; Sam hadn't tried to sneak anything past her in years, and he didn't know how out of practice he was. His earnest, unwavering eyes reminded her of nothing so much as Laszlo, age six, his face streaked with chocolate, swearing he hadn't eaten any brownies. "I'm with the kids on this one. Violins make me want to go into another room."

"If you heard Cecilia play, you'd want to stay and hear more."

"Sure sounds like you wanted to hear more."

He had the grace to laugh. "She sounds like somebody you'd hear on the radio."

"I turn on the radio to hear T 'n' T," Laszlo said. "Radio Jam."

"Marsha Marsha," Annie said.

"You're really not getting this, are you?" Vivy said to Sam, who had scooped the mountain of cheese into a bowl and moved on to chopping tomatoes. "If Natural High books acts regularly, we can start to bring the old business back. Alternative art, remember? 'On the streets, from the heart, for the people.'"

"Are you going to start up your own series of napkins?"

"Maybe. That was your line, by the way."

"I remember," Sam said. "I also remember that even when we were managing acts full-time, the old company went belly-up." Laszlo crashed to the floor, his hands drumming on his skinny stomach. "Yeah, son, just like that."

"Belly, belly, belly," said Annie.

"Call it auld lang syne, then," Vivy said. "I want to see our old friends. That's not so terrible. And when they play the store, Natural High benefits. Even Nancy admits that performers bring in customers."

"I'll be a performer," Laszlo said.

"What's your act?" Vivy said.

The boy squirmed for a moment. "I'm at level eight on Deathmaster VI."

"I'm not sure how much of a draw that'll be," Vivy said, and was surprised to see her son's face cloud over. "What?"

"I just want to do something," he muttered. He looked away from her roughly, and Vivy had to check her impulse to pull him to her. In the last few months he'd started to get moody, flinching away from her touch. Previews of coming attractions, she'd told Sam.

"We can work something out," she said, studying the back of his head and his reddening neck. "Maybe Fredd could teach you to juggle."

"Never mind."

"We could have a talent show for kids."

"I never said anything, okay?" He sidled over to the refrigerator and started pounding it with the side of his fist, thump-thump-thump, then thumpetty-tap, tap-thump, a little performance. Vivy flattened her hands on her hips. Nothing made her feel so helpless as her children. She looked at Sam, who shook his head and asked Annie what she'd done in school today. They were halfway through dinner she concluded her account of the songs, the butterflies, the teach moss collection. Somewhere in the butterflies Laszlo lifted his head and started eating, and the fist around Vivy's heart relaxed. Still, she wondered what new hunger the boy was feeling.

Not until after dinner, when the kids had crashed their way through cleanup and Vivy and Sam lingered over coffee, did Sam bring up Cecilia again. Vivy was startled. Lost in Laszlo's unhappiness, she had forgotten about Cecilia. "Just keep her in mind," Sam was saying. "Schedule her for some middle-of-the-week night when you can't get anybody else. You don't want to go only backwards, retrieving the old acts. You want to go forward, too."

"I am going forward. Fast-forward." Vivy leaned toward him and separated the dark curls on his forehead into separate ringlets. Seeing the sheen of moisture on his nose and cheeks, she fanned the air above his face. "I hope you're this gallant when I need defending."

"I'm way more gallant than this," he said, and then, after a moment, "You never need defending."

"Guess I'll have to work on that." She pushed back her chair. "Time for me to go earn the family bacon. Can you pick up groceries? We're all out of lettuce, and the kids haven't eaten anything green in a week."

"I'll go to Safeway if you'll think about booking Cecilia."

"I won't think about anything else all night."

In fact, she intended to think about everything except Cecilia, but once she and David were installed on their shift—early evening, mid-week, business slow despite the repaired air conditioner—Vivy found her mind circling back to Sam. Despite that plastered-on grin when he talked about Cecilia, his voice had been pleading. Ten years ago he would have managed the request with more dexterity.

Ten years ago they had struggled with accounts books and argued with boorish auditorium managers while lithe bodies slid into splits at their feet. In the mornings Vivy would stumble yawning into the living room and find half the members of Strikes and Spares, wearing only their skivvies, practicing handstands, their shapely legs scissoring

egs usually managed to wrap itself around her on
hen—sometimes it took her half an hour to get
those days she and Sam had juggled two or three
nd a pleasant, electrical thrill surged through their
:ing body was always stretching nearby, heating up
:d over into Vivy and Sam's sex life, and Vivy said,
laughing, that she couldn't keep track of how many people their imaginations pulled into bed with them.

Their marriage had never been fully open, but its door was left ajar. Neither Sam nor Vivy saw any reason to forego romance and excitement just because they were married. They sneaked phone calls, arranged lunches, collapsed into illicit, engulfing embraces from which they emerged tingling—never quite in bed, but not far from one. And when they weren't falling into those embraces themselves, they watched each other with quick eyes.

In those days Vivy thought of her marriage to Sam as a game that depended on hot grace as much as cunning; the winner of a round was the one who managed to signal an infatuation with the least fuss, the fewest clues. Or perhaps the winner was the partner who ignored signs of dalliance, too preoccupied to notice the other's sighs, long walks, lunges for the telephone. Either way, the loser was the one who broke down and demanded to know exactly what was going on, leaving the other to smile and say, "What are you talking about? You shouldn't get so worked up."

Vivy had loved the game, which kept her marriage just enough off balance that she could feel the tip and roll under her feet. Every day promised adventure. She and Sam fairly leaped out of bed in the mornings. But when the business dissolved, they lost their intimacy with muscular, sexy performers who didn't think much of such middle-class concepts as somebody else's marriage.

Instead, Vivy and Sam worked elbow to elbow with Nancy and Paul and David and Cecilia, who believed marriage was a state in which two people merged without boundaries or divisions. As if a little air and scandal, secrecy and fun in a marriage would destroy it. As if a good marriage required border guards and razor wire. Mottoes. Meetings. "We gather in order to build better marriages with our shared strength." She had gone into Life Ties with a willing spirit, but five years of meetings had taught Vivy that she and Sam had a better marriage back in the days when they could tantalize each other. Now every moment of every day was filled with duty, and Vivy felt as if the supple canoe that used to bear them had been turned into a barge.

Over the store stereo the carefully inoffensive CD—ocean waves, French horns, chanting—came to an end, and Vivy released a breath she hadn't meant to be holding. Sam might have an awkwardly lovesick heart, but he was right to point out that they needed some decent music in there. As the next CD started in with birdcalls and some kind of whistle, a kid at one of the tables cocked his finger like a gun at the speaker. Vivy called to him, "Have you got anything else?"

She had to repeat herself twice before the boy understood that she was talking to him. He shook his head. "I don't exactly carry spare CDs around with me."

Vivy ignored the sneer. "Bring something in next time. If I'm here, I'll put it on. If it doesn't chase people out, we'll play the whole thing."

"Deal." The kid smirked while the other boys at his table shoved him.

David, who was polishing the length of the counter with cleanser and a sponge, said, "I might be one of the people who gets chased out."

"Come on. Anything would be better than these symphonies for wind chimes and groaning whales. I hear those damn whales in my nightmares."

"I don't mind whales. At least you don't have to worry about the lyrics."

"You don't know that. Whales might be rapping. We could be listening to them singing, 'It's time to take a stand. Kill the fisher man. Huh.'"

"You're funny, Vivy."

"Just trying to keep the troops entertained."

He smiled and sponged around the freezers with his usual

meticulous pep, sweating lightly despite the regulated, seventy-two degree air. Leaning back against the counter, Vivy considered him: soft,
rounded body; brown arms; stiff beard that stuck away from his chin
like a shovel. He'd had that beard since she'd met him in their co-
ed college dormitory, a boy who could talk for twenty uninterrupted
minutes about plant propagation, pruning techniques, California's in-
digenous flora. Since half the students in the dorm were trying to grow
pot plants in their closets, people put up with his lectures. He held
consultations about drooping leaves and root rot and helped rig grow
lights. Although he himself never grew anything more contraband than
marigolds, he never turned anyone in.

He must have had girlfriends, although Vivy couldn't remember
any. Light, meek girls, proto-Cecilias, might well have padded around
after him and discussed the depletion of the water table, but Vivy's days
had been a raucous haze of rum and drugs and Sam, and David had
hardly made a dent in her consciousness. When Nancy proposed that
David Moore should join Natural High, Vivy had said, "Who?"

So now, trying to imagine life at home with David and Cecilia, all
Vivy could envision was long, quiet, extremely polite evenings. The
Moores weren't fighters, she was sure. David's hands, presently plunged
in the rinse water, lacked the spiny nerves required to pick up a plate
and fire it across a room. And if he and Cecilia weren't fighters, they
weren't likely to be much as lovers. They were so careful all the time.
When somebody at Life Ties told a joke, David would smile and Cecilia make a little snick snick snick sound, like scissors cutting through
chintz. Vivy could imagine their lovemaking as if she had a ringside
seat—neat covers, considerate division of labor. No more than fifteen
minutes, beginning to end, with both parties springing to their feet as
soon as they were finished. She envisioned David's scramble to wash
his hands.

"Ick," she said, imagining Cecilia handing David the hand towel.
Would she make artless, calibrated comments about Sam Jilet, as if he
were a lump of gold she'd just stumbled over? For the first time—she
was out of practice herself—Vivy wondered exactly why Cecilia had

played her violin for Sam, and she wondered if David had heard about the concert. Vivy and David, the excluded spouses, had been pushed into their own, special partnership, and she wondered whether David knew that.

"They say the heat's going to break soon," he said, running fresh rinse water and tucking the sponge up behind the faucet.

"Good. Laszlo and Annie are whining so much that I made them sleep out on the porch last night." She handed him a towel to fold. "How are you and Cecilia holding up?"

"She likes hot weather. So do my tomatoes. The ones on my porch are already knee high. The ones in my community plot are taller than that. I water them every night." He smiled, encouraging her to congratulate him on his tall tomatoes.

"So you leave poor Cecilia all alone?"

"I don't think she minds."

"I'd be careful. This is how thrillers all start—the young missus by herself in the early evening, unbuttoning her blouse in front of the window to get a breeze. Startled when a drifter comes to the door."

He laughed, then leaned on the freezer lid to latch it tight. "Cecilia hasn't told me about any drifters. There was a kid selling candy bars for a school trip. You want one? She bought six."

"There you go. A younger man."

Vivy paused, then said, "Sam came to see her the other day. I was a little startled to hear about it."

"She told me. He ran the new design to the copy shop for her. She was glad for the help."

"He heard her play her violin. Sam said she sounded like a professional. He couldn't believe you hadn't told us what an artist we have in our midst."

"She wanted to play with an orchestra once. I don't think she wants to anymore."

"Sam's all set to get her back on the road to stardom."

"You make him sound like he has a crush on her."

"He does."

"The fellow's got good taste." David turned to the mother and toddler who were approaching the counter. The boy, a shy child, twisted around his mother while she coaxed him into pointing at the flavor he wanted. In all, the transaction took close to five minutes, a track and a half of tooty Indian whistle and drums. By the time David had counted out change and rinsed the ice cream scoop, Vivy could see he had forgotten all about his wife, in whom he had untroubled faith. Many spouses at Life Ties wandered from their marriages specifically to jolt their partners out of such confidence, which was indistinguishable from complacency.

He reached into the freezer case to wrestle the empty Maple Walnut carton out, and Vivy said, "I'll get you another gallon from the back."

He shook his head. "All gone. Didn't you see Nancy's memo on this? The last two shipments of walnuts were bad, so we need to find a new supplier."

"How hard can it be to grow nuts?"

"Harder than you think, actually, especially if you want to stay away from sprays. I did a study in graduate school on borers," David said.

"You should send a copy to that orchard in Mineville. Maybe they'll take you on."

"What are you talking about?"

David's broad, mild face was curious, and Vivy briefly wondered what exactly filled up his brain. The fertile valley that held El Campo and Mineville and a handful of other towns was only sixty miles wide from the foothills to Sacramento, and didn't exactly bubble over with news. After reading the twelve-page *Valley-Herald*, Vivy felt as if she could recite every church's upcoming call for renewal, every diner that needed a fry cook. She said, "There's a spread up in Mineville that's looking for somebody to re-do its walnut orchards. Replant, prune, I don't know what all. Part-time. Pretty much a David Moore job, if you ask me."

"Nice of you to say, but David Moore has a job."

"Not one he did studies on."

"Thanks all the same." Wiping the clean countertop, his smile took on the crimp it bore whenever anyone presented him with a new idea.

"It's part-time. You wouldn't have to leave Natural High. And you'd get to do what you like for twenty hours a week."

"I like what I do now."

"Okay. You'd get to do what you love."

"You have quite a way of seeing things," David said, bearing down so hard she could see the soft muscles in his back shift from side to side. "I don't think everything in the world has to be a big quest. I like my life already. I don't have to change things."

"I just thought you should know what your options are."

"I'm not looking for options," he said. "I have commitments."

"A commitment doesn't have to mean you're locked in place. Just ask Sam and Cecilia." When David raised his startled gaze, she said, "Sorry. That was supposed to be a joke."

"It's kind of a compliment. Not many people would cast me as part of a romantic triangle."

He was right about that. Even though Vivy's frustration with him had momentarily ebbed, there was no overlooking his thinning hair, doughy waist, his nose as pudgy as a baby's fist. She said, "I know I sounded catty, but I was actually trying to help."

When he grinned he showed his gray teeth. Somewhere behind that beard lurked a dimple. "You're a good egg, Vivy. You think about people more than you get credit for. Would you be happier if I went up and looked at this job?"

"I don't really care who grows our walnuts. You and the job just seemed like a good match."

"Nice of you to think of me."

"I'm being practical. We need a new supplier for walnuts, and nobody would be more reliable than you."

"Well, now, don't get too excited. I'll go up there, but I may not want them. They may not want me." Catching the protest forming in Vivy's mouth, he added, "I've got a PhD that's five years old and no professional experience. Would you hire me?"

"I would if I knew how hard you work, and how dependable you are," Vivy said, avoiding his humid, affectionate eyes. "You should bring some ideas for long-term plans to the interview. Tell them what to do about borers. Five years as a partner here should have taught you how to do projections."

"It hasn't taught me to make plans on my own," David said, a bit of near-sarcasm that heartened Vivy. "Look, I know this is the kind of thing you love—new job, interviews, the whole thing—but I hate even thinking about it. My life is in order. I don't want to rearrange it."

"Jesus, David. How do you know you're not dead?"

"My tomatoes look terrific," he said.

Vivy glanced at him twice before she found the hint of a smile, an expression that quickly reverted to his normal, fond placidity. He was like some rounded-off life form, evolved beyond the skeleton and muscles of desire. She shivered. She would rather think of David as fiercely selfish, encircling every moment and squeezing it empty of possibility. At least selfishness had a little vigor.

"I'll bring you tomatoes in a few weeks," David said. "I planted Early Boys. Does Sam like tomatoes? I'll bring you a lot."

"He loves them. I won't tell him they come from you, though. If he knows they're connected to Cecilia he'll want to put them on an altar and worship them."

"Ha," David said. Turning to face her, he dropped one eyelid in a slow wink, like the gesture of a clumsy, fleshy uncle. A sleepy-eyed kid, one of two customers in the store, looked up and she frowned at him.

"We don't need two people up front," she announced, yanking the hot water nozzle to full spray and plunging her hands in. "I'll go chop almonds."

"Atoning for something?" David said. Often the partners prepared mix-ins after Life Ties meetings, pondering mistakes they'd made on the home front. After especially heated meetings Sam said the back room sounded like a flamenco troupe was practicing.

"Nope. This one's for charity."

David made a fond shooing motion, and Vivy wondered, as she slipped through the swinging door, how he had managed to jump straight into a grandfather's mannerisms without ever pausing at fatherhood.

Her sandals slapped across the isthmus of tile flooring between the chopping board and the enormous freezer. Vivy had arranged to buy that freezer, slightly used, from a restaurant that closed its doors after six months. The thing took up the whole back wall and saved the partnership over $1,000. Vivy briefly wondered, as she often did, whether she could apply the $1,000 to her and Sam's debt.

She pulled down the good knife, the one as long as her forearm, then reached in the freezer for a carton of almonds. She'd barely had time for the first rough chops when the phone rang—most likely Nancy, the only person who regularly called the store. Vivy was careful to sound cheerful when she picked up the phone and said, "Natural High Ice Cream," and so was reduced to a delighted sputter when Fredd's voice said, "Christ, Vivy, calm down. You sound like Shirley Temple."

"I had my tap shoes on."

"Take them off. You could scare a guy." Vivy could hear a clicking noise behind his voice, and wondered what he was juggling. Sounded like dried beans. "Listen, I heard about a festival down in Watsonville. I'll bet they need a juggler."

"So call."

"I was thinking you could do it for me. Take a cut. I'll feel better if you take care of the details."

"Flatter me, why don't you?"

"No problem. Seeing you the other day reminded me how much I need you in my life."

Vivy snorted. "Fredd, are you trying to proposition me?"

"In a way." Click. "I got to thinking about how things used to be. It was easier when you were around, reminding me of things, looking out for me. So I want you to go back to being my agent. All my gigs. Straight ten percent, right? This can be just between us. Nobody else needs to know."

"What the hell are you juggling over there?"

"Pennies. I'm practicing one-handed. What do you say? Get back in the saddle?"

"I guess you've overlooked the pesky fact that I already have a job." David's words rolled out of her mouth before she could stop them.

"Come on, Vivy. You don't need forty hours a week to book one juggler. You can make phone calls while you're cooking dinner. You don't even have to go to the gigs—I can set myself up. You'll still keep track of stuff better than I do, and you'll get some extra dough for whatever you want. Clothes, a car. You win, I win."

"We all scream for ice cream. If I went out and bought a car, my butt would be in a crack in a big way. Sam and I are in the hole eighty thousand bucks. No new cars until that's paid off."

"Well, this will help you start socking away some bread."

"I don't mean to make you doubt yourself, but I'll have to represent you for two hundred years to sock away eighty grand."

"That's the other reason I called. My nephew's in a band. Elphenevel. They play songs about Dungeons & Dragons games, with heavy metal guitar."

"Save me."

"No joke. Seventeen-year-old boys are nuts for this. The band played at a high school last week, and two thousand kids showed up. Two thousand kids, and the band brought home five hundred bucks. They need you."

"Heavy metal wizards? No thanks."

"You don't have to love it, Vivy. But they could fill the Civic Auditorium. You could catch them at the beginning of a real career. T-shirts. Posters."

"I get it," Vivy said.

"The guys are in college, in case music doesn't pan out. They don't want to play but a couple nights a month."

"I *get* it," she said. She ran her tongue back and forth across her teeth, an old nervous habit. This was a band that would call for big management, full promotion, the kind of work she and Sam had barely glimpsed before the old company slipped away from them. House managers, stagehands and the IATSE, contracts stipulating eight percent—was it still eight percent?—of the box office. The Civic Auditorium held five thousand, at no less than $15 a seat.

Fredd mumbled "Shit" and grunted—scrambling after one of the pennies, Vivy assumed. His voice sounded coaxing when he came back to the phone. "You're going to do this for me, aren't you?"

"Yup," she said. "For you and your nephew. But twenty percent, not ten."

"For crying out loud, Vivy, people have to make a living. I thought I'd be helping you, not bled dry."

"You want jobs? Twenty."

"Fifteen," he said.

"Done." Picking up the knife again, she lined up a handful of almonds and sliced them like a machine. Usually she couldn't manage such precision.

"Still a shyster. I feel better already."

"Checks will come through me," she said, missing the angle on one almond and watching it ping off the wall. "And nobody knows about this. Nobody."

"You're not even going to tell Sam?"

"I'll get around to telling Sam," she said. "I just want to wait a little. Right now he's developing his own act."

"He better not be juggling. I don't like competition."

"He's juggling, all right," she said. "He's juggling and walking a tightrope and balancing an egg on his nose."

"I didn't know he was so talented."

"You just forgot," Vivy said. "Stick around. The old acts are coming back to life."

FOUR

Sam

HOT, HOT, HOT. THROUGH May and into June, despite rumors of approaching rain that sprang up, spread, and dissolved like mirages, the temperatures in the valley around El Campo soared. Summer was always hot in this part of California; farmers planted long rows of apricot and pear trees, counting on sultry days to ripen the fruit. But these temperatures were too high, and blossoms were dropping before fruit could set. Nearly every afternoon passed one hundred degrees, and hardly any night dipped below eighty-five. Farmers were interviewed every night on the news. In grocery stores and beside swimming pools the heat was everybody's only topic. Natural High was doing land-office business, half of its customers, some of them old enough for retirement, coming into the store wearing bathing suits and flip-flops. Sam rarely looked twice anymore. Looking at skin—even thin, depleted skin that had no business showing itself in public—only generated more heat.

At home he and Vivy slept clinging to opposite sides of the mattress, their arms and legs carefully sprawled to avoid any touch. "It's not that I don't love you, honey," Vivy said one night when the air folded around their bodies like a heavy animal. She shifted her hip an inch further from Sam's arm.

"Right. It's not that I don't love you, too." He shifted and dangled his foot over the edge of the bed, letting Vivy hog the hot mattress. For a minute he entertained the notion that their arrangement on the bed was symbolic—Vivy spread-eagled, claiming three-quarters of the available space, Sam crowded to the very edge and hanging on. Then he let the thought go. Too hot to get mad, and way too hot for an argument. The thermostat was set at eighty, the lowest temperature they could afford, but somehow the house felt hotter than that.

Sleep loitered miles away. In a minute Sam would ask Vivy to turn off the bedside light, but for now he contented himself watching her study her scribbled-over list of acts. Occasionally, she inserted a question mark or an arrow. The list ran to three pages, a census of peculiar entertainments and rarefied skills. She'd told him about some band she'd picked up as a favor to Fredd, a band she said was going to make their fortune, but they weren't coming to Natural High. Instead, she had dug up acts he'd forgotten they'd ever heard of, and she caroled around the house every time she unearthed another magician or clown or acrobat. In just two months she had contacted almost all on their old list, and took for granted that Sam would be as delighted about this undertaking as she was.

To be fair, at first he had gotten a bang out of the whole thing. He and Vivy went out for a celebratory drink the day she located Sir Smokes, a guy they'd first discovered in 1979 on a street corner in Sacramento wearing a leather vest and breeches, eating cigarettes as fast as people would light them for him. When Vivy finally tracked him down again, he was busking only a block away from his original corner. "Actually, he was hard to find," she said now. "No phone."

"Now that you've found him, what are you going to do with him? You can't have a cigarette-eater play an ice cream store," Sam said.

"I feel better knowing where he is. Who would have thought he'd still be alive?" Looking distracted, Vivy drew another arrow. "We personally saw him eat whole packs of Camels and live to tell the tale. He'd play huge at colleges. He's the triumph of the individual over corporate America."

"He's a nut."

"A nut with an esophagus made out of cast iron. I wonder what else he can eat."

"No Marlboros—he said they didn't have a good balance of flavors."

"That's what separated him from the amateur cigarette-eaters," Vivy said. "Sir Smokes spent years developing his palate."

"Like us. We can tell fresh from two-day-old Triple Vanilla at a taste."

"Can you? I can't."

"That's how you keep your girlish figure," he said. Vivy lifted her eyebrows, then shrugged and turned off the light.

During the day she lived on the phone, single-minded as a bloodhound. She hauled one mothballed act after another back into daylight, and her delight didn't falter. She was even thrilled to zoom in on Warble-O, the birdcaller, a man neither one of them had ever been able to stand.

By the time she had scheduled six weeks' worth of entertainment, suspicion had set up residence in Sam's brain. The old vocabulary was slipping into Vivy's mouth—venues, percentage share—and she started more sentences with "We," the breezy old promoter's pronoun, meant to encompass the whole world. Did she actually think she could get the old business going again? All by herself, with no capital?

Sam watched the old lineup of talent creak back to its feet, miserably undead. He could hardly believe he and Vivy had once drummed up real audiences for these acts, had booked actual auditoriums. Now the performers' collective talent could barely fill a twelve-foot stage in an ice cream store. Except for Fredd and a few of the magicians, the old acts looked blowsy, their hands uncertain and their faces worried. Vivy had done her friends no favor by urging them out of retirement. Moves that had been daring or funny ten years ago now looked self-conscious and dated. Laurel LaRue was telling bra-burning jokes. Sitting at one of the back tables the night Laurel's act died, Sam drummed his hands on his thighs and watched Vivy scrawl notes as if Laurel had one fresh or surprising joke in her whole act, as if Laurel were actually funny, instead of dull and angry and probably deluded. Vivy wrote, "Get newer material." He plucked the pencil from her hand, scratched out "newer" and printed "GOOD" above it.

They barely waited to get in the car before they tore into each other.

"It hurt to watch," Sam said. "Was there one joke that made you laugh?"

"The store was packed," Vivy snarled.

"It was packed because it's a million degrees outside. How much did the store shell out for that performance? I'll bet there are twenty kids in town who can do better stand-up for free."

She shot the car out of its parking place, ignoring an oncoming van's wailing horn. "Laurel is a professional, in case that means anything to you. Not everything comes down to the goddamn balance sheet at the end of the month."

"You'd better give that balance sheet a thought, Vivy, because we're balanced in there too. And I don't think throwing Laurel up onstage did anything to help our line of credit."

Vivy let the comment ride until the end of the block. Then, over the engine's thunketing idle, she snapped, "What is it that's eating you so bad? Are you upset because Laurel screwed up some jokes or because you're afraid of what Cecilia is going to say?"

By the light of the dashboard Sam could see how Vivy's hair sprang wrathfully around her face—part Gibson Girl, part Medusa. Fleetingly, he thought of Cecilia's hair, which hung like a sheet down her back. "I hate this two-bit, shit-eating, no-talent talent that you book because the act is transgressive or naive or some other synonym for lousy. You know why you could get Laurel for twenty bucks? Because you get what you pay for."

Vivy hit the accelerator again. The Toyota shuddered. "Do you even look at yourself in the mirror, Sam? If you did, you might get a scare. You have turned into a company man. Everything comes down to the almighty buck."

"The money isn't what's bothering me."

"So what's bothering you?" she shouted.

Sam smiled. "I'm tired of having you waste my time."

Vivy drove home without saying another word, and in the morning she and Sam got the kids up without mentioning bookings or jugglers or schedules. In a spirit that might have been penitent or might have been just plain pissy, Sam continued to attend the performances at the store. But the argument with Vivy was banked, not buried, waiting for some fresh kindling to blaze up again.

Now, without apologizing, she turned on the light again, groping for her pencil. She looked, Sam thought without a trace of desire, terrific. The dry heat made her red curls froth around her face and brought a bright glow to her cheeks and mouth. She'd dropped a little weight—all of them had—so that her tiny chin looked more delicately chiseled, her shoulders more finely molded. She'd taken to admiring herself before the mirror and announcing that she intended to become a supermodel.

On those occasions Sam left the room. He didn't need to check his own reflection to know he looked like he was standing with one foot on skid row. Bags like little pillows pouched under his eyes. His cheeks had taken on a pasty tinge. Even his boxers chafed.

He and Cecilia, who were working first shift this month, compared notes: the heat made her drop things, she said, and patches of skin on her neck and arms erupted in prickly red scales. She looked like hell, frankly, but Sam felt protective when he saw her discreetly scratching her arms. At least she wasn't going to become a supermodel.

Still going over her list, Vivy noisily turned a page and poked her pencil into Sam's arm. "You're not asleep yet, are you? What do you think about having the Hula King come in between Warble-O and that guy who does imitations? I want to keep the talking acts spaced out."

"Warble-O doesn't talk. He chirps."

"Well, he isn't physical." She poked him again, and grinned. "Nancy's looking forward to him. She thinks he sounds like fine family entertainment."

She was inviting him to laugh, he knew; she was trying to do a little bridge building. If he could just laugh along with her, things between them might loosen a little. But he couldn't laugh. All he could think of was another evening lost, this time to a plump, nervous man dressed in a robin costume who molded his soft lips so that every call, seagull to jackdaw, sounded very much like every other.

"I might miss that one," he said.

"Don't be such a grandma. What else are you going to do with your evening?"

"Catch a ball game."

"You never watch baseball."

"It's America's pastime. It's time for me to get in step with my culture."

"You know, Sam," Vivy said, holding her pencil against her notepad so she wouldn't lose her place, "I don't ask you to do much. I find the talent. I work out the contracts. All you have to do is come. You get the cream. And then you complain."

"Maybe I don't like cream. Maybe I'm more of a skim milk guy."

"Then you'd better think twice about your line of work," she said, checking off something on her notepad and turning out the light again.

In the dark Sam tried to slide into sleep, but heat pulsed off Vivy's body. Every five minutes he tried a new position, peeling his legs off the exhausted sheets and flipping his pillow until he finally padded to the living room and laid a sheet down on the plush rug. When Annie crept in at dawn he jerked up, startled, his head filled with birdcalls.

He let Annie turn on the TV and made the kids French toast, which they loved, along with bacon—a noisy breakfast involving lots of pans and popping grease. Vivy slept on, or at least she didn't come out of the bedroom. Sam gave her a half hour, then poured himself coffee over ice, pulled on shorts, and left her French toast and bacon still in the pan. He had two hours before he was scheduled to open the store, time enough to walk, and he veered toward Cecilia's apartment, where he might be able to cadge some ice cream for breakfast, the only food he could contemplate in this weather. David would probably be out volunteering at the community garden plots, watering other people's thirsty pepper plants.

Sam had dropped by a few times, hoping to get Cecilia to play for him again. She always refused, but he kept finding reasons to return. Talking to Cecilia counterbalanced the hard, rented furniture and low ceilings, disheartened little spaces Vivy wouldn't have stayed in for an hour before she started fiddling with curtains and lighting. Cecilia didn't seem to notice her surroundings, or let them affect her. He admired that.

He was discovering in her a depth of personality he hadn't suspected, a surprising firmness of mind. He got a kick out of watching opinions rear up and blast their way through her meek demeanor. Once or twice Sam had caught himself wondering whether David appreciated Cecilia's tiny, contained bursts of anger as much as Sam did, but he put the kibosh on that kind of thinking. His visits to Cecilia were one hundred percent innocent, nothing that Laszlo and Annie couldn't witness, and Sam meant to keep it that way.

This morning she came to the door looking shipwrecked: her long hair soaked, her face puffy and splotched. As soon as she saw him she rubbed the heel of her hand across her eyes, but he could see she was crying, and his first, insane thought was David had hurt her, and Sam would joyfully hurt David worse.

"The heat, that's all," she said before he could say anything. "I'm at the end of my rope. I've taken about six cold showers, which cool me off but wake me up. I haven't slept." She paused, then curved her mouth mirthlessly and stepped back to let Sam into the apartment. "Gee," she said. "I guess that wasn't the most polite way to greet somebody."

"What happened to your AC?"

"Went out yesterday. The whole building."

"I'm relieved," Sam said. "For a second there, I thought somebody had broken in and beat you up."

"Just me. At around three o'clock in the morning I was so miserable that I started punching myself on the leg. I thought I'd go nuts if I didn't do something. David grabbed my hand until I promised to stop. He didn't want people thinking he knocked me around."

"A reasonable concern," Sam said.

"David," said Cecilia, and shrugged. Sam watched her mouth go soft as if she were going to cry again, and he said, "Let's get out of here. We can go to the store early and sit in the back and cool off. You can take a nap."

Cecilia nodded and pulled back her hair, tying it into a swift knot.

When she turned to pick up her purse and violin case, Sam saw how her hair, wet from the shower, had dampened the back of her T-shirt. Her shoulder blades jutted like bony wings. "Let's take my car," she was saying. "I have to run some errands after work."

"What errands?" Sam asked as they tromped down the metal staircase to the parking lot.

"Gas and groceries for sure. If I have time, I want to run over to a music shop in Sacramento. Something funny is happening with my violin. It might just be the heat, or I might be in trouble."

"Funny how?"

She unlocked the car door and waved it back and forth as if she really thought the air outside the car was much cooler than the air in. "There's a kind of hollowness in the tone. The sound flattens out in certain registers." She glanced at him. "You don't know what I mean, do you?"

"I get the general idea. But if you play for me I'll understand better."

"Please don't start, Sam. It's too early."

"We've both been up for hours."

"My fingers aren't awake yet."

"You can just demonstrate. In return for my sweeping you off to the land of air-conditioning."

She shook her head, shaking loose a few tendrils of hair. "Every once in a while I get a glimpse of what you must have been like as a promoter."

"I was good. The world just wasn't ready for me," Sam said.

"That's what I mean," Cecilia said, and drove the few blocks to the store in silence.

Sam rarely arrived at work so early—it wasn't even eight o'clock yet—and the sense of a day waiting to unfold made him feel tippy, as if he were trying to balance his weight on a ball. When they got out of the car Cecilia held her violin case and waited while he fished up the store keys, unlocked and unbolted the back door and flipped the lights on, then flipped them off again, because the store's cool seemed cooler with the lights off.

As they wandered into the main room, Cecilia lifted her face to the air and Sam flapped his shirt around his waist like a kid. Still flapping, he stationed himself under a vent, its rush of air as delightful on his skin as feathers, and shook out his damp hair. "Forget about a home life," he said. "I'm sleeping here tonight."

"It'll be a slumber party." Under another vent near the door, Cecilia spread her arms and twirled, making her long, light green skirt billow up to her knees. "Oh, my. This is better than a cold shower."

"Makes you wonder how our ancestors survived."

"Makes you understand murders and suicide pacts." She stopped spinning and flattened a hand on the refrigerator to steady herself. "Stays this hot, day after day, and everybody's brain melts. It's amazing we all show as much self-control as we do."

"Ha. When did your self-control ever lapse?" Sam looked at Cecilia's long skirt, her cheeks bare of makeup, her long hair still mostly held in the quick knot. Everything about her was lightly old-fashioned and proper, making her forthright, dry conversation that much more surprising, like an unlooked-for reward.

"True stories? Now we really are having a slumber party," Cecilia said. "When I was nine my mother took me to visit an old lady who had something to do with the library board where Mom worked. We were sitting on the couch, and the woman held out her candy dish and told me I could have one piece. The pieces were tiny, and I thought she was being stingy. When she walked my mother out to the hallway, I grabbed the dish and emptied every piece in my backpack. Ate them all that night, and didn't feel sick. What's the worst thing you ever did?"

"The worst thing you ever did was steal candy from an old lady? Oh, come on. You're not even trying," Sam said. He and Vivy used to play this game all the time, and would have scorned any story so mild.

Cecilia stiffened, although her smile, now steely, remained. "I guess I'm not up to your standards."

"Not even close."

"Are you going to tell me something involving dead bodies?"

"Only one or two of them were actually dead." Sam pointed at her violin case. "You promised me a concert. I'll tell you after you play."

"I promised you a demonstration," she corrected him. He could see she was annoyed, but even so he liked looking at her, the features that had looked so strained in the heat now pretty and simple. A good face to see after a long illness, Sam thought, and then, teasing himself: a good face to wake up to. She rested the violin case on one of the tables and unlatched it, brought the instrument to her shoulder, and began to play arpeggios, but Sam stopped her.

"Not in the middle of the room. There's a stage here."

"You're very bossy today," she said, but a tiny smile caught her mouth, and she crossed the room and stepped onto the stage, adding, "If you turn on those hot lights, I'll kill you."

"Some other time. Now play. Play, damn you," he said in a dark, European accent. All he needed was a cape to snap. He seated himself, and Cecilia began again with the arpeggios, which sounded like rippling silk. Slender as dragonflies, her fingers skimmed over the strings. Sound hovered, then lifted, then vibrated through the room. In Sam swelled a stillness so complete that the absence of emotion was like an emotion. An incoherent trembling seized him, and he wanted, for no clear reason, to cry. What he wanted from Cecilia was not flirting, and was certainly not sex. What he wanted from Cecilia was this intimacy so deep it had no words. When she lowered her bow and said, "Can you hear it? That flattened-out quality in the middle range?" all he could say was, "Please don't stop playing."

Cecilia stepped back. She raised her bow again after a pause and began to play a real piece, not just exercises. Sam didn't know the title or the composer; he didn't know much about classical music. But he could hear how skillfully she played, the notes cascading from her violin. For weeks Sam had sat through fumbling, ham-handed performances that substituted enthusiasm for talent and angry, reactive sarcasm for vision. Now Cecilia's music surrounded him, and he closed his eyes, feeling his legs quiver, imagining he could feel his blood purl in its course. When she finished the first tune she immediately began another, something livelier, and he bowed his head. His gratitude sang like wine.

Sam was never sure just how long she played before they heard the rattle at the back door. He was already preparing to say, "We weren't doing anything wrong," as instinctively defensive as one of his kids, when Nancy walked out from the back, looked at the two of them in the unlit room, and said, "Well, hello."

"Are you dying of the heat? We were." Sam strained to make his voice sound conversational. "And we've got first shift today anyway, so we came on in."

"Does first shift include violin playing? I don't remember that." Nancy looked unhappily from Sam to Cecilia, whose violin dangled from her hand. "Vivy isn't here," Nancy said.

"Cecilia's been having trouble with her violin. She was demonstrating for me."

"You didn't even turn the lights on."

Sam hardly recognized Nancy's voice, usually so very sure of itself. This moment, while she stared at them and faltered, was his opportunity to redirect her attention, but his imagination had evaporated as soon as he heard the key in the lock. Half turning away, Cecilia went back to arpeggios, frowning at her violin while she played the same sequence of notes three times in a row. Four.

"It sounds fine to me," Nancy said.

Cecilia played the sequence more slowly, stopping when she got to one of the middle notes. Sam caught its strange, closed quality, like a note played inside a box. "Can you hear it?" she said. "Both of you. Can you hear how it flattens out?"

"Sure," Sam said. "Clear as a bell."

Nancy looked first at Cecilia, then at Sam, her hand lightly touching her throat. At the table beside Sam's she sat down and let her head sink into her hands. "I can't hear any problem with your violin. But I hear something."

"Easy, Nance. You're letting your imagination run away here," Sam said. "My house is an oven and Cecilia's apartment is too, so we came to the store to cool off. Cecilia brought her violin because it needs to be fixed. I asked her to play for me to see if I could hear what's wrong."

While he was still talking Cecilia started to play something quick and intricate, a tinkling soundtrack to fill the spaces between Sam's words. He said, "Actually, I'm glad you came in now. I've been meaning to talk to you about scheduling Cecilia to perform. Vivy's been rounding up acts from far away, but I think we should showcase talent from right here in the company." Cecilia switched to a fiddle tune, and Sam started to tap his foot.

Nancy stared at Sam's foot, then at his Howdy Doody grin, then at Cecilia, who kept frowning at her violin. "What would you have done if David or Vivy had walked in?"

"Asked their opinion about Cecilia's violin. Nancy, nothing is going on."

"Don't you *listen* at Life Ties?" To Sam's horror, Nancy began to cry, not even raising a hand to cover her eyes. "We try so hard to learn from one another. But maybe it can't be done. Maybe every one of us has to make the same stupid mistakes."

"Sweetheart, listen—we haven't made any mistakes. I know what you're thinking. We wouldn't do that," Sam said.

Cecilia stopped playing and said, "'We believe that our marriages are the center of our lives. Every choice we make must consider our marriages first, last, and foremost.'" Sam couldn't make out her tone, and he could see from Nancy's face that she couldn't, either.

Nancy's tone was clear, though: she was pleading. "Look. Even if you're pure as snow, even if the only thoughts you had were about Cecilia's violin—do yourselves a favor. Don't see each other anymore. And take vacations with Vivy and David right away."

"I don't really think we can do that." Sam gestured at the front window, where already a group of kids with skateboards and baggy shorts stood jostling one another, jumping the curb, peering into the dark store. "Maybe after summer, when things slow down. Right now we need every set of hands."

"I would take on extra shifts for you. So would Paul. We would work around the clock. Your marriages are more important than Natural High." She swallowed. "I can't believe I'm saying this."

In the room's silence Sam clearly heard the swish of Cecilia's long skirt when she stepped off the stage and pulled up a chair next to Nancy's. She pressed Nancy's hand between both of hers and said, "I have worked hard to be happy. Do you think I would endanger that? I know that Sam has a little crush on my violin. I've told David about it. Sam hasn't said one word that I've kept a secret from David."

"And there's nothing I haven't told Vivy," Sam said promptly, a statement mostly true. She certainly knew about his crush, as Cecilia apparently wanted to call it, on her violin.

"You don't know what you could be getting into," Nancy said bleakly.

"We're not getting into anything. We're right here, with you, in the air-conditioning." Sam heard the coaxing note in his voice, not so different from the tone he used to soothe Annie back to sleep after a bad dream.

It worked, too—Nancy sat up and finally wiped her hands across her wet, tanned cheeks. "I guess I should be glad your instinct was to cool off," she said. Sam and Cecilia laughed, ignoring the quaver in Nancy's voice. "It seems stupid now, but I came in this morning to work. I need the file copies of the order sheets for the last three weeks."

"We're low on carob again," Cecilia said. "I don't know why it's so popular in this weather. I hate to even think about it—so thick."

"We hunger for what nourishes us." Nancy stood up and walked into the back room, Sam and Cecilia a step behind her, watching while she pulled a sheaf of order forms from the rickety file drawer. "Two of our suppliers want to renegotiate. Sunrise Dairy says they're only taking larger orders from now on, and Good Greens is closing out its orchard, replanting all the land. We'll have to have a meeting about this if I can't get it squared away." She frowned at an order form. "What is it about orchardists? Why can't we ever find a reliable provider?"

"As a matter of fact, Nancy, I'm working on that," Cecilia said. Sam, gazing at her bland expression and Nancy's startled one, felt a quick jolt of delight, the same keen pride he felt when Annie outspelled boys two years older at the all-school spelling bee. "I've got a lead out," Cecilia said. "I'll let you know as soon as I have things in place. It's a little delicate."

"Cecilia Moore. You're just no end of surprises," Nancy said.

"Each individual holds the wealth of the universe," Cecilia said. The words sounded like they came off a napkin, although Sam didn't remember it. Nancy produced a watery smile, then took a clean form from her clipboard, dated it, and handed it to Cecilia. She straightened the rest and slipped them into her deep jute satchel. "You've still got an hour before opening. If you want to put the time to good use—" She knocked on the freezer's dull metal door.

"Good idea," said Cecilia.

Sam waited until Nancy was gone before he said, "Shit," which at least got Cecilia to shrug and sigh, her flower-pink lips pressed together.

"So," she said. "What's the worst thing you ever did?"

"Got caught doing nothing wrong by Nancy Califfe."

"You like to push, don't you?" she said.

"Am I pushing?" he said.

"You can stop now. Hand me that sponge."

They worked together silently until ten o'clock, when they opened the front door. Their quiet seemed companionable to Sam. He and Cecilia were linked in misunderstood righteousness, a basic propriety that afforded them more dignity the more they were misunderstood.

He didn't share these thoughts with Cecilia. He didn't actually say anything at all until after the freezer shelves, already clean, were shining, and after she had turned on the lights and the CD player and the first round of customers had straggled in for ice-cream and coffee drinks. He contented himself with watching the simplicity of her gestures, the way her long skirt wasn't baggy, as Vivy said, but natural and graceful, of a piece with the woman who wore it. She had integrity, a word Sam had so little use for that he had to search for several minutes to come up with it. She was coherent, like the few adults he'd admired when he was a child, those grown-ups who didn't treat him as a kid or as an adult, but simply as Sam, a person they could somehow see, even if Sam himself mostly couldn't.

When she had finished clearing a table and brought the sticky glasses back to the counter, Sam said, "I think I can get you two more violin students, if you've got room for any more."

"Always need the money. Whose little darlings do you have in mind?"

"Mine." Catching her look, he said, "No joke. They're ten and seven—that's old enough to be learning about music. And I know there isn't a better teacher in town."

"As a matter of fact, you don't know that," Cecilia said. "I'm very mean. Sandy McGee told me so. Don't you want to run this idea past Vivy? You're going to be giving her a lot to swallow all at once."

"Vivy knows me better than Nancy does. She knows she can trust me."

Cecilia tilted her head and looked at Sam, her light blue eyes assessing. He gazed back as evenly as he could for a man whose pulse had, none too gently, started to hurry. "Sure," she said. "You can rent them an instrument at Marshall's Music downtown. Just let me know when you want to start."

"Right away," Sam said, and Cecilia laughed.

"Better check with Laszlo and Annie first. Kids tend to have their own agendas."

"I'll check. And they'll start right away."

"Made a decision, have you?" she said.

"And it's overdue," he said.

Entr'acte (2)

Hard Pavements Make Good Roads.
Secrets Are Toxic.
Consistency, Commitment, Contentment.
No Goal = Black Hole.

Sometimes new people admit they come to the meetings not for the uplift, or the challenge, or the community. Staring at their shoes, they whisper, "I just wanted to hear how things turned out." Like that makes them different. The stories are the best part.

Everybody comes here with lies, some of them spectacular. Regular group members become connoisseurs, assessing style and completeness, watching for innovation. Outsiders are amazed at how good we get at sniffing out falsehoods, but they don't understand: once you know what to look for, you can see a lie from miles away. Only the truth is transparent, like glass, and even glass can be streaky.

Most people tell boring lies, so formless and obvious that a kid would spot them. A really good lie feels like a right angle: clear, symmetrical. The best lie we can remember came from the man who, when confronted, admitted he was sleeping with his wife's sister. It took us weeks to find out he was sleeping with her mother. Vivy was so impressed she whistled.

People lie about adultery, of course. They also lie about their jobs, saying they make more than they actually do, or less than they actually do, or not letting on that they've been fired—a common lie, right up there with sleeping with the neighbor. "I have to work late." "I didn't get the bonus." Work is like a greenhouse for lies, providing all those hours away from home, all those paychecks, bonus checks, raises, and cutbacks.

More often than you'd think people lie about money. One woman inherited $200,000 and never told her husband, just spent it a little at a time, when she took the notion. She spent $150 on a Baccarat glass that she kept on her nightstand, in case she woke up thirsty. He was out busting his can every day so they could pay the mortgage, and she was keeping two hundred grand like pin money. He might never have found out except she forgot to put aside money for taxes one year, didn't want to cut into her principal, and came to him for a loan. We liked this one so much we named a whole category the Baccarat Lie.

Then there are the lies people don't know are lies, the self-deception buried under layers of wishful thinking. These lies turn people into actors who give Oscar-level performances because they don't know they're performing. Huddling, sharp-eyed pinch-purses brag about their generosity. World-class narcissists explain how they work for— live for—others. A needle-thin woman who regularly puts in ninety hours a week at her law firm insists her greatest pleasure is lazy mornings with her cat and a mug of tea. Sometimes we have trouble keeping straight faces.

One man started coming to Life Ties with his fourth wife. God only knows whose idea it was. His first wife, he told us, had divorced him. His second ran off—we all loved this—with the milkman. Who even has a milkman anymore? The third got a sex-change operation. The latest quivered beside him at meetings, her lips swollen and purple, and wouldn't speak. "What is wrong with women?" he kept asking.

"I don't think the problem is women," Nancy said.

The man stood up and walked toward her, stopping when they were almost nose to nose. "Then what is wrong with you?" he snarled and stalked out, his little pooch-mouthed wife scuttling behind him.

We got up a pool, and several of us lost big when he and his wife came back the next week. He didn't say a word until the end, when he turned to her and croaked, "I—"

She nodded at him, and he said it again: "I—" He needed two weeks before he said, in front of all of us, "I like coming into the kitchen and seeing you in the mornings." They still come back from time to time.

As Nancy says, we want to be found out. We're here because we want to hear our own mouths speak the truth. We want to see our lives as we've never seen them before.

Every Lesson, the Same Lesson. Every Place, the Same Place. Every Goal, the Great Goal.

FIVE

Vivy

"No way," Laszlo said.

"Oh, way, all right," Sam said. "Serious way. Extreme way."

Vivy, who had been reading a contract for Elphenevel at the kitchen table, watched her son root through the freezer for a Popsicle. Sam stood one step behind him. He'd already tried to dragoon Annie, but she'd zipped off to her friend's house as soon as she heard Sam calling. Whenever she sniffed unwelcome news she turned into Houdini. Laszlo, every inch Sam's son, turned into a mule.

Sam said, "Playing the violin will be cool when you start to get good. You'll be a hit at parties. You'll be able to play whatever you want."

"I want to play Deathmaster VI."

"No problem. Right after you finish practicing your violin."

Laszlo sighed, impressing Vivy with the amount of scorn he was able to pack into the sound. "Where do you come up with this stuff?"

"It won't be so bad," Vivy said. "Cecilia Moore will be your teacher."

"Oh. Cecilia." Laszlo leaned back against the refrigerator and fluttered his hand above his heart. "Teach me, Cecilia."

Sam paused only a second before he stepped next to Laszlo and fluttered his hand in unison with his son's, the two of them fanning themselves like a couple of belles. Vivy kept a close eye on Sam's theatrically trembling eyelashes. She didn't know how much it cost him to clown like this, but she was interested in finding out.

"I yearn to play the violin. I long to play the violin," Sam crooned. "Teach me, Mrs. Moore, I beg of you."

Laszlo giggled. "In case you're interested, Dad, you're really weird."

"In case you're interested, son, you're going to be taking violin lessons. Your instrument is already on order."

"My instrument." Laszlo snorted and cut his eyes at Vivy, calculating what he could get away with. "My *instrument*."

"Your sister will be sharing it with you," Vivy said blandly.

"No sister shares my instrument!" he shrieked and whirled out of the kitchen, almost certainly to run to his friend's house to play a video game that featured five or six busty kickboxers. Vivy looked at Sam. "That didn't work so well."

"He's a kid. What did you think he was going to say, 'Hooray'?"

"Cecilia's going to have her work cut out for her."

"Cecilia has plenty of kids who don't want to be there. She calls them 'reluctant learners.' All we have to do is make sure Laszlo and Annie put in their half hour a day."

"This one's your lookout. I've already got my hands full." She gestured at the messy table: Elphenevel's contract to play an auditorium in Placerville, her laptop, her crowded notebook-calendar bristling with yellow Post-its, her scrap pages of notes and reminders, including a phone number for a new act, Norma's Big Band, which did steady business at VFW halls and was looking for more regional representation. Sam reached across the table to tap the calendar affectionately, another gesture that must have cost him.

"You of all people should see the value in music lessons."

"I do see the value. I just don't see the time."

"The kids can miss half an hour of Cartoon Network. Anyway, I'm not expecting you to be the one cracking the whip on them. Just don't undercut me, all right? Don't come in when they're supposed to be practicing and take them out for McDonald's."

"Jeez, Sam. Thanks for the vote of confidence."

He shrugged. "You're impulsive. That can be great sometimes. But I'm asking you to control your impulses around the kids."

"You make me sound like a child molester."

"I'm not talking about you, I'm talking about Laszlo and Annie. Self-reliance and self-control need to be built into a character. Music can teach that."

"Yoo-hoo. Sam. You can come down from Mount Olympus now."

"I've been thinking, that's all."

"I can see that," Vivy said, letting the point in her voice hover until Sam looked back at her.

"Coming on too strong?"

"A tad."

"Sorry." He raised an eyebrow. "One more thing? I think we should leave the radio on the classical station. I think it would be helpful." He opened the refrigerator and rummaged. "Is there any tea left?"

"Laszlo finished it. However, making more will help you build self-reliance."

Vivy kept her place at the table while Sam pulled the big tea pitcher from the sink, rinsed it out, and set water to boil. She pretended to study her calendar while he banged through cupboards looking for teabags. The silence in the kitchen was thickening. Sam wasn't an idiot. He knew he hadn't gone around preaching self-reliance before he fell prey to the charms of the superbly, self-reliant Cecilia Moore.

Any other man ripe for an infatuation would find a nymph, a creamy-faced, long-legged, high-assed creature who would flirt with him, madden him, give him a few dreams worth having. Vivy wouldn't have minded Sam dreaming about a nymph. But the notion that he was sighing over prudent, frugal Cecilia, devoted Life Ties member, once-a-month soup kitchen volunteer, earnest stick of a woman who dressed like a Puritan and belonged to the El Campo Arbor Society unsettled Vivy. What in the world could he be hungry for, if Cecilia Moore satisfied the craving? The best Vivy could do was hope the taste was fleeting and easily sated, like his occasional yen for pickles.

Pushing down her unease, she looked back down at the Elphenevel contract, the band's biggest so far. This time they would be opening for Recoil, a San Jose group with a local following. Recoil had gotten some national airtime with a song called "Bloody Dice." Laszlo had started shouting the refrain as soon as Vivy mentioned the gig. When Laszlo finished, Sam said, "Warble-O's looking better."

She'd been lucky to get Elphenevel the booking. Recoil's usual opener, Splended Citeez, refused to play Placerville because their drummer had been arrested there twice before on vice charges. Vivy had been interested. Who knew there were hookers in Placerville? The booking agent hadn't wanted to talk about it.

"The first year will be tough. Lots of scales," Sam was saying while he poured steaming water into the pitcher. "But once they get some skills it will be nice to have homemade music at night."

"Hope you still think so when Laszlo perfects his rendition of 'Bloody Dice,'" she mumbled. The contract went on page after page, a snarl of union stipulations and contingencies. Elphenevel would be bringing home $2,550 after Vivy's fifteen percent. Fredd's nephew told her admiringly that she was a shark.

She said, "This gig in Placerville—Laszlo wants to go, but I don't love that idea. I don't want to get there and find out there's chicken wire in front of the stage."

"I'll find a classical concert and take him to that. It'll be a whole new world to him."

"Forgive me if I'm raining on your parade, but our children like their old world." The phone rang before he could restart the rhapsody; he said, "Just give them the chance. That's all."

"Okay," Vivy said into the phone.

It rang nonstop all day—new acts, old acts, the fragile, widening web of community arts directors and managers. "You bet," Vivy said. "A family act with visual appeal. I have just the thing. You can count on me." She scheduled Fredd at grade schools, Norma's Big Band at a Labor Day bash. The calls tripped over one another, shoving Sam off to the side of her concentration. "I need a unique act people will remember. I hear you're the one to call," said one woman from the Feather River Arts League, and Vivy felt a bright spark of satisfaction.

At three o'clock, after Laszlo called to say he was with Annie at the rec center pool and they'd be ready to come home in an hour, she took a shower. When she turned off the water the phone was ringing again. Marteeny was already talking when Vivy picked up the receiver, rattling along so fast that words tangled in her mouth.

"I don't want to put you out because you've done so much for me and held out a hand to me and acted better than a friend, and I hate to ask you to do even more, but my fiancé keeps saying he wants to come down to El Campo with me even when I told him it's not right to thunder in on you this way with two of us instead of one. He doesn't even know you, but he keeps wanting to come, and said if he has to he'll stay in a motel, but he wished I'd just ask."

"For crying out loud, Marteeny. Of course he can stay here. We'd love to meet him."

"It's an imposition, I can see that, bad enough to have just me, but here I come with baggage."

"You're our friend. Don't you think we want to meet the man you're going to marry?"

"Just say the word. He can stay in a motel. He said so himself."

"Look, do you not want him to stay here with us?"

"It's just—" Marteeny said, "you don't know him. You don't even know me anymore. I'm afraid you're going to be awful disappointed. I've stiffened up, Vivy, if you know what I mean."

"Tell me about it. Sam and I are a hundred years old."

"I'm just not sure the gal you think you invited is the gal who's going to show up. And here I am lugging along this rancher you don't even know. Did I tell you he's a rancher?"

"It will be fine. He's not a space alien or anything, is he?" Vivy glanced at her watch and picked up her keys. By now Laszlo and Annie would be past impatience, into a ten-point sulk.

Marteeny paused to take a breath, then drawled, "Well, he wants to marry me. So he can't be exactly normal. Listen, you're sure about this?"

"Positive. Tell him we can't wait to meet him. Our casa, his casa. Don't worry about a thing."

Vivy ended the call and ran out to the car, knowing that Marteeny would, despite Vivy's assurances, keep worrying. For the next seven days Marteeny would sit in her kitchen and jitter, remembering all the people who had petted her tiny, tight, upside-down butt, many of them the same people she had, upright, gripped with her strong legs and kissed. Folks didn't forget an encounter like that.

Vivy remembered the grip of those legs herself. Clad in tie-dyed purple tights, Marteeny's quadriceps had felt as smooth and hard as two warm stones around Vivy's waist. Also warm were Marteeny's tiny hands massaging Vivy's shoulders. Marteeny's toes, flexible as blunt fingers, kneading Vivy's back. Marteeny's arm snagging Sam's wrist and pulling him to her. The noisy, bright memories tumbled out. Vivy closed her eyes and smiled.

As always, her past seemed very close. Like an overstuffed backpack, its contents jammed and poking out and tied with shoestrings, her old life rattled with every step she took, and Vivy would sooner die than put it down. She loved to remember the bad decisions, the insane ambitions, every folly and impulse. She liked to imagine her young self walking next to her and giving a little advice, a better friend than Vivy had found in life. That young Vivy had laughed when Nancy put "The Present Is Our Platform To Tomorrow" on a napkin. The present was nothing; a person could change it with a breath. Only the past was sturdy enough to stand on.

But now that she was a fiancée with a rancher and prospects, Marteeny wanted to pry her own past apart. She wanted never to have been that ardent girl, and she wanted all of those memorable embraces never to have occurred. As much as Vivy would have liked to console her friend, nothing could make her forget her memories of Teeny Marteeny, age seventeen, kissing everything in sight.

Vivy threaded her car through the blocks of traffic the bypass was supposed to have corrected. She was glad the rancher was coming. She was curious about him. How many men would set their cowboy hats for an expert kisser barely taller than the bedpost, a woman who, in the kitchen, hinged her elbows backward to grab the salt? Sam had

always said Marteeny was the closest he and Vivy came to running a
geek show.

Vivy expected a good return for Marteeny's performance at Natural
High. If things went well, Vivy would book her to come again in two
months. If things went very well, Vivy would pour some coffee and
remind Marteeny about the old days, the sheen her smile had always
taken on when the applause began. This fiancé might want Marteeny
to keep her loose ligaments offstage permanently. But if he didn't, Vivy
was prepared to hoist her back up onto the boards. Right off the bat,
Vivy could think of two venues that would like a contortionist.

She was getting into the rhythm of the old work, the details and
the little battles, the endless phone calls, the pink sheets documenting
load-in, load-out, head counts, and vandalism. The gossip. The lingo.
The checks. She hadn't needed long at all to get used to writing numbers in the deposit column. She'd bought sandals for Laszlo, three pairs
of shorts for Annie, and a blouse for herself. The rest of her promoter's
salary, close to $3,000 so far thanks largely to Elphenevel and in small
part to Fredd's state fair gig in Nevada, had gone straight to a savings
account, the first she'd ever had. The friendly bank teller had chattered
about her own two savings accounts—one for a car, she said, and one
for a house. What was Vivy saving for?

"Nothing specific," Vivy had said, smiling brightly at the teller's
bright smile. "Just saving. Jane Bryant Quinn says no household is secure without savings."

"It just helps you sleep better, doesn't it?"

It certainly did. For the first time in years Vivy was remembering
what security felt like. Every penny she put up made an exit from Natural High more possible. Already she was negotiating $15,000 plus con-
cessions for an Elphenevel concert in Vacaville; she had paid a design
student at the university $500 to design T-shirts. If she sold forty-two,
she'd be in the black. At night she pleasured herself by calculating her
and Sam's diminishing debt, a long, steep walk to daylight. Every time
she saved another hundred dollars, she took another step.

She still hadn't told Sam about this walk. She wanted to wait until she was sure of his attention. Twice she had told him Elphenevel was bringing in real money, but he made cracks about pimping for the fantasies of adolescent boys, missing the point. When Vivy mentioned finding a new house, one with two bathrooms, he hardly looked up from the TV. "Beyond our means, babe." As if their lives had been stuck on a pin, and they were allotted one bathroom and two crapped-out cars in perpetuity. Vivy had stared at him, then left the room. That moment had frightened her more than twenty speeches about Cecilia. Since then both glee and fear rang through her every time she filled out a deposit slip.

When she parked at the rec center and confronted her children's angry faces, she agreed to Cokes from the drive-through and fries, too, a rare concession. She drove home the way Annie liked, over the bumps, and let Laszlo turn the radio up. When they got back she reminded them only once to hang up their wet bathing suits, even though she knew she would be the one to fetch the suits, forgotten and sodden, from the bottom of the kids' backpacks. Whatever other pieces of her life weren't fitting together, at least she could give her children a good day.

They were giggling in front of the TV when Sam came home. "Yo," Vivy said from the kitchen. She heard Sam hit the mute on the TV and turn on the stereo, twiddling the dial until he could get K-Camp broadcasting some gluey symphony. The kids, of course, yelled. She strolled to the living room doorway in time to hear Sam say, "Give your old man ten minutes of pleasure. Then we'll revert to life as usual."

"We were *watching*," Laszlo said. "I want to see how it comes out."

"I was *listening*," Sam said. "In the car. I want to hear how it comes out."

"I'll bet you were listening because Cecilia told you to," Annie said.

"Very funny, miss. I don't only do things because somebody tells me to. Sometimes—once a year or so—I do things because I want to."

Sam had his eyes closed, and one finger traced tiny lines in midair in time to the music. Scowling at the silent TV, Laszlo got to his feet in front of Sam and mirrored his gestures, his finger filigreeing the air, his face a mask of solemn rapture. Annie giggled. Sam's eyes popped open. Caught, Laszlo swept his arms as if he meant to dispel a fog in the room.

"You could try listening," Sam said. Anger was packed into his voice like clothes in a suitcase. Hearing it, Laszlo swept his arms again.

Sam said, "You could try opening yourself to something new."

"Like you're giving me a choice."

"I'm giving you a gift."

"I wanted to see the end of my show," Laszlo said.

"Fine." Sam picked up the clicker and turned the sound back on, over the stereo. Noise—talk, bouncy advertisement music—filled every corner of the room. "There."

"It's over," Laszlo said. "You made me miss it."

"We're both in the same boat then, aren't we? Except yours will be on reruns." Sam looked up at Vivy. "What?"

She shook her head. Updates she might have provided about Marteeny and the fiancé stayed locked in her mouth. She stared at Sam until he plopped onto the sofa beside Annie—Laszlo, still angry, shifted away—and stopped looking strange to her.

A WEEK LATER, IN the afternoon, Marteeny called from a gas station half an hour north of town. "We're almost there! It's really happening! Last chance to send us to a motel!"

"Do you want to break my heart? I *vacuumed*," Vivy said. "Hurry on in, now." After she hung up she checked the bathroom to make sure the kids hadn't used the clean towels. Once Marteeny arrived at the house she would relax. They would have a few drinks, get to talking, and the last five years would melt. The fiancé didn't have to change everything. Vivy had rehearsed several stories that would be safe to tell him.

When she heard the rough crunch of tires in the driveway, she hurried out, and stopped two steps out of the door. The stout woman in a blue pantsuit who lowered herself from the dinged-up, dusty pickup was some stranger. She looked like a bake sale organizer. A PTA member, a subscriber to *Life,* a garden club secretary. She didn't look like Marteeny, that was for sure. She looked like Marteeny's mother.

The woman paused beside the truck, and Vivy watched her take in the little bungalow. Through Marteeny's eyes Vivy scanned the crunchy grass and the grease spot on the front steps where Laszlo had tried to fix the chain on his bike. Beside the stain sat the basket of lavender-blue impatiens Vivy bought that morning. And then Vivy herself, standing half in the shadow of the concrete porch. "Viv-VEE!" Marteeny cried, the old scream, and Vivy ran toward her, arms wide.

"Look at you! Just look at you!" Marteeny half-wept into Vivy's arm, although she was holding on too tight for Vivy to see anything. Being hugged by Marteeny was still like being hugged by a python. "You haven't changed at all."

"Sure I have. I have crow's feet."

"You're skinny as a mink," Marteeny said happily, backing off to gaze. "A sight for sore eyes. Good enough to eat."

"Down, girl. You don't want to wear out all your compliments before Sam gets home."

"Sam!" Marteeny hugged her plump arms and rocked from side to side. Vivy grinned back, an expression she was pretty sure reflected pleasure less than shock. From her dumpling feet in their tiny high heels to the top of her head, which bore a permanent wave so recent each curl was still clenched, Marteeny was a solid packet of flesh—dense, round as a cherry tomato. The sexy sprite who used to pass the time balanced on her neck while working her legs into half hitches flashed through Vivy's brain, then flicked away like a TV image gone dark.

"Time to meet mister man," Marteeny said, taking Vivy's hand and leading her to the truck where the fiancé stood waiting for them. He was stout too, his belly pushing out the front of his white, snap-down shirt. But even with the gut he had the air of a powerful man, someone who could lift and haul. Black pants and black beard and black, thinning hair and black string tie: he looked like a cowboy singer. Better: a cowboy singer's agent.

The man waited until Vivy was directly in front of him, then held out his hand. "Court Hellerman. Tina's been telling me about her days onstage. Pretty interesting. I wish I could have seen it." He slapped Marteeny's rump. "She's a good dancer—you don't have to show her the steps twice. So I wasn't surprised when she told me she used to be part of a circus."

"Don't you start, now," Marteeny said.

He said to Vivy, "At first I called it her days with the freak show. She set me straight."

"That's right," Marteeny said.

"Real, decent entertainment that anybody could bring a family to see," he said.

"That's right," Vivy said, intercepting a nervous look from Marteeny and ushering the couple out of the hot sun before they all got heat stroke. She had beer in the refrigerator but Court asked for soda, if it wouldn't put her out, and Marteeny said the same for her. Vivy suspected Marteeny could use the beer, but she brought out two Cokes and a Bud for herself on a tray, along with a bowl of pretzels. Marteeny took a handful and piled them neatly on her napkin, sucking the salt off one pretzel at a time while Court talked.

"People have short memories. This isn't the worst heat we've ever had. Five years ago, the drought started in February and I was selling off stock in June. That was a hard year. But people don't remember. They think this is the worst we've ever lived through."

"Well, it's pretty bad," Vivy said.

"I'm just saying we're all survivors."

"Survivors. I like the sound of that," Vivy said. "Makes me feel like a pioneer."

"You would have been good in a covered wagon," Marteeny said. She sat with her head cocked, as attentive as a wren. "You would have kept everybody's spirits up. 'You don't want to quit before you see what's on the other side of that mountain, do you?'"

"You never know. Something terrific might be over there," Vivy said, then added, looking at Court, "Marteeny used to call me the curious cat."

"Tina says you're the best friend she ever had."

"She's one in a million. But I guess I don't need to tell you that."

"Sure you do," Marteeny said. "You should tell him I'm one in two million. That's what Sam used to say about you, remember? 'Vivy's a limited edition. Go down to L.A. and comb it end to end, you won't come up with but two or three more like her.'"

"Of course, L.A. is bigger now," Vivy said.

"Haven't changed," Marteeny said. "When is Sam getting home?"

"As soon as he can get loose from the store. He can't wait to see your show—he was asking me whether you're going to do that old trick where you stand on one arm." What Sam had in fact said that morning was he hoped Vivy wasn't planning to make her fortune off Marteeny's visit. "Who wants to see a fat contortionist?" he had said.

"Me," Vivy had said. "More than ever. Don't you?"

Now Marteeny blushed and bit her lip, and Court said, "You could stand on one arm?"

"These folks haven't seen me in years," Marteeny said. "They remember when I didn't weigh but eighty-six pounds."

"I'll bet you can still do the split, though," Vivy said brightly. "That used to hurt to watch."

When Marteeny paused, Vivy's heart dropped. If Marteeny couldn't stand on her hand and she couldn't do the split, what exactly did she plan to do on the stage tonight?

Marteeny swallowed the pretzel she'd been licking, then stood up as if to leave the room, stepping around the coffee table. Positioning herself in front of Vivy, she rolled up her pants, stepped out of her shoes and said, "Like this?" while she dropped smoothly into a ruler-straight split, her right leg pointed ahead of her, her left behind. Through the trouser fabric, tight as casings, Marteeny's plump thighs looked relaxed, even though Vivy's own thighs twitched just looking at her.

Court whooped and applauded. "Isn't that something? Isn't that something? This girl just kills me."

"Or like this?" Marteeny said serenely, pulling herself upright again only to slide back down, this time straddle position, her legs pointing to her right and left like oars.

"No one else can come close to this," Court said, beaming. "Sometimes Tina will get all weepy and blue because she can't cook. 'Hell, honey,' I tell her, 'I can fry up a steak. But you're the only girl I ever knew who can point her legs all around the compass. You're a treasure.' I'm right, Viv, aren't I? Tell her so."

"You're right, all right," Vivy said, resisting the impulse to lean over and give the man a squeeze.

Wearing a dreamy smile—maybe she was listening to their talk, maybe not—Marteeny reached over and wrapped her hand around her right foot, then lifted her leg straight off the ground. Vivy remembered when Marteeny could lift the leg without the help of her hand, but the move was still amazing. Without any visible strain she pulled her leg straight up, so it grazed her ear, then bent her knee and tucked the leg quickly behind her head, letting out a grunt so soft only someone standing right beside her, as Vivy was, could have heard it.

Then the kitchen door banged and Sam sang, "I know who's here!" the sudden noise startling Marteeny. She jerked, lost her balance and faraway expression, and, before Vivy could grab her, the tiny woman pitched forward onto the carpet. As Sam came whistling into the room, Vivy tried to pull Marteeny up again, but she couldn't get the leverage she needed, and Marteeny's arm just rotated in its socket. Vivy tugged again, but the woman, helplessly laughing into the carpet, was dead weight. Not until Court kneeled on the other side could he and Vivy pull the snorting, hiccupping Marteeny up and help her unhinge her leg.

"Oh, man. What do you think? Was that embarrassing enough?" Marteeny said, scrambling to her feet and straightening her clothes and stepping into her shoes more or less in one motion. Her face was red as a plum, but she still managed to hold out her arms to Sam. "Let's hope it goes better tonight."

"I've burst in on you lots of times. You never used to be scared,"

Sam said, bending to kiss her cheek, then wrap her up in his long arms. Watching their cheerful embrace, Vivy felt her low hum of unease subside. Sam could grouse as much as he wanted; he still remembered who his old friends were.

Vivy said, "Sam, this is Court, Marteeny's fiancé."

"You are one lucky man," Sam said.

"I like to think so," Court said. "It's nice to meet you. Tina says you and Viv hung the moon."

"I didn't think word had gotten out about that," Sam said.

"No secrets," Vivy said.

"We didn't stop until we were sure the moon would shine straight down on Marteeny," Sam said.

"Get out," Marteeny said.

"Best work we ever did," Vivy said.

Court looked from face to face as if he were following a tennis match. "I like to watch people who've known each other a long time. You learn things."

"Let us know what you find out," Sam said. "Vivy and I spend half our time missing our lessons. Who can I get a drink?"

"I could do with another soda," Court said, resuming his heavy place on the sofa, Marteeny perched beside him. "If it wouldn't put you out."

"Coming right up," Sam said, heading out to the kitchen and returning with a huge bowl full of Cokes and beers and ice, his old party tactic, so nobody had to keep making refrigerator runs. Holding out a fresh Coke, he said to Court, "You surprise me. I always heard ranchers liked whiskey."

"They do, mostly," Court said. "I've seen more than one man drink his ranch right out from under him. I decided to be more careful than that. I have a bride to think of."

"Riskier than a ranch," Sam said.

"That's what I thought," Court said while Vivy said, "Now, Sam. Don't frighten the man."

"I don't scare easy," Court said.

"Good. That's the number one rule for marriage," Sam said.

"You never get scared?" Court said.

"Not so far," Sam said while Vivy said, "We're working on it."

"Two peas," Marteeny said.

"Black-eyed and snow, maybe," Vivy said. "So how did you two meet?"

Marteeny wound through a story involving neighbors, somebody's sister, and a potluck supper while Court quietly beamed at her. The wedding would be small, Marteeny said shyly, a private gathering in Court's living room. "I wish we could have some kids there, though," she said. "It doesn't feel right without any kids."

"You can rent ours," Sam said. "We'll charge less if you keep them."

"Get out," Marteeny said.

"They're at a pizza party, but they're coming to the show," Vivy said. "Laszlo swears he remembers you. He says you gave him a Milky Way backstage once and made him promise not to tell me."

"I never," Marteeny said.

"Sounds just like you," Sam said. "Winning over a new beau."

"She wouldn't do it now," Court said, and swigged from his Coke. "She wouldn't go behind your back."

"That's true," Marteeny said, ducking her head as if she were admitting something. "I'm all on the up-and-up now. Secrets are—" She paused, searching for a word.

"Toxic," said Vivy and Sam together. Vivy glanced over and put on a rueful face to match his.

"You guys working up a new act?" Marteeny said.

"Sprucing up the old one," Sam said.

"We go to meetings. There are all these slogans," said Vivy.

"What kind of meetings?" Court said. "I like stuff like this."

"Kind of a support group. Through a church," said Vivy.

"You testify?" Court's face above the wiry black beard was bright, and his smile showed big, straight teeth.

"You could say that," Sam said. "Sunday night meetings. People come in and tell their stories. You hear some amazing things."

"You guys are kidding," Marteeny said. "Court, don't listen to them. They're pulling our legs."

"Actually, we're not," Vivy said. "Scary, isn't it?"

"This must be some group," Marteeny said.

"Honey, give them a chance," Court said, leaning forward now, rolling his sweating Coke can between his hands. "So what do you talk about?"

"People talk about what's going on at home. If you like gossip, it's unbeatable," Vivy said.

"Most of the time couples come because things have gotten rocky, but that isn't a requirement. The idea is a whole group of people can solve problems better than just two angry people by themselves." Sam flicked his gaze back to Vivy as he spoke, and she nodded.

"That sounds like a real resource," Court said. "I've always held for the wisdom of the group over the impulse of the one. When you work by yourself, you think about these things. One fellow by himself, with nobody to talk sense to him, will go off half-cocked. I'll bet 90 percent of murders wouldn't be committed if there was a group of people to think about the killing, not just one."

"Court, Vivy and Sam don't need to hear your speech," Marteeny said.

"Aw, honey. Everybody needs to hear my speech." He squeezed her thigh, then nodded apologetically. "These things are important to me."

"Do you want to come with us? You could come to a meeting. You don't have to pay or sign up or anything," said Vivy, catching too late Marteeny's frozen expression. On her napkin lay the shards of several snapped pretzels. "You don't even have to talk. Most newcomers don't. But it's fun to hear what people have to say."

"Court always talks," Marteeny said faintly, and then more vigorously, "Today is Thursday. We can't stay here till Sunday."

"Why not?" Sam said.

"You could. You'd be welcome." Vivy tried to meet Marteeny's eye, but she sat unmoving beside Court, her face stiff.

"I think this is the kind of thing Tina and I need," Court said. "I'd like to know how she's really feeling about being a rancher's wife."

"I tell him all the time," Marteeny said. "I tell him I've dreamed of having a quiet life, living with real ties to a place. Shoot, cooking all day sounds good to me. As you can see." She flicked her hip. "But he keeps thinking there's something more, that I've got secret feelings I'm hiding from myself."

"I've lived up there a long time. I've seen marriages give out. A man wakes up to a note that his wife has gone back to cable TV and coffee shops. It's hard country—not much for women," Court said.

"Court, what if we go to this meeting and I swear in front of Sam and Vivy and everybody that I want to marry you? If I swear I want to share your life and hear about cattle every night and live a hundred-twenty miles from the nearest department store? If I promise I know what I'm looking at and it still doesn't scare me off? Then will you believe me?"

"Going to a meeting like this is an opportunity," he said. "No telling what we might find out. It's never a bad thing to learn."

"As you do love to tell me," Marteeny said, finally smiling and tapping her fingers on the back of Court's broad, raw-looking knuckles.

"Well, this is a bonus for us," Vivy said. "I just hope you don't get too bored. After Marteeny's performance, there's not going to be much shaking around here. El Campo isn't exactly Manhattan."

Marteeny hooted. "This is the bright lights. You don't know where we live."

"See? That's what I'm talking about," Court said. "That right there."

"I wasn't complaining. I was stating a fact. You yourself said that after a while the cows know more about you than your friends do."

"I was making a joke. You—you're thinking about it, going out to the pasture and eyeing the stock like you're figuring out who's going to be your best friend. That doesn't tell me you're feeling good about the future." Court looked at Sam, then Vivy, and spread his hands before him. "We're some kind of guests, aren't we? First we force you to let us stay here two extra days, then we have a fight in your living room. Guess you won't invite any other ranchers in."

"Ha," Vivy said. "That was a fight? You two are pikers."

Marteeny said, "I used to hear you and Sam clear across parking lots. Once you guys were backstage while I was doing my act and Vivy yelled, 'Well then, *take* the goddamn G-string' just as I was switching arms on a handstand. I started to giggling and came down like a sack of potatoes."

"I remember that," Vivy laughed, and then looked at Court, whose mouth was set unhappily. "The G-string was on a raccoon. It was very funny at the time."

"I can see that," he said.

Vivy pointed at him and said to Marteeny, "You have gotten yourself a very polite man."

"Tell me about it," she said.

Vivy looked at Sam. "We should take lessons."

"Nobody's politer than we are," he protested, sitting up straight and making a solemn, butler's face. "Gallant Sam, Gracious Vivy, beloved by the multitudes. Especially if the multitudes get to eat."

"I'm fine," Court said quickly.

"Sam's just trying to get me hopping," Vivy said, standing. "A little husbandly nudge. I hope you both like lasagna. I got some early garden tomatoes that want to be used."

"Tomatoes! In June. Imagine that, Court," Marteeny said.

"Where'd you get tomatoes?" Sam said.

"David. He planted early ripeners. Would you like to hear about them?"

Sam laughed. "How do you suppose Cecilia stands it?"

"As I understand it, by playing her violin."

A sudden tension, new and glinting, quivered between them. After a moment Court said, "We won't see tomatoes until August, and then only for three weeks. You folks are living in the Garden of Eden."

"Watch out for talking snakes," Vivy said.

"See many of those around here?"

"Yesss," Vivy said, so she could exit on a laugh. Still, she couldn't help noticing that when she poured oil into the hot pan the whole kitchen hissed.

SIX

Cecilia

AT FIVE MINUTES TO eight on Sunday night, Life Ties was just about ready to start. The couple assigned setup had arranged the metal fold-ing chairs in a semicircle and distributed this week's pamphlet. At the refreshment table, Cecilia poured water into the coffeemaker and slotted the filter into place, listening to the rustle and talk from the group—twelve couples tonight, a good crowd. They laughed quietly, exchanged names. The ones getting along with their spouses held hands or slung their arms across chair backs. David was sitting in that group too, pointing at her and smiling. She smiled back and held up the carafe: did anybody want some, while it was fresh? David nodded, so she poured him a cup. They were getting along.

She'd already told him the story about her improvised concert for Sam, a story that took as long to tell as it had taken to act out. Ten minutes of Bach, Nancy's stunned face, how foolish Cecilia had felt, although David protested that she hadn't been foolish at all. According to David, she had done nothing less than decent. According to David, playing the violin for Sam had been an act of kindness.

Cecilia had not gone on to tell David how hungrily Sam had looked at her, and how she'd felt her skin shine under his gaze. She did not discuss the way she'd played an extra piece even though Sam would have settled for one, and she didn't mention that she revisited the memory two or three times a day. She wasn't about to talk about the memory tonight, either, but she was glad to be at the meeting.

94

Uplifting talk would be good for her. Good for Sam, too, if he ever arrived.

Battered copies of the Statement of Beliefs were already being passed around before Sam hurried in with a bearded man in worn black pants and a white shirt: the contortionist's fiancé. Vivy had introduced him after the show on Friday night, but Cecilia had been staring at the contortionist's strangely long arms and missed his name. Now the man looked around the store with an eager face, and Sam leaned over to confide something to him. A beat later Vivy scrambled in, her arm around the contortionist's plump shoulders. Marteeny, Cecilia remembered. Wearing tight purple trousers and clutching an egg-shaped handbag, the tiny woman had the look of something encased, nothing like the witty, freewheeling spirit who had, upside down, drunk half a glass of tea and then strolled across the stage on her hands. Cecilia dropped into the seat beside David and pointed toward the newcomers.

"This should be interesting," she said.

"How do you mean?"

"How often do we get showbiz people in here? I hope it's not one of those meetings where we wind up picking apart the slogans. I'd hate for them to get bored."

"They won't get bored," David said.

Cecilia sharply stopped talking. Her husband's face, gazing at the group, was an arrangement of even surfaces, with no place to hide an emotion or secret. If he were unhappy, she would know. Still, her small guilt flicked like a feather.

Nancy, the group leader for the night, strode to the front of the store, called out, "Greetings!" and then led off reading the Statement of Beliefs: "We believe that we are put on this earth to improve it. Through our marriages, we become models."

Sam and Vivy and their guests were seated directly across the semicircle from Cecilia and David. Sam recited the Statement from memory while Vivy shared her copy with Marteeny, who sat upright as a stanchion, her feet two inches above the floor. From time to time the fiancé, on her other side, touched her arm.

"Every choice we make must consider our marriages first, last, and foremost." The fiancé nodded as if the words were old friends; he tapped the paper for emphasis. Some people new to the group used the Statement as a lash, staring holes through their partners during all the parts about sacrifice and commitment. But the man's pitted, rough-featured, purely interested face apparently saw nothing but promise in the pledge. After the Statement was finished and Nancy asked if anyone was ready to speak, he came right to his feet.

"I'm Court Hellerman and I'm here with my wife-to-be, Tina. I know you all are here to talk about marriages-that-are, not marriages-to-be, but I'd just like to tell you I like the things you say, and I hope Tina and I can make the kind of marriage you're talking about."

David murmured, "Nice guy," and Cecilia agreed. Just having the man in the room made the rest of them sit up straighter, as if they weren't a bunch of exhausted warriors negotiating their bits of battle-scarred turf. When he went on to thank them for letting him come and said how much he hoped to learn, she had to pinch off her impulse to clap. Two others went ahead and did. Startled, Court smiled, then tipped an imaginary hat.

"This is nice," Nancy said. "It's good to be reminded of where we started."

"Before we learned," cracked somebody on the far side of the circle, and people laughed.

Nancy shrugged and said, "Right. Before we learned."

"Girlfriends," said a woman whose name Cecilia could never remember.

"Boyfriends," said the man next to her.

"Girlfriends *and* boyfriends," said Louise, who had been coming once every few months for years. Cecilia had the quick desire to get Court and Marteeny out of the room. They seemed too kind for the restless mood that crackled around the room.

"Laugh if you want," Court said. "I want to learn. Tina too. That's what we're here for."

Nancy crossed the room to stand before him. Her smile was tender.

"What kind of marriage are you looking for, Court?"

"I like the clarity you all have," he said. "And community. Every-body standing together. Brick on brick: that's how you build anything."

"Every brick level and secure," Nancy nodded. "By coming here before your wedding, you and Tina can make sure your foundation is perfect."

"Hang on to a couple of those bricks," a man said. "You'll want to throw them later."

Ignoring him, Nancy kept smiling at Court. "It takes work. Are you ready to work?"

The room slowly quieted until the only sound was the whistle of the air-conditioning. Already the coffee, sitting on the burner, smelled sour. Court said, "Ma'am?"

"She means, what questions do you have for Tina?" asked a man with a goatee, a Life Tie-er for six months or so. He leaned toward Court. "Do you have any fears you haven't shared?"

"Are there things you haven't asked about?" added the man's wife, a tidy woman with neat hair and shoes.

Cecilia had heard the questions dozens of times, but never before had they sounded so bullying. She tried to send a sympathetic glance to Court, but he wasn't looking her way.

Nancy said, "You don't need to say anything, of course, unless you're ready to. But this is a safe place, if you're ready."

"She's the girl for me. When she said she'd marry me, I couldn't believe my luck."

"But then you wake up the next day, or a month later, and you start to wonder, 'Who is this person? Do I really know what I need to know?'" Nancy said, inexorable.

Court's pleasant expression took a few moments to dissolve. He frowned and twiddled his thin beard. Beside him Marteeny sat im-mobile, her jaw so tight that she could have driven nails with it. Even David, when Cecilia glanced at him, looked disturbed. "There's plenty that I don't know about Tina," Court said slowly. "There's plenty she doesn't know about me. That's all right. We've got a lifetime to find things out. Where's the fun of waking up with somebody every day of your life if she doesn't stand a chance of surprising you?"

Vivy said, "That's all you need to know, Court. That's more wisdom than anything else you'll hear here. It will get you through the first ten years of marriage, and by then you'll know if you need anything else."

Court twisted a few strands of his beard into a spike and kept looking at Nancy. "But I know what you're getting at. Tina's got a past. I've wondered about that. I figure she'll tell me whatever she thinks I need to know."

"Are you asking her now, Court? Is this your way of asking her to tell you?"

Marteeny's eyes were closed, and her hands were clamped along the top of her handbag. Vivy was the one who said, "I didn't hear him asking anything. I hear *you* asking."

"Often we need help expressing ourselves, especially at first," Nancy said. "Not everyone communicates as freely as Vivy." She got a small laugh for that. Everybody was looking at Court, who was looking miserably at Marteeny, who was looking at the ground.

"I guess we're in it now," he said. "Tina? You know everything there is to know about me—my high school sweetheart went down to the city, and then I was lonely until you. Is there anything you need to tell me?"

Marteeny's voice was so tiny that everyone in the room leaned toward her. "I used to kiss people."

Court's face took a moment to shift expressions. Then he looked like the sun coming up. "I was ready for worse," he said.

"I mean, it started with kissing. And it was a lot of people."

"How many people?" asked the tidy woman.

Marteeny's voice grew even smaller. "A hundred?"

Court opened his mouth and shut it again. The radiance began to drain from his face. "That's a little hard to hear," he said.

"I—that was a different person."

"It was," Vivy said.

Court rocked lightly forward on his chair. "Did you kiss Sam?"

Marteeny nodded. Court needed a long moment before he asked, "The juggler?" and she nodded again.

"Court, all this is old. Gone. It belongs to some different Marteeny." Vivy's face was blazing. "Look at her. You know this woman."

Marteeny patted Vivy's arm. Then she raised her face to Court, her lips parted, her eyes wet. "That's what there is to know."

"Truth is the start of healing. Secrets are toxic," said the man with the goatee, whom Cecilia wanted to slap. Court was having his face mashed into the start of healing. He didn't need a slogan to help him identify the experience.

Court lifted his face and looked not at Marteeny, but at Nancy. "I guess this was what you were driving at."

Nancy's face—broad at the brow and cheeks, narrow at the chin, a perfect valentine—was so inviting that Cecilia realized anew, pointlessly, how beautiful the woman was. What a horror she was. "Don't think that we only share the hurtful things. We share our uplift, too. Our vision. Lately I've been visioning snowshoeing with Paul up a mountain, both of us helping each other, pushing each other until we get to the top, where we can look down and see the whole world. We pitch camp there, and then have sex that lasts all night." She smiled as if she were giving Court a gift. Court, like most of the people in the room, looked at the floor.

"Do you see what I'm saying? You can tell Tina and all of us where you hope to go with her. You need to tell her that."

"Right this minute, she can snowshoe to the top of your mountain all by herself and stay there," Court said. "Since you ask."

"Court, don't do this," Vivy said.

"You all expect a lot out of a man, you know that?"

Nancy talked into the long pause that followed. "We trust the wisdom of the group to see what we by ourselves can't see. We come here for hope and encouragement. Why else would we come?"

"To keep from killing our husbands when we find out that they've spent half the savings account," said a woman in running shorts sitting beside Vivy. She and her husband had been to Life Ties a few times before—Eloise? Elena? She stood and nodded at Court. "Are you finished? I don't want to cut you off. But if you're done, I have something I'd like to share."

Court managed to nod, and the woman said, "'Every decision made alone is a betrayal.'" Then, ticking off items on her fingers like an accountant, she listed the many financial betrayals of her husband, a balding man in jeans and a button-down shirt who sat without expression as the list continued. The woman's confident voice filled every corner of the room with its faintly threatening Slavic accent. If she'd noticed that Court and Marteeny's lives had just exploded, she didn't appear to care.

The real estate limited partnership, the woman said. The shopping center. Shares in an industrial park. Not once stopping to consult her, even though he knew she could help him make an informed decision. *Because* he knew she could help him make an informed decision.

Cecilia let her gaze light back on Court and Marteeny, their eyes glassy and faces gray. They had never been more united. If Cecilia had seen them beside the road, she would have called an ambulance, describing two people who looked hurt, perhaps beaten, perhaps robbed.

Other couples came to Life Ties in the grip of raw discontent, fueled by some event terrible enough to push them into this room full of strangers. They came enraged, craven, their mouths twisted with disappointment. Their lives, once so simple, now bulged with suspicion. Life Ties helped those people. Like a scalpel, the meetings peeled away malignancies—resentment, anger, peculiar and destructive fantasies. But Court had brought delight to this meeting. Cecilia looked at David, who listened without expression.

The woman jackhammered away, from bad real estate investments to the cheap gabardine suit that hadn't lasted a season, his bowser of a car, strawberries on sale that went bad before they could finish them. "Oh, come on," Cecilia said, and David slid his hand across hers. Hush.

"It's a pattern," the woman insisted. "It's a faith issue. He doesn't want to have faith in me. And now I can't have faith in him." She turned so Cecilia could see the sculpted muscles in her thighs; she was probably off training for marathons while her husband made another despairing purchase. "Just last week he comes home and tells me, 'Harmony Orchards,' as if the name will make everything okay. The place is a payroll shambles—it didn't even turn a profit last year. He didn't buy into an orchard, he bought into the trees in some guy's backyard."

"Actually, it was a shrewd purchase. The company is changing its management," David said. "You'll want to hang on to those shares."

Cecilia stared at her husband, who gazed back with the minute smile he used when he wanted to surprise her. Across the room the financial woman's face was angry and pinched.

"I was talking."

"I have information that can help you."

"I don't need your information."

"Fine." David shrugged, and his mouth flattened out. This was how he fought.

"David, would you like to speak?" Nancy said, and the other woman said, "I was *talking*."

"As good a time as any," he said, rising. "I started going up to Mineville a few weeks ago. I heard about an opening they had for an orchardist, part-time. I knew Cecilia would want me to take the job, but I didn't want to say anything to her until I'd seen the place. It's a very solid operation that just needs a little time. I'm excited about the possibilities there."

"You already knew? I was working out all kinds of strategies to coax you into going up there." Cecilia giggled, a first in this room.

"What exactly are we talking about here?" Nancy said. Her voice was going up like an express elevator, and bright, rosy patches appeared high on her cheeks. "You announce you've secretly taken a new job as if Cecilia should thank you."

"Thank you," Cecilia said loudly, hoping Court and Marteeny could hear. But they weren't showing any interest in David's new job. Marteeny had slid down half an inch in her chair. She popped her thumb in and out of joint.

"I'm telling you there's a difference between a secret and a surprise," David said.

A woman laughed. "My husband would agree with that. He secretly refinanced our house so he and his girlfriend could spend two weeks at Club Med. Then I found out. Surprise!"

David was saying, "That's not what I mean," while Paul stood up. His face, always stark, looked like pure bone, free of flesh or muscle. He said, "David, I wish you'd come to the group and said, 'I'm thinking about taking a new job.' I wish you'd let us know."

Paul walked toward David, and Cecilia glanced again nervously at Court and Marteeny, who should not have to witness this. If Paul came within five feet of David, Cecilia would step between them.

Paul typically held his peace at meetings. Sometimes three or four weeks of meetings would pass when he seemed to doze, or woolgather, or let his silent presence offer whatever support anyone might find. He was content to let someone else do the leading. But when he was led into a discussion of his own marriage, his anger ignited, carbonizing any subject in reach: chores, bills, shirts that shouldn't have gone in the dryer. Cecilia had seen him leave Nancy staggering, literally unable to speak. When she finally found words again, the screaming could be heard across the street—as could, still later, the sounds of their love-making, or at least so a few Life Tie-ers always claimed.

"What you did is completely against the spirit of the group," Paul said. "You, me—all the partners are pledged to the company. That means the company comes before anything else."

"The store needs a steady supplier," David said.

"We need trust and communication more. That seems to be the topic of tonight's meeting." Paul looked at Court and Marteeny. "Does anybody here agree with David?"

"No," the financial woman said crisply. "No," echoed a couple sitting beside her. "I can't believe you didn't know better by now," said the man with the goatee, who'd gone to get some of the brackish coffee.

"Oh, Jesus, Paul," said Vivy.

Cecilia looked across the room at Sam, who was looking at her, and she looked at Marteeny, who was plastered against the back of her chair as if she'd been slammed there. Pale as a moth, Court drew himself to his feet.

"I'm a newcomer here, and I may be out of line." His voice shook.

Still looking at David, Paul said, "I think an apology is in order."

Court went on doggedly, "But sometimes an outsider can bring a fresh vision. I'll just tell you, I think being able to trust a fiancée is about the most important thing I know. I admit that right now I feel like I just swallowed a boot. But I'd still hate to find myself in a spot where, if I was married, my wife couldn't go off and try a job that appealed to her. It's a marriage. She doesn't have to punch a time clock."

"That's right," Vivy said. "Court has it right, and he hasn't even been married yet."

"I really don't see any reason to apologize," David said.

Paul broke in again. "If you tell Cecilia you went to the hardware store instead of coming straight home, why should she believe you? Secrets lead to secrets. You've come to meetings long enough to know that. Now that you've secretly gone out and gotten a job, what will keep you from going out and secretly getting yourself another woman?"

Her voice burning with laughter, Vivy said, "Paul, that's the most hilarious thing I've ever heard. Even from you."

"You could try to be helpful here," Paul said to her.

"I am being helpful," Vivy said. "Shoot, I'll be more helpful. I will personally put up five hundred bucks that says David is faithful to Cecilia and Cecilia is faithful to him. A thousand."

Cecilia bridled, although she knew Vivy meant to be on her side. Was Cecilia supposed to be pleased that people saw her as some kind of nun?

"It looks easy from the outside," said the financial woman, her voice bitter. "It looks easy before the first betrayal."

"Or the second," said a fat man in a tank top, and then the meeting was a free-for-all, voices outshouting one another, agreeing, contradicting, bringing up cherished resentments and failed hopes. A man on one side of the room and a woman on the other were each crying, the man saying, "The goddamn *contract*." The symphony of disappointment at Life Ties was usually enough to reassure Cecilia. So many people cared so much. No one would go through these meetings if they didn't hope so desperately. But tonight was different, and not reassuring. Marteeny flinched as if rocks were being thrown. Nancy practically had to yell before she could make herself heard.

"I wasn't going to mention this, but now I think I should. David isn't the only one with a secret. I came into the store last Thursday and found Cecilia up on the stage, giving Sam his own private violin concert. You can tell me there's nothing wrong with a little music, but no one else was in the store, and all the lights were off. It's bothered me ever since."

Cecilia pressed her lips together and closed her eyes. Here it came.

"Nancy, do you think this is late breaking news?" Vivy said. "Everybody in town knows Sam's got a thing for Cecilia. My kids know. Court and Marteeny know. If we had a dog, it would know."

The man with the goatee asked David, "Do you know?"

Cecilia stared at the flowers sprigging her dark blue cotton skirt. She could hear David's nod. "Sure," he said.

"And what does that mean to you?" the financial woman said.

"Like I already told Vivy, I admire Sam's taste." Cecilia exhaled as if she'd been punctured. A single voice laughed. She lifted her head in time to see Marteeny, blushing, press her fingers to her mouth. Sam, two seats down, kept his eyes fixed on the opposite wall, the tiniest smile playing on his mouth.

"Well, you're very trusting," Nancy said. "If I tried to spring something like this on Paul, we'd be seeing divorce lawyers, not a marriage group." A few people chuckled, although Marteeny, watchful this time, did not.

The man with the goatee shrugged and said to David, "You guys have work to do."

"Hard work," said the financial woman with satisfaction.

"Oh, brother," Vivy said, voicing Cecilia's feelings precisely.

Paul's face tightened even further, the skin stretched so hard over the bony ridges it looked like a mask of itself. "It just kills you to take anything seriously, doesn't it? You can't stand the tension for two minutes."

"I take seriously what should be taken seriously," Vivy said. She didn't stand, and she didn't take her hand from Marteeny's knee. "Nobody's asked you to run the world, Paul."

"If you don't believe in what we're doing, the door is right behind you."

"I'm not ready to leave yet," Vivy said. "I hate to miss the end of the story."

David leaned over and whispered, "She's the one who usually makes the story," and Cecilia mutely nodded. She was half appalled at Vivy's behavior. She was also delighted.

"When it's your marriage on the line, your hopes and faith, I'll remind you," Paul said. "We'll be here to watch."

"Thank you. I like an audience."

Paul and Vivy craned toward each other, the space separating them surging as if it were crowded with laser beams. Nancy stepped into the space and Cecilia was almost surprised not to see her singed. "I think we need to stop right here and gather ourselves." Cecilia gave her head a tiny shake. No matter how often she was reminded, she could never get herself to remember that Nancy played the *good* cop. "You, all four of you, need a chance to think over what direction you're facing. Think about where your present roads will take you."

Revisiting the scene later, Cecilia couldn't ever piece together what came over her. Some misplaced sense of justice, some gratitude to Vivy for standing up for herself. Some anger at the group for wounding Court and Marteeny. A lunatic impulse, near suicidal, and loud. Cecilia lifted her chin and said, "I think this whole group needs to do a little thinking. I don't know how you all feel about what's gone on here tonight, but I think we've done real harm. To Court and Tina. I feel like I've joined a beating."

"The truth needed to be told. Secrets are toxic," said the financial woman.

"Easy for you to say," Cecilia said. "You don't think you have any secrets."

"Go, girl," Vivy said.

Paul said to Vivy, "Sometimes I think you would sell tickets to a beating if you could call it entertainment."

"I only sell tickets to acts worth seeing," Vivy said.

"I mean it," Cecilia said, unable to shut up and let Vivy take her usual heat. "Court and Tina came here in good faith. Now they can't even look at each other. We did that. Should we be proud of ourselves?"

"Why are you speaking for them?" Nancy asked.

Cecilia glanced over. Court was studying his finger with fierce attention. Marteeny was studying her handbag. "Because they need someone to speak for them. Look what speaking for themselves has gotten them."

Court and Marteeny seemed to be on the verge of hyperventilating. Sam, beside them, watched Cecilia, his eyes bright as sparks. "They probably don't ever want to see this place again. That's no big loss. But they don't want to see each other again, either."

"Well, now," Court said.

"If you think the group should apologize to Court and Tina, I'm certainly willing to put that to the group," Paul said, while the financial woman was already shaking her head: no way. "But I'd like to know why their cause is so important to you. Frankly, I don't think it's a coincidence that Cecilia is showing a new interest in sharing."

"Sam—Sam is developing a real interest in music." Cecilia's voice came out sounding scraped. She knew if she were listening, she wouldn't believe this person with the raw holes in her voice. Sam smiled at her, which didn't help. "He wants to learn something new. We should be encouraging him."

In the clumsy silence the man with the goatee and his wife and the man who made investments stared at her with newly interested eyes. She felt them take in her blush and her trembly fingers. She wondered if they also felt the snap of one of the filaments that bound her to hard roads and total union.

And then David spoke up. "Cecilia's right. If I learn something new, I bring it back home and talk about it. Sharing is the real pleasure of marriage. I learn what Cecilia knows. She learns what I know. That way we're bigger together than we are apart. 'Two Minds, Two Hearts, One Life.' Isn't that right?"

He waited, his face bright with confidence, for Cecilia to agree with him. Every gaze in the room dragged on her while she tested out responses, finally saying, "It's important to try. Every day."

"And the trying itself. Doesn't that bring joy?" David said.

An image arced across Cecilia's brain: David's hot arms wrapped around her shoulders, his wide, heavy face buried in her throat. She fought to inhale. "It's better than not trying," she said.

"Are you all right?" Nancy asked. "You look pale."

By focusing on David's disappointed eyes she could almost forget Sam's, which glistened. "I don't know. I haven't been feeling myself," she said. David's look turned to cautiously hopeful inquiry, and she shrugged and brushed her finger across her lips, a gesture that probably looked as though she were removing a hair.

Nancy suggested Cecilia stay seated during announcements and the Gathering of Hope: "That we be lights to ourselves and one another. That our actions bring us to new life, new vision, a new world." At a meeting some months ago Vivy, standing behind Cecilia, had hummed "Deutschland über Alles" through the Gathering of Hope. Cecilia hadn't failed to think of the anthem since. Tonight she took bitter pleasure in its stalwart rhythm, and kept humming while the group collected backpacks and notebooks. David hurried for the door. He wanted, Cecilia knew, to water his tomatoes while there was still a wash of daylight left. "Bye," he called. No telling what hope he was carrying out into the hot twilight.

At the back of the room two clusters had formed, one around the financial woman and one around Sam, who was telling a story with lots of gestures. Court and Marteeny stood at the edge of Sam's group, wordless, their hands like paddles at their sides. Sam's voice was genial, telling a joke she'd heard before about a teacher, a judge, and a goat. A long joke, good to get lost in.

When he gestured at her to join them, Cecilia didn't hesitate. She plunged out the door to walk the two miles home. Taking huge strides, she marched through the murky air, darkening by the minute.

Picking at her long skirt, which kept clinging to her legs, she swung away from Oak Street and its coffee shops and video store, onto Sixth, a pretty little residential side street lined with old houses and duplexes. During the school year, college students filled up these blocks. Shaggy, untended olive trees hogged the yards, the soft fruit they dropped leaving purple stains on the sidewalks.

When Cecilia first came to El Campo, she and David had spent most of their evenings strolling these streets, peering at the houses and imagining the lives that went on within—students reading *Critique of Pure Reason* and listening to the Grateful Dead, young parents urging their toddlers to eat barley and carrots. Cecilia had enjoyed passing one tableau after another, believing all of these unruly lives fit together into a pattern all the more comforting because she couldn't discern it.

But recently David had steered away from the rough old student streets. They should buy a house, he'd said more than once, in the good school district. He asked Cecilia to take drives with him through new subdivisions, and instead of gazing into windows and guessing about the lives behind them, he eyed rooflines and noted the condition of downspouts. Several times he pointed out olive trees, with their messy habits and greed for water and nutrients, were poor choices for landscape planting.

Cecilia couldn't help herself; although she also wanted to buy a house, some part of her brain went into hard reverse. Every time he saw an attractive floor plan she wondered what atrocity had pushed the owners to sell—bankruptcy, divorce, death of a child. Murder! As if David's refusal to think about the people behind the downspouts forced her to entertain the most lurid possibilities.

David laughed at her, though fondly. The yards they saw were well tended. The shingles and siding were in place. These lives looked fine, he said. But it was easy to make a life look fine. She and David, old Life Ties hands, knew the tricks. A low-hanging pine branch caught the end of her hair. Cecilia snapped it off and rhythmically swatted her hand as she walked, taking angry pleasure in both the sting against her palm and the sharp, sweet smell of pine sap.

She tossed the branch aside when she got to the apartment building, a cube of concrete fronted by a parking lot, hideous, the apartment chosen by David before she'd come to El Campo to join him. Now she trudged up the noisy metal stairs, let herself in, and glanced at the meager mail on the lamp table. She pawed through the envelopes—bills, flyers, trash, nothing—and threw each one onto the floor. David came in from the kitchen. "You're home." Pointing at the mail by her feet, he added, "Madame is displeased?"

"Thank you for going to Mineville. I'm glad you took the job," she said.

"You don't sound happy."

"Never mind. I'm still thanking you." Pulling him by the hand, avoiding his eyes, she towed him into the bedroom and started unbuttoning his shirt.

"What's this?" he said softly, resting his hands on either side of her neck.

"This." She rubbed her hands up his smooth back, pushing at the dense flesh. "And this. And this." She lifted her blouse over her head and let her hair spill across her shoulders and catch in her mouth—in his mouth, too, when he kissed her. They tumbled onto the bed, and when he asked her what she wanted she said, "Everything." She pressed her face into the base of his throat, hard.

After they finished, breaths steady and legs companionably interlocked, she lifted damp, curly hairs from his chest one at a time. "Randall Thorpe-Jones," she said. "Agatha Louise. Cyril."

"What are you talking about?"

"I'm rehearsing baby names Nancy will hate. Lancelot Beauregard d'Anvilliers."

David laughed, but he still said, "You sound like Vivy."

"Vivy has two children."

"And a husband who looks nervous."

"Funny. I think he looks relaxed."

"All right," David said. "Maybe that's just projection. I think he should look nervous." He pulled Cecilia closer to him, despite the sweat that still shone all over his body. "I hope this isn't how we make a baby. Anger isn't the way to get him started."

"Oh yes it is," Cecilia said, fingering the hairs on his chest, trying to get them to curl up evenly. "I want him to come into the world spitting fire. Like his Aunt Vivy. Like his mama."

Entr'acte (3)

WHEN GOOSEY NEWCOMERS LOOK ready to bolt, we lean over and whisper, "He totaled her car. She poured wine onto his computer. He broke every bottle in the house, including makeup and bath oil. She shot his dog."

"And they're *here?*" the new members ask, looking at the couple holding hands, laughing. "They're still in the same state?" After a moment they add, "If people knew things like that about me, I'd never be able to look them in the face."

They're wrong, of course. Seeing recognition in strangers' eyes is exactly what brings people back. "When I found out about the other women, I waited until my husband was out of town and then sold his truck. I sold the next one, too. Then he quit leaving the trucks at home." "I took a hammer to my wife's collection of antique cameras. It seemed like a good idea then. I wouldn't do it now."

When the newbies look unconvinced, we remind them that, no matter what they think, they're barely past their own first acts. They shouldn't rule out the possibility that guns or large animals might appear in the next scene. The mildest-looking Life Tie-er can turn to his wife and tell her he's been running drugs, or intends to start. Nobody wants to miss a meeting like that.

While we're waiting for somebody to astonish us, we watch Vivy and Sam, our longest-running show. More than once they've kept restless new members from leaving. Sam will drawl the name of a man who used to water the lawn by hand every night for an hour, hoping Vivy would walk by. Vivy will interrupt Sam, correct his details, remember how many nights she shared a drink from the man's flask. Gin in the

111

hot months, then brandy. "It got to be October, and he had the green-est grass you ever saw. He told me it was very soft, if I wanted to lie down on it." Didn't you ever get jealous? newbies will ask Sam, and he'll say, "What do you think we're doing here?" an answer that isn't an answer.

Vivy herself never opens one of these conversations, but she'll an-swer a question once it's put to her. If Nancy asks her to report on the past week, Vivy will admit she forgot to put gas in Sam's car, a confes-sion about as grudging and teenage as you can get. Why is she even here? the newbies will say indignantly. She isn't trying. Then Sam will pick up the story, pointing out that since she forgot the gas—the gauge is broken, stuck at three-quarters—he wound up stranded halfway out to the mall. When he called her she flew up in the Fiesta ten minutes later, eighty miles an hour, hardly stopping the car long enough for him to fling himself in and see her bare breasts, above which she'd written "I'm sorry" in pink lipstick, a message he eventually nibbled away.

One new woman was so shocked by that story she went into the bathroom and splashed handfuls of cold water on her face. She didn't want to even think about such things. If she keeps coming to meetings she'll realize the story is exactly what she needed.

At first, all we can imagine is what other people must be thinking about us. But after a while we start to think about the things people say, and we start imagining their lives. Little by little, we spend more time thinking about other people than we do about ourselves. We start coming to meetings so we can find out more details, test our theories. Other lives become more interesting than our own, and this is an im-portant step toward healing.

One couple started coming to meetings after the wife found out about her husband's girlfriend. Standard fare. The interesting part was how she refused to say a word about it—not to him, not to us. The abject husband was the one who told us the details while his wife sat beside him, her back straight as a knitting needle, and saw no reason to respond to any of our questions.

She became our obsession. We discussed her after meetings, and then, as time went on, in phone calls and over lunches. Was the woman in denial? Was she plotting her revenge? Was she truly ready to put the betrayal behind her, dipping into some Christlike fund of forgiveness? No one believed that.

After ten months, her back still straight, she revealed her own affair with the same woman, which had ended the night before. We kept a safe, riveted silence while the group leader, poor thing, had to ask the questions, quote the slogans, suggest the woman put together a list of chores for atonement. Some chairs in the kitchen needed refinishing, the woman said mildly.

The phone calls started as soon as we got home, and picked up again around breakfast time. We tried to imagine the silence at the couple's dinner table and in the bathroom. The slightest gesture either party made would touch off memories—the same memories, but not the same. We imagined them getting dressed in the same room, then different rooms, then never bothering to undress at all. It was his fault. It was her fault. We played out every scenario we could think of, and why not? The participants themselves had given us the details. They had invited us to join their story, and we did. We kept that story alive months after the couple themselves left Life Ties, through separate doors.

Even that story eventually died. They all do. By now we've thought everything there is to think, even about Paul and Nancy, David and Cecilia, Vivy and Sam, our most valiant members. They have made so many bad choices, and we're grateful for that. But they haven't surprised us in a long time, and we're getting bored.

SEVEN

Vivy

COURT AND MARTEENY LOOKED subdued at breakfast the next morning, picking at their waffles and smiling wordlessly at the kids. Vivy's heart, which already felt as if it were caught in a vise, constricted another degree. She should have thrown herself in front of the door to keep Court and Marteeny away from Life Ties, that sideshow act, that last resort. She must have been out of her mind to suggest they go. As if Life Ties might be charming. A unique entertainment for the out-of-town guests. Court had been so inspiring when he talked about the wisdom of a group. He hadn't figured on the wisdom of a group containing Nancy. And Paul. And, of all people, Cecilia.

She glanced across the table. Sam brooded over his coffee, the bags under his eyes like tiny balloons. He'd hardly said a word. Vivy knew he was whipping himself, taking his own responsibility for the meltdown at Life Ties. They could talk about responsibility later. For now, she wished he'd help her out here and try to talk. Her words, unaccompanied, wobbled and sank in the kitchen's angry air. "Who needs more syrup?" she said, though a bottle, still half full, stood in the middle of the table.

She and Sam had sat through difficult Life Ties meetings before. Once Sam had to go to the emergency room with a bloody chin when a wife pitched a Coke can at her husband and missed. A few times the yelling was so loud the police came, separating husbands and wives who strove to land punches, sometimes expertly. But Court and Marteeny had strolled into the meeting as shyly happy as malt-shop sweethearts, and the group had shoved them into the boxing ring anyway.

Once the meeting was over Vivy couldn't stop apologizing. When they got home Court pulled out the foldaway in the living room, and Marteeny moved wordlessly to Annie's room, where she had been sleeping. Vivy followed her. "Do you want me to say anything to Court?"

"All the saying's been said." Marteeny picked up her comb and put it down again. Resignation dragged at her round face. Vivy would rather she'd looked furious.

"None of this should have happened," Vivy said.

Marteeny shrugged. "It's up to Court now, isn't it? If he can't live with a gal with a past, he'll tell me. He doesn't keep secrets. He's good that way." Her face crumpled and Vivy moved to embrace her, but Marteeny shook her head and Vivy backed out of the room.

Now, from her seat opposite Vivy, Marteeny cleared her throat. "It's about time for us to hit the road. If we have any more coffee we won't make it to Oroville without having to stop."

"I'm not ready," Court said.

"You look ready."

"You know, I've changed my mind," Court said, and held up his cup. "I'll take one for the road."

"Honey, you'll regret that."

"I think I can manage an extra cup of coffee. I'm not an old man yet."

Sam announced that he had to take off, and Laszlo and Annie gazed at their plates with new attentiveness. Vivy poured Court more coffee, then resettled the coffeepot on its warmer. If there was a fleck of truth in the Life Ties dictum that people's clearest emotions always make themselves known, then Marteeny would have heard Vivy's heart thundering *I'm sorry, I'm sorry.* Of course, Marteeny might have been broadcasting responses of her own: *Look. Just look at what you've done.*

"I'll help you with your bags," Vivy said when they finished, and Marteeny said, "Thanks," at the same time that Court said, "No need."

He ostentatiously picked up both suitcases and lugged them out to the truck, but Vivy hung back with Marteeny, pressing her hand against her friend's dense arm. Bad as this timing was, Vivy needed to talk business. Marteeny's performance at Natural High had been Vivy's first unqualified success there since Fredd; even Sam had praised her. He was surprised, he said, and Vivy forbore from saying he was no more surprised than she was.

Who could have guessed Marteeny's extra flesh would make her act better than ever? Instead of a giggling elf on the stage, Marteeny had become a queen. She swiveled her legs and arms backwards with—there was no other word for it—elegance. When she tucked the first knee behind her head, the applause started, and it swelled when she notched the other knee in place, hoisted herself onto both arms, upside down, and strolled to the edge of the stage. She had to wait a minute for the sound to die down before she started talking, which Vivy had never heard her do onstage before.

"My mother screamed the first time she saw me do this. She dropped right to the floor. She wanted me to think she'd fainted, but my mother's no fainter. I walked over and looked at her until she opened her eyes. She said, 'Don't ever let anybody know you can do that.'" Inverted, Marteeny shrugged, her arms flexing and straightening beneath her. "Too late.

"When I was in school, kids would give me a quarter to bend my arm backward. I got invited to parties if I would walk on my hands. Dads would come in and say, 'Take a look at that.' Moms would hold their hands over their eyes. The pretty girls in class told me I was an exhibitionist, which wasn't exactly right. I did what felt good. If people liked to watch, that was fine by me."

She unhooked her left leg and, holding it straight, tapped the floor in front of her and behind her before tucking it back in place. Somebody in the audience wolf whistled. Marteeny smiled, an expression made somehow sly because it was reversed. "Girls like me don't get whistled at if we're standing on our feet. There are people whose shins I know better than I know their faces. When I finally met a man who whistled at me right-side up, I was so confused that I tripped and fell right in front of him. Bad as my mother. He helped me up and two months later he asked me to marry him."

This time the smile was impish, a flash of the old Marteeny, and applause started up again. Swaggering now, Marteeny dipped her head and drank iced tea from the glass Vivy held for her. "I said yes," Marteeny said, and the applause grew cacophonous.

Now Vivy held her friend back until Court was out of earshot. "Listen, honey, I know performing isn't at the front of your mind right now. But you were amazing. Better than good. I could book you again tomorrow."

"It was fun. You're right—it isn't at the front of my mind."

"I'm just trying to make sure you know. You're the real thing."

Marteeny shrugged. "Like Coke. But not so fizzy."

"I'm serious. I see a lot of acts. I don't see many like you."

"You go to a girl's head." Marteeny's eyes swept toward Court out in the driveway. "I don't think I want to make my living as the world's fattest Gumby."

"You've got a gift. That's all I'm saying. And you can do whatever you want to do with that gift. But if you decide you want to perform again, you should let me know."

Marteeny peered up at Vivy, half frowning. "What was this, a secret audition? I came down here because you told me your ice cream store needed help. Now you're going to put me on Ed Sullivan? I hate to tell you, but he's dead."

"You've always been good. I didn't think you might have gotten better." Vivy paused, considering her words. "There's work out there. Shows, you know. New kinds of vaudeville. TV, if you want it. I've got new connections. I can make the arrangements."

"Let me think," Marteeny said. Her voice dropped a register, to a gravelly tone Vivy had never heard from her before. "Court might like the idea. Or he might have liked it yesterday."

"He might," Vivy said, watching her friend not cry. "It's nice to have some of your own money. Gives you a little room to move. Whether you share it or not, you know it's yours."

"I can't believe that's a Life Ties–approved sentiment."

"It isn't," Vivy said.

"Jeez, you haven't changed."

"That's what Sam says when he's mad at me. Will you think this over?"

Marteeny nodded while Court strode back to them, his mouth already full of thank you and goodbye, the road to his ranch easy to find. He rocked a little, uneasily balanced on his cowboy boots. Vivy said, "It was wonderful to meet you. Marteeny's very special. I should have known she'd want to marry someone very special, too."

"You've been very hospitable with two hoboes who overstayed their welcome."

"We'd kidnap you, if we could," Vivy said. Court was too polite to actually look over at his truck, but she could see his eyes drop and feel the shift of his shoulders toward the street. Two nights before, they'd sat up late drinking soft drinks and yelping with laughter. *Life Ties*, Vivy thought, the words spitting across her mind like a curse. "Will you come again? We won't make you come to any meetings. We won't *let* you come to any meetings."

Court smiled then, and clasped her hand. "Come to our wedding," he said.

To her amazement, tears rushed to Vivy's eyes. "Try to keep me away."

She waited until the truck turned the corner and disappeared before she wiped her eyes, returned to the house, and made a quick call to Fredd. She had scheduled him a fair date in Yuba City that he had, typically, forgotten. "What would you do without me?" she asked.

"I'm the grasshopper. You're the ant. I'd never make it through winter."

"I'll keep tossing crumbs your way," she said.

"Speaking of crumbs. I talked to my nephew last weekend. He said Elphenevel is going to get four thousand dollars. My last gig got seven hundred bucks."

"You, dear, have a refined skill. You're a connoisseur's taste."

"That's your way of saying I'm stuck at seven hundred dollars?"

"I'll try for a grand next time," Vivy said. "It's time to start promoting you bigger." She went on, suggesting new tricks, maybe some music. Talking eased the ache that swelled in her lungs, and she spent five unnecessary minutes debating whether Fredd should hire an assistant, just for the comfort of his lazy presence on the other end of the line.

Still pondering his complaint that audiences didn't know how to appreciate an act anymore—"They ask me whether I had a happy childhood. Who cares about a juggler's mom and dad?"—she left the waffle iron for Sam to clean up and got in the car, hurrying now. Mineville was a good forty-five minutes northeast. She had arranged to meet David at the orchard office, where he had put aside an order for Natural High: $500 worth of walnuts and blackberries. For a few miles, speeding between beet fields, Vivy wondered if she should feel miffed about becoming the de facto delivery girl. Then she rolled down her window, turned up the radio, and let the wind churn her hair. Around her the foothills lept into the clear air, looking promising and conquerable, as they must have looked to the forty-niners. Just driving out of El Campo made Vivy feel as if her leg-irons had been loosened. She took a breathful of hot asphalt and sugar beets and watered, worked soil.

A half-familiar song came on the radio. Now that Vivy was spending two nights a month driving all over north central California with a van full of college boys, she was familiarizing herself again with radio hits. Mostly, underneath the fuzzed-out bass lines, they were songs about sex, violent with adolescent longing.

You wanted to deepen it
But now you're keepin' it
For yourself.

As Sam pointed out, no grown-up listened to lyrics so bad. Vivy agreed, then sang vigorously along.

The concerts themselves, which she had dreaded, were turning out to be fun. Backstage she swore amiably with the union guys while Elphenevel crashed through "The Sword Sings" and "Dwarf Victory"; when the band finished its set she and the drummer drank root beer in the dressing room and played Scrabble. Each concert grew a little bigger and a little more complicated—at Placerville she and the IATSE thug had gone head-to-head over the placement of an amp at the edge of the stage—but every concert was paying her better, too. Sometimes, on shift at Natural High, she felt a brief and fierce dislocation, as if she'd been hurled backward into a life she'd finished long ago.

No one was aware of this except Vivy. Sam talked about symphonies, Laszlo about Nintendo, David about the hours he had spent fixing irrigation lines and thinking about grafts. He still hadn't committed to the job long term, he said. He still wasn't completely sure. But the night before, on shift, he had issued her a printed Mapquest page of directions to Harmony Orchards, with landmarks and mileage highlighted. "One point six miles after the silo. If you watch your odometer, you'll see." Even so, she might have missed her turnoff if she hadn't glimpsed the stingy cardboard sign on the mailbox. The driveway, a buckled asphalt footpath, was dusty and disintegrated at the edges, and the only plants that grew along it were the same spindly gray weeds that lined the highway. Vivy supposed hard-core orchardists had more important concerns than landscaping, but the opening glimpse of Harmony Orchards was not reassuring.

Dust settled behind her car as she pulled in front of the office—a revamped garage, she saw when she walked inside, the pea gravel underfoot imperfectly hiding old, oil-stained concrete. Heavy smells of fertilizer and motor oil clung to the cinder block walls. "Hey," David said, waving at her with his beaker. A dozen pots straggled along the rough wooden bench before him, two or three dozen more on the shelves near the door. "Hang on just a second."

"No rush." She watched him trickle water into one of the pots, then make a note on his checklist. He trickled water into the next pot and made another note. Here was the result of years of study and desire: days spent calibrating drops of water from a glass beaker. Sighing, she looked at the plants before her. They looked identical—twiggy, thorny, ugly, labeled unhelpfully with their Latin names. Somebody had to be pretty snooty to assume customers who knew their plants down to species and variety would want to come to an overheated shack to buy their bushes.

"That's cotoneaster," David said, crunching over to join her and wiping his hands on his cutoffs. "Nice shrub for fall. By November it's full of berries. The birds love it. Want me to put one aside for you? Two would be better."

"Thanks all the same."

"How about a potentilla? Covered with flowers from May to September. Instant garden."

"I thought you were supposed to be growing trees here, not bushes."

He shrugged happily. "It's not hard to grow these things. Now, pick something. I want to send you home with a present."

"You can send me home with walnuts and berries. The store is about cleaned out."

She'd meant to hurry him along, but already he was leaning against the wall and talking, his hands fluttering like leaves. "I want to give you back something. I would never have found this job on my own. Even if I'd seen the ad, it wouldn't have occurred to me to apply. You were the one who pushed me, the one who acted like a real friend." He beamed moistly at her. "You brought something back to my life that I'd thought was gone for good. You can't be surprised that I want to give you something in return."

"For now, nuts and berries. I'll let you know when there's something else I want," Vivy said. Her embarrassment made her try to cut him off. She wasn't Albert Schweitzer just because she thought people ought to enjoy their jobs. As far as Vivy could tell, every habit and hobby people found for their spare time—falling in love, starting families, trying to find some earthly reason for their lives—seemed to guarantee disappointment. Work, at least, could be a haven.

He laid his forefinger alongside his fleshy nose, another of those corny stage gestures, and slipped out the door. In a moment he was back, staggering a little, a burlap bag slumped over his shoulder and flats of berries balanced on each arm. "I sorted them," he panted, sliding the flats onto the unfinished board counter. "It took half an hour. Take a look. Every berry there is good."

"I'll take them on faith," Vivy said.

"Here," he said, plucking a shining blackberry and holding it out to her. "We'll call this a celebration."

"What are we celebrating?"

"New life. New start. And it isn't just the money. It's—things seem more possible now. 'Opportunity Is the Corner of Fate and Desire.' Maybe we're finally there. Cecilia and I are thinking about a family. We're working hard to get there. It's good work."

His face glowed and Vivy dropped her eyes, unable to keep her rowdy imagination from careening straight to his bedroom, that cross street of fate and desire. She saw the queen bed taking up most of the stuffy space, the sheets turned back, the green chenille bedspread thoughtfully folded in the corner. A plant propagation manual on his side of the bed, sheet music on hers. Cecilia waiting beside the bed, her long hair hanging straight down her bony back.

"Well, that's terrific," Vivy said. "Really."

"Our sex is starting to get—I don't know—urgent. It's a shift. Like we say on the napkins, 'Truth and Hope Bring Life.' If Cecilia and I have twins, we can name them Truth and Hope. Actually, I'd like that."

Vivy produced another helpless, frozen smile, undone with sudden longing for Sam, who could have riffed for half an hour on names for Natural High twins—Cleanliness and Timeliness, Obsession and Compulsion. But David's meager store of irony saw no humor in saddling babies with names straight out of the Scout handbook. "Nancy would like that, too," Vivy said. "She'll also like these nuts. I've got to get moving."

David wouldn't let her go until he'd fussed around her like a grandmother for another fifteen minutes, tucking a jar of honey under her arm, making her stop to taste new strawberries, the products of grafts—were they sweet enough, did she think? Oh yes, Vivy assured him. She wouldn't want them one bit sweeter. She nodded, smiled, backed out of the office three times. When she finally got the car door closed, David still talking, she roared back down the driveway like Mario Andretti.

The vision of David's barrel shape joined to Cecilia's near-skeletal one made Vivy flinch. Some things shouldn't be shared, if not for the sake of common decency, then for the sake of aesthetics. But every confidence David uttered bound her to him more durably, as if they were dancing to a song that wouldn't end. How long would it take him to notice that Vivy wasn't telling him about her days or nights with Sam? Not that, lately, there was much to tell.

It was close to noon by the time she got to Natural High, pulling up to the back door to unload all the goods. Up front, she overheard Sam say to Paul, "You are so right. That's exactly how it is." To let Sam know she'd heard this ennobling scrap of conversation she coughed from the storeroom, then hauled in the sack of nuts and long flats of blackberries. Sticking her head into the main room, she said, "Delivery."

"Took a while to get here," Paul said.

"David was showing me around his establishment."

"Hey, Vivy. We were talking about you," Sam said, his tone broadly warning. She flicked her hair back and leaned into the room.

"What did you decide?"

"You're the girl mothers warn their sons about."

"That's fun."

"Not every woman would be pleased," Paul said, and Vivy stood up straight.

"What was your mother like, Paul?" she said. "I'm curious."

"She only had two rules, but she made them stick: clean up after yourself, and pay as you go." He frowned, and Vivy wondered whether his mother had ever tried to teach him a third rule: smile when you're being unpleasant. So helpful in dealing with people you dislike. He said, "They're good rules. I was just telling Sam."

"Do you need help with the supplies?" Sam asked her.

She smiled. "You guys keep jawing. I'll clean up after myself."

Letting the door smack the back of her leg, she tromped back into the storeroom and dropped the burlap sack of nuts on the metal freezer floor. Just as it hit the floor, the sound like a detonation, she realized that David hadn't written up any bill of sale. The $500 in fifties she'd taken from the store's tiny safe still sat untouched in her purse. With the realization, a door she never guessed existed slid open in her brain. She paused only a moment, rubbing her eyes to steady her vision.

From the used metal desk where the partners stored records, she pulled out the store ledger and wrote a $480 debit to Harmony Orchards. The sum, on the line below $625 for cream, would raise no eyebrows. Then she slipped a twenty from her wallet into the cash box, leaving the fifties at the bottom of her purse. Vivy finished the notation and underlined it. If she thought about how much Natural High owed her, the sum came in well above $480.

Vivy's hand hesitated for a minute before she closed the ledger; her heart was galloping, and she nearly crossed out the whole thing and put the money back. From the outer room, she heard Sam's weary voice again: "Isn't that the truth, though. It's like you keep saying."

Her hands damp, she called goodbye to Sam, slipped back out of the store and drove home with special caution, holding to speed limits and stopping to gas and wash the car. When the kids came home from the pool, squeaky wet and sharp with chlorine, Vivy had peanut butter sandwiches and cut up apples waiting for them. "Wow," Laszlo said. "Just like on the commercials."

Which was more or less exactly what Sam said when he came home after his shift and she met him at the door with a piece of cheese on a cracker. He lifted the cracker as if to toast her. "Livin' large."

"Don't spoil your appetite. Here's my surprise for you: we've both got tonight off."

"Stop the presses. Somebody must have been asleep at the switch when the schedule was laid out."

"It gets better. Both the kids are going to sleepovers."

"*Honey.*"

Vivy smiled at him sideways. "The night is ours."

"I'll go to Safeway, eh? For the wine. We can rent a video. Action? Comedy? Yours for the asking."

Vivy took a moment to register that Sam was serious. "Oh, come on," she said. "Let's live a little. At least let's go out to dinner. We haven't been out for months."

"Video'd be cheaper."

"*Out.* O-U-T. Someplace where somebody else will cook the food and wash the dishes."

"Cash. M-O-N-E-Y. We're only halfway through the month, and we're not exactly flush."

"It's not so bad. And you don't want to turn into a skinflint at this late date," she said. She could tell he caught something off in her tone. His expression shifted and focused, and she took a short, self-protective step back.

"You know," he said, "I was just thinking that we hadn't talked much about money lately. Cecilia was telling me she and David go over their accounts every night, making sure both of them know where every penny is. I said, 'Gosh. I just leave that all up to Vivy.'"

"I can't believe you. After days talking with your girlfriend, you want to spend our one night alone going over the bank statement?"

"Maybe," he said. "Maybe I just want to know how much you've racked up to Visa."

The Visa was clear. The Visa had been clear for two months. "Nothing," she said. "Do you want to run and tell Cecilia?" How had they drifted so quickly into a fight? She had meant to give him something nice after that browbeating from Paul, but now they were standing two feet apart, their hands actually clenched.

"Really. How much?"

"I told you. It's clear. Check it yourself."

"Vivy, I've known you a long time."

She felt her eyebrows arch, making her eyes round and full of promise. Her mouth, though, took a moment to unhinge. "Well, I guess you know everything."

"So you figure now's a good time to go out to dinner."

"Baby," she said, "it's my night off, and I'm going out. I want you to come with me, but I'm not asking more than three times." His face was a mask, the mouth curved into something like a smile, the eyes above them furious and betrayed—although she'd like to know what *he* could feel betrayed about. "C'mon," she added. "My treat."

He snorted. "We're not done."

"We're not started," she said.

After that neither of them was inclined to move with special speed—Vivy washed and blow-dried her hair, Sam went into the front driveway to shoot hoops. By the time they got to Chanticleer's it was nearly eight o'clock, and the restaurant was stuffed. It took Vivy five minutes to get the hostess's attention, and then she had to shove a path to the bar, where she yelled for two margaritas. By the time a table opened up for them, it was past ten and she and Sam were sloshed, Vivy slumped on Sam's arm. She hadn't forgotten she was mad at him, but she'd had three margaritas and the spins were setting in.

She was hungry, too, or thought she was. Sam pointed out the vegetable fajita plate that was a good value, and that Vivy had ordered on other nights, when she and Sam were getting along better.

She planted a finger on the menu. "Prime rib."

"You'll never eat it. You don't even like red meat."

"And a baked potato. And the salad bar. And a side of baked beans."

"Anything you don't want?"

"Ice cream."

She felt a pleasant shimmer of vindication when Sam ordered prime rib, too, and when he didn't object to her bottle of Merlot, although surely he knew as well as she that wine was the last thing they needed. Drinking together was a kind of pledge. They were stumbling toward some common ground, a thought that moved Vivy. She dabbed at her eyes.

When the busboy arrived with the bread, Sam snatched up the basket and tore into a roll while Vivy flirted with the boy, leaning toward him, asking his name, pointing to Sam and calling him a caveman. The boy backed away and Sam hammed it up, cramming another roll in his mouth and grunting; always they were at their best for an audience.

The salad seemed to arrive in the next second and Sam said, around a mouthful of lettuce, "Cecilia thinks we should try offering salads at the store. She says not everybody eats ice cream, and we could widen our clientele."

"Salad at an ice cream store? People don't come to an ice cream store because they want to look at bean sprouts. I guess you told her that was a swell marketing idea."

"Nope. I told her it sucked," Sam said, and Vivy giggled into her wineglass. "Turns out David is bringing in a bumper crop of peppers and cucumbers and they don't know what to do with it all. So they talked about setting up a salad bar at the back of Natural High."

"I'll bet they did. I'll bet they built little scale models, complete with sneeze guards."

"David would be the one," Sam said. "Fiddling with toothpicks and cardboard after work. Cecilia would say, 'How was your day, dear?' and David would say, 'Oh, very busy. At eight fifteen, I poured a cup of coffee. At eight sixteen, I took three sips.'"

Vivy said, "Here's Cecilia: 'At nine o'clock, I urinated six point two ounces.' What do you suppose they do for a big night? Use two differ-ent kinds of lettuce in the salad?"

"Followed by little bowls of Cherry-Berry Swirl that the store would have had to throw out for freezer burn."

"Followed by a seven-and-a-half-minute romp in bed, which will give them enough time to get dressed again and watch the news. You know, if they do have a baby, I hope it grows up to be a biker."

"Son of a gun. Are they trying to have a baby?" Even through the haze of restaurant noise and the alcohol zigzagging through her system, Vivy heard again the elaborately false note in Sam's voice, so stagy it was insulting.

She squared her elbows on either side of her plate. "Only every night for the past year and a half, Mr. Observant. At first they thought the baby would just come if they kept engaging in the connubial act, but month after month nothing happened. So they started with the manuals and all the little rituals to get Cecilia to relax—scented can-dles, long baths, having sex with her hips propped up on every pillow in the house. David must feel like he's assaulting Everest."

Sam's face, she noted with satisfaction, was flattening into solid stone. She went on, "He keeps trying new things to get her interested. Games, toys. Back rubs. He comes in to work and his hands smell like apricots from the massage oil. She gets headaches. He says he has to be careful how he approaches her."

"He's just telling you all kinds of things, isn't he? What're you telling him?"

She smiled. "That I've never had any trouble getting pregnant. And that I like sex. A lot. I like a lot of sex a lot."

"What does he say then?"

"I think I should take him on," she said, looking with surprise at the full plate of meat that had materialized before her. "He's never been with anybody but Cecilia. I'd be doing him a favor."

"Guess I'll have to take on Cecilia, then," Sam said. "Just to keep things balanced out."

"Have fun," Vivy said. "Bring that measuring cup every time you go to the bathroom."

"You're pretty sure of yourself. She may have banked fires."

Vivy threw her head back and hooted. "And you're the man to fan the flames? Guess again, Romeo. I know Cecilia's type. She has little sneeze guards on her lettuce crisper at home."

"So when did you become an expert on Cecilia?"

"When you started looking at her like there was a test coming up and she was it."

"I like to notice what's in front of me."

"And this, my love, is exactly why we've got to get out of Natural High."

Sam cut a piece of meat and put it in his mouth, an action that made Vivy queasy. "What if we don't want to go?"

"We can stay here and scoop ice cream orders for the rest of our lives. That's the choice, Sam. Those are our options. I don't mind telling you, I'm looking for the exit sign."

"Send me a postcard," Sam said.

"Girls in grass skirts." Vivy pushed her chair back. "I'm ready to see the world." She watched Sam eat half of his prime rib before he pushed the plate away and allowed the waitress, who'd been hovering, to come with the check. Sometime while they'd been arguing the restaurant had cleared out; the roar of conversation and rattling dishes had been replaced by the hoosh of water from the kitchen, a radio in there playing KHTZ.

"Here," Vivy said to the waitress, digging in her purse and pulling out two fifties. She ignored Sam's startled look, but sat quietly until he was ready to go, and then quietly beside him on the ride home. Her mouth suddenly seemed a very unreliable instrument.

In the morning they made breakfast for the kids with a minimum of fuss. Vivy's head felt like a cracked egg. Still, after Laszlo and Annie took off, Vivy pulled down her shirt collar and showed Sam a glimpse of a bra he'd never seen before—green lace that made her breasts look like cups of eggnog. She'd bought it months ago, but never got around to wearing it.

"Ooh la la," Sam said. "Giving me something to look forward to?"

"Just showing you what I've been using the Visa on," she said.

"I guess I should start to worry."

"Oh, man. Six hundred Life Ties meetings, and you still don't get it. You should have been worried all along."

EIGHT

Sam

As WAS HIS CUSTOM when he was furious, Sam worked with precision, glad Cecilia was late for their evening shift. He didn't want her to witness his glittering punctiliousness and his savage, pointless sarcasm. He knew he was at his worst, and self-consciousness only made him more brittle, more angry. Every scoop he handed across the counter was a baseball-sized globe exactly centered on its crisp wafer, the Platonic ideal of an ice cream cone. And every word flew out of his mouth like a whip crack. "That should tide you over till the next snack," he told one chunky teenage girl, whose face crumpled. He watched her drop the double-dip cone in the trash can outside the store, a waste of everyone's time and money. After she left, he went out and rubbed a smudge off the trash can.

The store shone. Every unoccupied chair sat six squared-off inches from its table, and the bleached oak floor gleamed from baseboard to baseboard. The countertop also gleamed, as did the glass freezer cover. Sam couldn't stop rubbing things, straightening, scrubbing, aligning. The napkins on the counter were flush with the metal edge, "Our Goal Is Not Gold" on top, and the sink holding the scoops was filled with clear, scalding water. He changed it in the lulls between customers and entertained himself by imagining dunking Vivy's head beneath the surface.

He didn't suppose she was actually out to bed David. Sam knew Vivy too well. No matter how much she wanted to needle Sam, David's

Baden-Powell good cheer made Vivy squirmy as a pup. Vivy and David together would be like Betty Boop and Dudley Do-Right, the fast head cheerleader and the president of the Latin club. She might force herself to tease him. She might flash that green bra. But she would stop short of screwing him, as she had always stopped just short of screwing other men.

Or so Sam had always believed. What did he know? Using a paddle and all the strength in his wrists, he smoothed the top of the ice cream in each carton. That morning, after Vivy sped out of the house, pointedly not saying where she was going, Sam went to the rickety desk where they heaped their bills. He found the phone bill—not too high, considering all of Vivy's texts to her lousy, no-talent talent—three grocery receipts, and the PG&E statement, which was through the roof, as usual. But no Visa bill. They'd never bothered to set up their online account, so he couldn't check by computer. Instead, he flipped through the stack again, then rummaged in the drawer for the checkbook. At least he could see how much she'd been paying, if not the running tab. But the checkbook wasn't in the drawer where they usually tossed it, and the side drawer, when he pulled on it, was locked. Sam pulled harder, thinking at first it was simply jammed. He'd never realized the drawer had a lock.

Since that moment sweet anger had gathered in him. With one turn of one key Vivy had bounced the high wire they had walked for fifteen years. Always before this she would tell Sam whatever he asked—about money, about men. Often enough, Sam hadn't wanted to ask, enjoying the little thrill of suspicion that he could obliterate or ignite with a single question. She understood the tension as well as he did. "Just ask," she would say, sparkling. It wasn't as if Vivy ever withheld anything.

But now she had presented him with a locked drawer. He thought of every time she'd gotten into money trouble, every stupid, impulsive purchase—1940s circus posters, crystal martini glasses. And these were the purchases she admitted to. Feeling his pulse drum, he considered the way she pored over the store's balance sheets at night—looking, she always told him, to see how many new acts they might bring in.

This new idiot rock-and-roll band. All that money running through her fingers. For the first time he was truly afraid of what she might be doing, and what she might be pulling him into. His name was right alongside hers on that Visa account, and hers next to his on the Natural High incorporation papers.

He was letting this insight burn like a red wire into his brain when Cecilia rushed into the store. Her hair and white blouse clung to her sweaty back, and she was laughing, breathing hard, apologizing. A late lesson, a phone call, every red light in El Campo. Sam said, "Don't even try to talk to me. I'm a bear today."

"We can be bears together. I'm supposed to teach music to every tone-deaf and constitutionally tardy child in El Campo. Grr. Why are you a bear?"

"Nothing. It's complicated."

She glanced at him hard and lifted her eyebrows, then silently looked around for some chore, but he had beaten her to every one of them. The few customers checked their phones, and the CD, surf and reed flutes, tootled along. Cecilia hovered at the opening between the counter and the rest of the room. He felt the pressure of her expectation alongside her eagerness, which he'd already managed to slap down a little. He hadn't meant to. "Should I go into the back?" she said, when the silence between them stretched wider.

"No."

"I didn't think so."

"Tell me about your students."

She straightened, clasping her hands before her like a nineteenth-century schoolgirl, and sang "Twinkle, Twinkle, Little Star," intentionally getting it all wrong—missing rests, wavering between two sour notes, breathing three times in a phrase. Sam snorted, and Cecilia, encouraged, gathered steam.

"'My fingers hurt,'" she whined, folding her arms and tucking her hands out of sight. "'My wrists hurt. You make me practice too much. My neck hurts.' If one, just one of them practiced half as much as they all swear they do, I would personally eat a twenty dollar bill. Cheerfully."

Sam could see she was hamming, trying to get him to smile, and the effort touched him. "Just wait until you get Laszlo and Annie," he said.

"Are they going to be my ticket to Carnegie Hall?"

"Not likely. But they'll lie more creatively about practicing. It's a skill they've inherited from their mother."

"Creativity is good," Cecilia said. "When they put a little effort into their lie you know that you register somewhere in their psyche. You know what I mean?"

"Don't I," Sam said.

She ignored his acid tone, kept smiling and kept talking—Vivy's old tactic, but without Vivy's confidence or dash. Stammering, soft-spoken Cecilia halted frequently; he could see her searching for a safe rope that would pull him out of the fires of his anger. Weak joke after weak joke, her steady effort practically courageous—for the first time all day Sam began to soften, pondering the slight overlap of her two front teeth and the play of bluish shadows across her skin. When she tilted her head, inviting him to laugh with her, her straight sheet of light brown hair curtained her shoulder, an effect both prim and alluring. He laughed, a little roughly.

Later, he would remember this moment as the pivot, even though he knew attraction was complicated and shifts and tilts between people were constantly degraded and renegotiated. Nevertheless, from the moment he relented and laughed, he felt anticipation whistle along his nervous system.

And he needed only to look at Cecilia to see she was feeling the same whistle and spark. Her stammering fell away and her laugh, frequent now, was full. She twirled around him to get to the Mocha Crunch; he sidled closely past her and restraightened the napkins, though they didn't need restraightening. All of a sudden he and Cecilia were aligned, generating a bright electrical current. Cecilia brought in more carob chips just as Sam scooped up the last handful from his aluminum tray. "Do you want—" Sam asked a customer, and Cecilia finished, "—wheat germ with that?" They both raised their eyebrows, and then they both laughed.

Drama was in the air. At seven-thirty a crowd of teenagers, straight from some play rehearsal, banged into the store, yelling, "For *I* have known joy, known ecstasy—" and then convulsing with laughter. Huddled by the window over matching mochaccinos, a purse-lipped man and woman who looked forever married scowled at the kids and then at Sam, as if he should muffle them. He shrugged. He wasn't the kids' dad. The store did a whole lot better off of ice cream than it ever would from coffee drinks. "Who can I help first?" he asked.

One after another, loudly, punctuating their statements with cries about joy and ecstasy, the teenagers ordered elaborate desserts. Sundaes with three toppings, soda drinks with flavors and whipped cream and shavings. Even the girls, who often only wanted iced tea when they were out with boys, were crying for extra scoops and bigger portions. Sam wondered whether they'd all gotten sky high backstage at their rehearsal, or whether they'd stopped for a smoke on the way to Natural High, somebody's car windows still opalescent and sweet smelling.

"Don't be stingy," said one of the girls, her hair dyed black, her eyes lined with purple, and her Greta Garbo accent terrible.

"You're lucky you got me tonight," Sam told her, rounding off a scoop of Mocha Crunch the size of a grapefruit. "I'm feeling generous."

"He's right, you know," Cecilia said, working on a scoop of her own, her delicate face so animated and pretty that Sam wanted to kiss it on the spot.

"For *I* have known joy, known ecstasy—" cried the girl, eliciting an approving howl from her friends. The couple with the mochaccinos pushed back their chairs and left, shaking their heads at Sam as they slammed the door closed. He shrugged again. The kids were making too much noise. On the other hand, the man and his wife were a couple of prigs.

"You should come in on Thursday and Saturday nights," Sam said to the purple-eyed girl. "We have entertainment."

"Oh God, don't I know it! I arrange my *life* around Saturday nights here." She leaned across the counter toward Sam, her breath a thin cloud of cigarette smoke and a spicy breath mint. "Did you see the comedian? She was the best thing I've ever seen. And there's going to be a drum orchestra. I'm going to get here at three in the afternoon to save a seat."

Her dilated gaze drilled into Sam's forehead. For the life of him, he couldn't read her tone. She might have been looping him into depthless teenage sarcasm, or she might have genuinely loved the way Laurel stumbled over her dusty material, then reminded the audience it was okay to laugh. "You should audition," Sam said. "The woman who does the hiring will be working tomorrow, and she's always looking for new talent. You guys could do a scene."

"Are you kidding?"

"A river of tomorrows will not bring this day again," declaimed a boy who had been jamming Triple Vanilla into his mouth. Beside him, another boy held up his spoon: "—when I have known, as in the beat of a wing—ah, shit. Something something everlasting."

The kids whooped, firing napkins at him and shouting bits of dialogue. The girl in front of Sam tapped her finger on the counter. "Still want us?"

"See the redheaded woman tomorrow. I think you're just what she's looking for."

By the time the rest of the orders had been taken and the kids sprawled across five tables, the noise in the room had risen to the level of actual discomfort. A boy had fished a CD from his jacket by a band called Mutually Assured Destruction, and suggested Sam give it a try. Now the room throbbed like a sore, but Sam kept the CD on; the crashing, incoherent guitars fit his anarchic mood and gave the kids an air of wanton menace he wanted to encourage.

"I'll go in the back to chop," Cecilia shouted, gesturing at the speakers, and Sam, drumming his hands against the edge of the sink, let her go. The atmosphere in the store was becoming less wholesome by the minute. In the corner, by the community bulletin board, the girl with purple eyeliner was dancing by herself, thrashing her arms as if she were working a churn. Twice adults holding children by the hand opened the store's front door, looked in, startled, and backed out again.

Sam watched with a satisfaction that surprised even him. Cecilia was scheduled to work till closing, and she wouldn't go anywhere. For now, by turning the store into a mosh pit, Sam was addressing some deep karmic need. Five years of relentlessly upbeat energy, the nonstop emphasis on building and betterment, had produced in him a sudden appetite for destruction. He was ready—more than ready, hungry—to let down his guard, allow in the negative vibrations, let the goddamn chips fall. He would blow up a building if he could, watching with pleasure the collapse of support beams. Then he'd go rescue Cecilia, who would be grateful to see him.

Two boys had joined the girl in the corner. They angled their shoulders to bang off the wall and against one another, but Sam could see they weren't really hurting themselves. Pretend anarchy. Mutually Assured Destruction seemed to be singing "Back tack, back tack," although the chorus might as easily have been "Slag rack, slag rack." Sam knew the kids would flee the store if he joined them in the corner, even though he could bring more pure rage to the dancing than they had ever thought about—and he also knew, in the tiny surviving responsible sector of his brain, that he had no right to inflict his disgruntlement on them. This was their show, not his.

But it was his store. He skipped a carob chip under the feet of the dancers, and then another one. He had tossed out five chips before one of the girls sitting at the closest table noticed what he was doing and nudged the boy lying half in her lap, whom she had been feeding Very BlueBerry. The girl frowned at Sam. He skittered another chip into the corner. Next to catch on was one of the boys, wearing a Terrapin Station T-shirt—a relic from his dad's bottom drawer, Sam bet. The boy plucked a walnut from the puddle that was left of his sundae and pitched it at the dancers. Then a smashed berry, which caught the girl on the ankle before she flicked it off and ground it under her canvas shoe.

As the kids at the tables skittered more nuts and chips along the floor, the dancers made their own game, pulverizing the nuts and kicking the chips at one another, then slinging fingerfuls of ice cream. Blobs of ice cream smeared the floor and baseboards, the dancers swore, yelled, laughed until more kids got up from their tables, crowding the little space, kicking and jostling each other even after the CD screamed to its finish and the store suddenly seemed to chime with quiet except for the frantic scuffling and shouts.

Behind the counter, Sam rested his chin on his fists and watched, the very picture of the kindly, old-fart soda jerk. Except, of course, he wasn't kindly, especially since he knew he was the one who would have to clean up the mess he'd provoked. When a thin boy whose acne ran in red, inflamed lines like tears down his face wavered up to the counter and wanted, after great hesitation, Carob Ripple with chocolate chips, Sam snapped, "We don't have chocolate chips."

"What are these?" The boy pointed at Sam's tray of carob chips.

"Rabbit turds."

"Whoa." The kid squinted at the chips, then looked back up at Sam. "Really?"

"What do you think? I'm going to stand here and lie to you?"

The kid was staring at the chips again, transfixed. "Let me taste one."

"Penny apiece."

The boy fished up a nickel from his slack pocket. Sam picked out five chips and set them on the counter, and the boy hesitantly set one on his tongue. "Doesn't taste like chocolate," he said.

"I told you," Sam said, and the kid grinned.

"Give me a double helping," he said. He watched as if Sam were TV while Sam scooped and spooned and sprinkled. Then the boy made his extremely uncertain way—he was *wrecked*—back to the table. Most of the seats were taken again, the other kids red-faced and panting, fanning themselves, their legs and arms flung across nearby tables. Sam was just about to put on Mutually Assured Destruction again when a girl shrieked, "You got *what*?" and the boys at the table roared.

"That's not funny," she said, standing and grabbing her backpack. "You guys are gross." She flounced out of the store, two of her girl-friends trailing her like threads. The boys looked at each other and shrugged, but in a moment they were standing too, their tables a still-life of sticky spoons, overturned dishes, banks of napkins. "But they're *good*," protested the Terrapin Station kid as all the boys started pushing chairs out of their way.

"Chicks," said another one of the boys, and the last boy sighed and got up. In a surprisingly considerate gesture, he eased the door shut behind him.

The silence in the store trembled like a held breath. The kids' mess looked like the result of battle—chairs overturned, walls and windows smeared, the floor streaked and dotted. No real damage had been done, but the room held the sense of damage, and Sam's wild spirits began to seep away. In a moment he would weep.

"What came through here, a rodeo?" Cecilia's voice was rich and amused. She had put up her hair, but strands near her face hung free, and Sam felt the strong, distinct desire to wrap those strands around his fingers.

"My fault. I made a riot."

"You did a thorough job of it."

"Anything worth doing is worth doing well. You don't have to help with the cleanup. It's my mess."

"What's a partner for?" Cecilia tucked one of her desirable strands behind her ear. "Come on. Many hands make light work."

Sam handed her the rags and spray-on cleaner for the tables while he attacked the floor, the kind of substantial job he'd been craving all night. Even at the end of a normal day the light wood showed every scuff and bit of lint. Now it looked as if the teenagers had been shooting BBs. The strawberries left shadowy pink clouds, and the carob chips were flattened against the hard finish. Strewn across the floor like freckles, every chip had to be picked at and scoured away. Who could have known carob was so hard?

"Shit, shit, shit," Sam chanted.

"What's wrong?"

"Nothing that two weeks on my hands and knees won't fix."

He heard the swish of her long skirt as she crossed the room, and then her long silence. "You know, if we just get up the worst of this, nobody's going to even notice the rest. We don't usually get on our hands and knees to clean the floor."

"That's for sure."

"Anyway, wood floors get marked. Those dents and dings show that the floor has been used. That's part of their appeal."

"So we should deliberately mess up our floors?"

"People do."

"You're good at this," Sam said.

"Good at what?" Wide eyes innocent, she shrugged.

"And you never saw any kids pogoing over here."

"As a matter of fact, I didn't. The last thing I saw was kids flopped around the tables eating enough calories to sustain an African village. I left when the soundtrack started."

"Smart. I should have, too."

"Not enough room in back for two," she said. He watched her pleat her cotton skirt around her pale fingers, skinny as pencils. The moment when he might have said something suave and suggestive about tight quarters passed; he watched her work the fabric up and down. Looking at her fine motions contented and excited him.

"Come on, lazybones," she said. "We're still not done here."

While Sam went back to the baseboards, his tongue thick in his mouth, Cecilia moved all the ice cream back to the big freezer. She put away the mix-ins and washed their trays while Sam cleared the tables and loaded the dishwasher. She set the chairs upside down on the tables while he mopped the floor. He didn't look up, but he sensed her watching him as he finished. He could feel her standing very close to him. When he turned to look, though, she was all the way across the room, by the light switch. She nodded at him, then turned the lights off.

"Thanks," he said. "You made things easier."

"That's what I wanted to do. Is there anything else?"

"Sure." In the dark room she looked like a slender column of shadow that he moved toward. She stiffened when he put his arms around her, but she didn't pull away. He pressed his face against her fine hair, which smelled like fruit. "I just want you to know that you've been the one thing in my life that's been keeping me going. You make me able to stand my life. I think about you all the time. I need you."

"You say things." Her voice was high, but she didn't push him back. "You turn a girl's head."

"I'm telling you the truth, Cecilia-girl. You don't have to believe it. But it's still the truth."

Holding her was like holding a tall, wild bird. Her weight was nothing in his arms. Her bones could be hollow. He could snap her in half. "Do you believe me?" His voice cracked like a boy's.

She laughed then, and leaned against him so he could feel her sharp shoulders and tiny breasts. When he tilted up her face, searching for her mouth in the dark, she guided him, then kissed him back.

Entr'acte (4)

MANY EYES, MANY EARS. A group has collective knowledge, long on memory and sharp of eye. We observe and remember. We surprise ourselves with all we know.

And people are so easy. Eyes that drop when one person talks suddenly lift and spark at the sound of a different voice. Shoulders tense, elbows draw back, a mouth loosens no matter how its owner tries to control it. At one meeting a woman's toes reached out like tiny water creatures every time her husband opened his mouth. When you know people, you care about them. When you care about them, you pay attention. When you pay attention, you learn things.

The slogan says secrets are toxic, but here's the quiet corollary, more correct: around a group like this, there are no secrets.

NINE

Cecilia

CECILIA LET TWO WEEKS pass before she went to the Rite Aid. There she bought two home pregnancy testing kits, different brands. She had read stories about missed diagnoses—one teenager in New York had clung to the promise of her negative result for eight months, despite her ballooning belly and its strange new flutterings. When she was taken to the emergency room she threatened to sue the admitting physician, insisting she was suffering appendicitis, not labor.

Cecilia read the instructions twice before she tore open the pouch that held the testing materials, and read the instructions again after the patch at the end of the stick turned blue, meaning positive. Then she buried the carton at the bottom of the wastepaper basket and started again the next morning with a different kit, different instructions. Same result.

The bathroom wall where she rested her cheek was cool. When she warmed the first spot, she moved to another, pressing her face against the smooth plaster. For the two weeks since her encounter with Sam she had dropped cups and pots, tripped over perfectly flat carpet, snapped two violin strings. She had avoided Sam, who shot her collusive smiles at Life Ties. At night she had lain beside hot, peaceful David and rehearsed every scenario that might be true: a baby. No baby. David's baby. Sam's baby. Cecilia's own, private baby, nobody's business but hers.

She hadn't had a secret for so long she'd almost forgotten how it felt, this sizzling power line wrapped around her spine. Cecilia shook her head, thinking of the dozens of people who came to Life Ties after carrying secrets for years. How did they do it? She was already exhausted.

The thought of David's soon-to-arrive joy made her more exhausted still. No one could be as delighted as David, and his delight would shine forth when he looked upon her and, later, when he looked upon the child. Who might be his child. David looking, day by day and year by year, for his traits and characteristics—while Sam looked on too, with his own hungry eyes, always remembering the one crucial fact David did not know, and that changed everything. Cecilia bit the inside of her mouth until it hurt, and then bit harder. She could make her husband happy or she could tell him the truth. Both choices would hurt him, who deserved no hurt.

Forcing her unwilling legs, she crossed the hall into the bedroom. David mumbled, his damp mouth smashed against the pillow. She sat down, turned on the bedside lamp, and watched his blinking eyes focus on the sky-blue stick she held. "Wait," she said. "Before you think anything." Then she told him about Sam.

He lay still, not once interrupting. When she stopped talking he continued to gaze at her, his face empty of expression, so lacking its usual confident drive that it seemed less a face than a prototype of one—eyes approximately here, jaw roughly thus. He rolled out of bed, avoiding her outstretched hand, and pulled on yesterday's shorts and a fresh T-shirt. For ten minutes—she kept her eye on the bedroom clock—he didn't open his mouth, and Cecilia's trembling turned to a light hum.

When David did speak, his voice was pinched; he almost sang. "I didn't expect to begin the morning this way. I'm watching my life rearrange itself. All of the pieces are changing places. I'm thinking new thoughts. If we hadn't come back to El Campo, this wouldn't have happened. If we hadn't gone to Life Ties, this never would have happened. I don't think I should have to be thinking that." Even in his rage he spoke in good "I" statements, just as Life Ties had taught them.

"I can't begin to tell you how ashamed I am," Cecilia said. "I was sorry as soon as it was over."

"I'm sorry too. That's what the damaged spouse generally says, right? I haven't paid close attention to the speech. I didn't expect to give it."

Cecilia bent her head. His outrage stripped the remaining webby clouds from her thinking. Their bedroom, which had seemed indistinct an hour ago, revealed itself as it had always been, a collection of hard lines and sharp corners. She felt as if she were waking from a disorienting dream, and like a wakened dreamer she pinched her hands and shook her head. The oak veneer headboard, the chenille spread: they were dependable, if not beautiful. Dependable *was* beautiful. She gripped the thought like a life preserver. As if in response, she remembered the brush of Sam's wet mouth against her throat, and jerked to a different position on the bed, hating the treacherous thoughts her mind now contained.

"I feel unprepared for this," David said. "Genuinely unprepared. Do you want to know what I want right now?" Cecilia nodded. He said, "I want to be sure this can never, ever happen to me again."

"It won't," Cecilia whispered, opening the door for David to ask *How can I know that? How can I trust you now?* And he did. Pacing the far side of the bedroom he asked all the furious, frustrated questions, and Cecilia lifted her head and responded to every one of them. She felt as if she were being dragged along rough pavement, bumped indifferently over rocks and curbs, exactly the treatment she wanted. Every touch of Sam needed to be scraped away, every sign of him removed from flesh and memory, and if the removal hurt, then so much the better. If David wanted to hit her, she would take the hit. If he asked her to move out, she would pack. Only one thing did she truly fear: that he would expect her to share this grotesque misstep at Life Ties.

Apparently, the thought hadn't occurred to him yet. He had lapsed back into wordlessness, and held his blazing silence until Cecilia stood up. Then he snapped, "Where are you going?"

She sat again. "To make coffee. Don't you want some?"

"You know, it may not seem this way to you, but I feel insulted when you ask if I want coffee but not if I mind you having sex with Sam Jilet."

Cecilia traced her finger over the bedspread's curved lines. For a long time, probably further ahead than she could actually see, she would be functioning on David's rhythm, not her own. Still, at the moment she was desperate for caffeine, and after five more minutes she got up and went into the kitchen. She snatched the first half cup before the machine finished brewing, not caring about the sputtering mess and the puddle of hot liquid on the counter. Some women gave up coffee when they got pregnant, she thought, sucking down the half cup and pouring some more. She wouldn't be one of those.

When her hands stopped shaking she brought David a cup, setting it on the table beside him. He didn't touch it or look at her, but as soon as she turned to leave the room he said, "Now I'm wondering where you're in such a hurry to go."

"I didn't think I was the person you most wanted to look at right now."

"You're not. But if you're not here, I'm going to wonder where you are."

"I'm in the kitchen."

"Oh, I'd say you're farther away than that."

She passed the morning drinking coffee and halfheartedly sketching handbills. The round scoops of ice cream kept turning into round baby heads; she drew babies crawling, babies smiling, babies drooling. Cartoons. She tried to draw a baby with David's broad nose and deep-set eyes, but the proportions went wrong, and the face came out looking lumpy, as if it had emerged from a street fight. Cecilia crossed it out, then crossed it out again, then scrubbed the pencil back and forth over the image until not even an outline could be made out. She remembered enough from her college psychology course to know that compulsive, destructive actions tended to follow trauma. She folded the paper in half and started ripping it into the tiniest bits she could manage.

"What are you doing?" David's voice was tired.

"Just—" She shrugged. "I didn't like what I drew."

"Huh. Me neither. What can I rip up?"

Cecilia held the stack of drawings toward him. He glanced at the sketch on top, a baby's head snuggled into an ice cream cone, and ripped the whole stack in half. "Doesn't help," he said, letting the pages fall to the counter.

"Sorry," Cecilia said.

"I'm having real trouble with this. I'm—" He swallowed and shook his head, his eyes squeezed shut.

"David, I would do anything to undo it. I hate myself."

"Yeah, well. Hate. Would you like to know what I just realized? I'm on shift today with Sam."

"Call someone. Get out of it."

"I've been on shifts with him." His voice was raw. "In the last two weeks. 'How's Cecilia?' He actually asked me."

"She's rotten."

"Standing there, washing scoops, like it was the most natural thing, asking about the wife. I wouldn't have been able to do it."

"No," Cecilia said.

"If someone had brought this story to a meeting, I would have thought the guy was nothing but a jerk. Now I have to remember that he's the man my wife chose."

"David!" Cecilia cried, or tried to cry. Her mouth was dry as sand. "Are you trying to hurt me or hurt yourself?"

"You. Definitely. I'm just along for the ride."

"You can't work with Sam today."

"Who's going to take over for me, you? There's a concept."

"I'll call Nancy," Cecilia said, avoiding his gaze.

"Maybe it's not such a bad idea. You and Sam. Six happy hours together."

"Don't do this, David. It's ugly. It's beneath you."

His look was so bleak that she recoiled. "Don't say one more word."

Trembling seized her fingers and held them. She trembled as she showered, trembled as she walked back to the kitchen, where David hadn't moved. "Are you going to go in?" she said.

"I don't know what I'm going to do. I'm waiting for a good option."

"Yes," Cecilia said. When David didn't snap at her again, she risked glancing at his eyes, which were red and directed toward the bookshelf. His botany textbooks, her slender theory workbooks and battered scores. Scarcely a volume in common. *The only way out of pain is through pain,* she thought, a Life Ties standby that David didn't need to be reminded of.

They hardly spoke on the walk to the store. Although the spring heat wave was now history, it had merely given way to summer, and day after day after day dawned clear, any overnight dew already baked away. The heat made Cecilia feel as if she were living on a treadmill. Every morning she put on a T-shirt, every night peeled it off again. Somewhere people were wearing sweaters, a thought she entertained as if it were heaven. She wondered if they knew how lucky they were, then shook her head. No one ever knew.

She nodded at toddlers splashing listlessly in portable pools. Their mothers, sprawled in folding chairs, nodded back. The older kids, whose shouts and skateboards and boom boxes usually took over neighborhoods, were off at the mall or the movies or Natural High, anyplace with seats and air-conditioning. Sam said they should be paying rent. Cecilia winced and shivered, and David folded his lips and walked a little faster. He knew the kind of thought that could make Cecilia shiver on a ninety-degree day.

The store, when they got there, was close to full. Vivy's bright sign in the window read Crystal Billy the New Age Clown. Cecilia had forgotten this was an entertainment Saturday, and she wasn't sure she had it in her to sit through the comic stylings of a New Age clown.

"What are you waiting for?" David asked, so she pushed open the door to the cool, noisy, sweet-smelling air. Sam looked up and waved an ice cream scoop at them. Cecilia turned to face the other side of the room, where she caught a glimpse of Vivy's face, an angry mask.

From the stage Crystal Billy was talking in a high-pitched, wispy voice. "Everything ties together, once you know how to look. All life is in harmony. Can you hear it? *Many* lives come together in har-*many.*"

A droopy specimen even by Vivy's standards, Crystal Billy wore a faded rainbow Afro wig over a face painted as a mandala, black on one side, white on the other. The black and white dots were prominently placed on his cheekbone and jaw, but the dividing line bulged over his thin nose, giving him a deformed look. He wore a white T-shirt, green surgical pants, and canvas deck shoes that had been cheap and out of fashion since Cecilia was a girl. All in all, he looked as if he'd spent ten minutes assembling his act, which seemed to consist mostly of talking.

"What is evil divides us. What is good creates union. U-nion, like an on-ion, right? An onion is made of many layers. U-nion; on-ion." While he talked he picked up a bright green, skinny balloon from the table beside him and started to twist it. Half entranced by the man's sheer dreadfulness—his voice squeaked like a cheap flute—Cecilia watched, assuming he would create some kind of balloon onion. But instead he knotted the balloon at each end and twisted it in the middle, forming a crude Y.

"This is the ancient symbol for the Tree of Life. It stands for wholeness. If we remember we are all arms on the Tree of Life, then we will treat each other like family. *Tree* of Life, *treat* like family."

He held out the flimsy balloon, ready to place it in an eager pair of hands, but the kids sitting near the stage were talking and didn't look up until Crystal Billy tossed the balloon onto a nearby table. One of the boys sitting there batted it away.

As far as Cecilia could tell, she and David and Vivy were the only ones listening as Crystal Billy prattled on. A boy sitting by the window picked up a yellow balloon twisted into a double horseshoe, unwound it, and wrote LED ZEP along its side in black felt-tip. Three girls chattered tightly at a table next to the water fountain, one of them throbbing with laughter. From time to time she threw back her head and sucked in air as if she were surfacing.

"To be *whole* means you are wrapped around a *hole*," Crystal Billy said, holding up a red balloon tied in a circle, a long tail dragging at its side. Glaring at the stage, Vivy made a slashing movement at her throat.

"I've had enough," David said. He edged around the room and slipped behind the counter, ignoring Sam's grin. Cecilia watched David's heavy back disappear into the storeroom. When Sam tried to catch her eye, she looked back at the stage.

"If we act from our centers, we will be free." Holding the red balloon before him, Crystal Billy stuffed the free end through the hole in the middle, a stunningly obscene image. The girl sitting by the water fountain glanced up and choked on her iced tea. At the sound, some of the other kids looked up. Raw laughter crashed through the room, Crystal Billy frowned in confusion, and Vivy jumped onto the stage.

"*Thank* you, and let's all hear it for Crystal Billy," she said, grabbing him by the elbow. Two boys scrambled for the red balloon while she hauled the clown, his rainbow frizz bobbing, to the side of the little platform. He went meekly, and Cecilia wondered how many times he'd gotten the hook before.

It was only twelve thirty, which meant a half hour of his allotted performance time still remained. Customers took the schedule seriously. Two weeks ago a mother had straggled into the store at twelve fifty-five and dressed Vivy down when she found the act for that day—the Hula King—was already packing up. "It's no pleasure getting three kids in here on time, you know," she snarled. "Your ad said entertainment until one o'clock. What are you going to do about that?" Vivy bought them double dips, which the kids—boys blessed with their mother's bruised-looking mouth and angry eyes—seemed to appreciate well enough. Even so, the mother said to Vivy, "I don't think you understand your responsibility."

She did today. No sooner had she parked Crystal Billy at the edge of the stage, where he sulkily swung his legs, than she bounded back before the crowd, her eyes and smile kindled. Cecilia recognized the look from her own audition days, the cocky students impatient to show the judges what real talent looked like. Cecilia had always been careful to take the stage modestly, letting the music speak for itself. Look where that had got her.

Prowling the front of the stage like a barker, Vivy smiled at a cranky boy squirming in his mother's lap and picking his nose. "Pretty inspiring talk from old Crystal Billy, huh? But sometimes you don't want to be uplifted. Sometimes you just want to fool around." Partially inflating one balloon from the stack Crystal Billy had left on his stool, Vivy made a fast wiener dog and tossed it at the boy. "Woof."

Her hands were quick as birds. She made a rabbit, a poodle, a race car, lobbing them into the crowd as she went along. The kids were giggling, and Vivy, a big kid, giggled along with them. Cecilia had hurt Vivy, too, and she'd know it soon enough.

"I used to spend a lot of time behind stages," Vivy said. "I got bored, so I taught myself to make things with balloons. First I learned the classics—" she held up another dog, purple this time, and handed it to a woman at a table with a sticky toddler "—then I branched out." Her motions blurring, she twisted a blue balloon into a round fist, the middle finger shooting up like an arrow. She waited until the teenagers began to laugh, then refolded the shape into a coiled snake; she pulled a pen from the pocket of her shorts and drew a smile on its face.

"I know the rules. I know what I'm supposed to do. But don't you get sick of people telling you how to run your life? 'Be careful about this. Watch out for that. Practice half an hour a day. Don't waste. Don't spend. Don't move. Don't breathe.'"

Nobody was laughing, but nobody was leaving either. Near Cecilia, a girl leaned over and asked her friend, "Is this supposed to be funny?"

Out of a red balloon, Vivy twisted a quick set of horns and set it on the head of a chunky boy. That got a laugh. "Play a little. Tell a few jokes. Haven't you all heard? You'll live longer if you laugh." Crystal Billy sniffed pointedly. She clapped a balloon between her hands, but it was too underinflated to burst. "Boom," she said.

Cecilia swallowed dryly, alarm tightening her eyes and lips. She recognized this mode, Vivy reaching for any handy words, any complaint or accusation. No telling what she would say to keep her audience. Feeling her heart hammer as if it wanted to break through her rib cage, Cecilia wondered what Sam might have told his wife about breaking rules and blowing things up.

"We don't need to be on leashes all the time," Vivy said. "We don't need to be on leashes half the time."

Cecilia moistened her lips. As loudly as she could, she sang, "Oh give me land, lots of land, under starry skies above—don't fence me in."

Vivy's head jerked up. "Finally. My backup singer is here."

"Let me ride through the wide open country that I love—don't fence me in." Cecilia didn't have to turn her head to know Sam was watching her with a delighted smile. David was right behind him, neither delighted nor smiling.

"Shoot, girl. And here we thought you could only play the fiddle," Vivy said.

"I can carry a tune," Cecilia said, her long skirt brushing the backs of chairs as she made her way to the stage, then turned to face the crowd. "And I can lead a sing-along. Vivy's just about out of balloons." She lowered her voice threateningly. "But I know lots of songs."

Before any of the dismayed-looking teenagers had a chance to jump up and leave, she began on "Summertime." She wished she had her violin—her singing voice was nothing more than passable, but she loved to play Gershwin. Still, the tune was a good choice. Lots of people in the crowd knew it, including a half dozen of the teenagers, who brought some real soul to the singing.

She could hear Vivy beside the stage quietly paying off Crystal Billy, evidently giving him less than he'd contracted for. He argued pretty spiritedly for a man who didn't think money was a true value. Cecilia swung into "Let's Call the Whole Thing Off," getting a couple of the littler kids to laugh at the "po-*tay*-to" "po-*tah*-to" bit. Two teenagers pushed back their chairs and launched into a ragged, self-conscious foxtrot. Tardily, she recognized them as part of the theater group that had declaimed about joy and ecstasy the night she and Sam closed the store. Heat rushed to her face and neck. "What else?" she called to the crowd while the dancers, proud and embarrassed, flung themselves back into their chairs. "What do you want to sing?" Cecilia asked.

"'Free Bird,'" called several boys.

"Get real," Cecilia told them.

"'Row, Row, Row Your Boat,'" shrieked a little girl who immediately began to chant, "Merrily, merrily, merrily, merrily, merrily, merrily," until her beaming mother hushed her.

"'This Land Is Your Land,'" suggested a woman with a long gray ponytail and Birkenstocks.

"'Old Man River,'" boomed a father by the door who could obviously carry the low notes. Cecilia was ready to go with that when Sam strolled out from behind the counter and drawled, "Try something with a little jump in it. Everybody knows the Beatles. Let's do 'All My Lovin.'" The "Old Man River" man groaned.

"I don't know it," Cecilia said. She shrugged. "Classical education."

"'A Hard Day's Night.' Everybody knows 'A Hard Day's Night.'"

"Not singable," Cecilia said, turning back to "Old Man River," but already the theater teenagers were howling away on the Beatles, most of them singing the melody, while a few others approximated the harmony on a song about the love that waited at home after a long day at work. She should have gone with "All My Lovin." She should never have started this.

Cecilia stood in place, feeling her hot blood beat against her cheeks and throat. She and David seemed to be the only ones in the room not singing. Sam had been right—everyone, even the woman in Birkenstocks, knew the words to "A Hard Day's Night." Cecilia knew them too, but the choir on this needed no help from her, and she had been trained to keep still when it wasn't her turn to play. So she didn't try to find David and make any despairing, apologetic signal. She didn't try to catch anyone's eye. Instead she pondered dignity, and wondered whether she would ever claim that trait again.

"A Hard Day's Night" wasn't a long song, although it felt so. By the bridge it was already falling apart, people laughing and forgetting words. This was Cecilia's chance; she stepped forward and started warmly singing, "Row, row, row your boat."

She gestured to the kids to join her, and by the time she got to "Life is but a dream," a wiggling knot of the littler ones had scrambled into a ring on the stage. Teenagers hightailed it for the door. Cecilia smiled. The children's voices careened in every direction, as unmusical as the worst of her students—one of them was her student—but Sam had drifted back behind the counter, and she took a careful, satisfied breath.

She let the kids sing as many rounds as they wanted, which was a lot. She lost count at nine. When they finally wound down, the littlest girl still stuck on "merrily," Cecilia's voice had gone thin, and the store was half empty, every note of the Beatles blotted out.

"Are you going to do this again?" a girl's mother asked Cecilia. "It's a fine idea. I can't remember the last time I sang."

"To tell you the truth, it was kind of spur of the moment," Cecilia began.

"Sure," David said, walking toward them. "Why not?"

"We'll have to clear it with our director of entertainments," Cecilia said.

"I'll take care of that. I'm going up to Mineville with her now. You and Sam can man the fort." He didn't bother to meet her eyes; she didn't bother to keep the unhappiness from tightening her mouth. The girl's mother pretended to busy herself, digging in her purse, but Cecilia could see the naked interest on her face.

Cecilia said, "Are you sure you have to go?"

"Vivy needs to pick up supplies."

"You don't need to go with her."

"Yes, I do. She won't know what to pick up unless I'm there to tell her." He paused flatly. "Don't worry. You can trust me."

Cecilia pressed her lips together. She nodded when David said maybe he'd be back in time for dinner, maybe not. She watched them leave the store, Vivy looking skittish as a pony. After the door closed behind them the room seemed to fall silent even though there were still customers around. These days, there were always customers around.

"Cecilia? I could use another scooping hand back here," Sam called. His slightly harassed voice had a broad, winking quality, his Ozzie inviting her Harriet. Cecilia muttered a ten-count before she moved.

The space behind the counter had never seemed so narrow. She kept dropping the scoop, dropping spoons. She chipped weakly at the surface of the ice cream. "Here," Sam said. "Let me." Standing an inch behind her, he closed his hand around hers and plunged the scoop into the Mocha Crunch. "Man's job," he said.

"Fine. I'll go do some women's work." She gestured at the dish tray, half filled with sticky beige bowls, but he didn't move. "Come on, Sam. Let me work."

"All work and no play."

"—would make me very happy right now. I already played."

By "play" she meant the sing-along, but she could see from Sam's pleased expression what he was thinking. She said, "I want to wash dishes. I yearn to wash dishes."

Before Sam could make a crack about yearning, grubby, ten-year-old Kenny Fagus—Cecilia's student, with breath that could knock her out of her chair—came to the counter and dropped a limp dollar bill next to the cash register. "Carob Carob-Chip," he said, looking at neither of them, speaking to the air.

"You're very bossy. What's the secret word?" Sam said. Reasonably sure the question would stump Kenny, Cecilia turned to the next customer. People kept coming in, a steady parade, enough to require two sets of hands. She said to Sam, "I'll ring up orders. You scoop," and moved to the register without waiting for his reply.

Sam didn't try again to touch her, but she felt his presence all the same—felt it, in fact, more piercingly as he maintained a scrupulous distance and related each order. The cash register sat in the center of the counter, with the ice cream set out on either side. Order after order, Sam trotted in neat half circles behind her until Cecilia felt connected to him, like a planet to its moon, or a trainer to her horse.

Only when the last customer in line had been served did Cecilia turn. As she'd expected, he was studying her, and she managed a fleeting smile. "There. Everybody happy."

"We're a good team."

"All us partners are a good team. I scoop ice cream in my dreams."

"I don't," he said.

"You'd better start. It's your life," she said.

"Don't you tell me what to dream. My dreams are my last refuge."

"'Children of the night, of indigestion bred.'" She couldn't remember where the quote came from, but there it was, a little nosegay of words in her mouth.

"Jesus, Cecilia."

A woman with a coffee drink looked up from her magazine, and Cecilia couldn't keep from reaching toward Sam, if only to get him to quiet down. Her hand hovered between them, the gesture half finished. She said, "Nothing personal. I'm not attacking you."

"I don't know what you're doing."

"I'm trying to work my shift."

"Well, that's fine. I'll nominate you for worker of the week."

This time she did put her hand on his arm; half the room was glancing at them now, sitting very still. "What," she whispered, angry with herself for not having put on a camouflaging CD. "What am I supposed to be saying?"

"Do I have to give you a script?"

"Apparently. You're letting everybody in here know you're not happy with what you're hearing."

"What do you think?" His whispered words foamed up now, and Cecilia had to lean close to hear. "I want to know what's going on with you. I want to know where we are. You won't even let me talk to you. I don't know what to think."

"Sure you do. You just don't like what you're hearing."

"You're going to shut me out? All by yourself? Just like that?" He looked down and whispered so furiously she could barely make out the words. "All I've been doing is thinking about you. I thought at least you'd be thinking about me."

"I have been. As of this morning, so has David."

The look Sam gave her was so shocked and stricken that bitterness flooded Cecilia's mouth. As if *Sam* could imagine himself the injured party. She said, "'We believe that marriage is a total union. We share our thoughts, fears, emotions, and intentions with our partners.'"

"Please stop that."

Every customer in the store, even Kenny Fagus, sat as if carved in place. Cecilia imagined she could see their ears cupping around each syllable.

Sam said, "I'm trying to share my thoughts and emotions with you. But you won't let me."

"No, I won't."

Sam reached over to the cash register and punched the drawer open, then slammed it back, punched it open, slammed it back. "This is all getting pretty goddamn funny. That night you'd do anything to make me feel better. Now you won't even look at me."

For a moment Cecilia thought about whispering *I'm pregnant*, but doing so seemed too cheaply dramatic, especially with customers listening as if she and Sam were Peyton Place. She and David had this one secret left. David, off driving through the foothills with Vivy, did not seem precious to her now, but the secret did.

"I suppose you're going to be volunteering this story at Life Ties," Sam said. "Waving your hand, wanting Nancy to call on you first."

"I promise you that won't happen."

"Then maybe I should be the one. Stand up and say, 'Hey, everybody—I have something to share.'"

"I can't stop you," Cecilia said. Her voice, despite her efforts at control, caught in her throat.

"You're not leaving me any place to stand," he said.

"Then walk," she said, wiping her hands roughly on her apron and dodging Sam to get to the storeroom fast, before the tears overcame her.

TEN

Vivy

"WELL, THAT WAS A bust." With David in the passenger seat beside her, Vivy sped to the bypass north of town. She had to punch the accelerator to get around a slat-sided pickup trailing cabbage leaves, a move she had no business trying in a twelve-year-old Fiesta; she had barely slid back in her lane before a Firebird wailed past. "I only hired him in the first place because I thought an act with 'New Age' in the title would please Nancy. But she wasn't even there. Crystal Billy." Vivy pronounced the words acidly. "Mr. Rogers' cousin from the commune. At least I got him out the door for only seventy-five bucks. I should give the other seventy-five to Cecilia. She provided the afternoon's entertainment."

"Don't bother," David said. "She does what she wants whether you pay her or not." He gazed out the window at a white frame house with a patchy lawn, at two girls with bikes, at a bean field that could use some water. Vivy doubted he was seeing any of it. In the store, the tension between Cecilia and him had hissed like steam. Every time David left the room Cecilia's head had jerked up, and every time he reentered he stopped in the doorway, searching for his wife. At the time Vivy had wondered whether they'd just fought or just had sex. Now she wondered what the fight had been about. It looked like a world-beater.

"I thought you guys were looking for a little extra cash."

"We don't need it."

"Lucky you."

"Don't call me that." This time the snap in his voice was sharper, and Vivy closed her mouth, although she kept sneaking glances at his fixed glare, his jaw set so hard she could make out the straining cords of his neck through his beard. Who would have thought he had such anger in him? She felt a stirring of new appreciation. "Talk about something," David said. "Other than me."

Obligingly, cutting her eyes every few minutes to check his immobile profile, she chattered. Whatever had happened, his unhappiness now was obvious, and she was willing to fill the space between them while he regrouped.

She talked about Crystal Billy, a topic requiring no input from David. Crystal Billy's appearance demonstrated the difficulty of finding not merely new acts for the store, but quality acts. "Sam and I fight about this all the time. Fredd, Marteeny—those are performers worth my time. But so many of the old acts are gone or gone sour. I have to find some new source. Amazing performers used to be on every street corner. Now the only guy on a street corner is Crystal Billy. Christ on a crutch. The kids weren't even bothering to make fun of him."

"Huh," said David.

"I'm standing out there in the audience, thinking, 'I vouched for this guy. I brought him here. I'm *paying* him.' When you and Cecilia came in I wanted to crawl under a table. Then when she started to sing I wanted to kiss her."

"A common reaction."

He stared out the passenger window and hummed a single note. Vivy recognized the tactic—she used it herself when Annie burst into the kitchen reciting every word from the TV show she'd just watched. Right now Vivy could confess a murder and he'd say "Huh." She said, "Can I tell you something, David? Can I confide?"

His hands tightened on the edge of the seat. "What."

"Even on a lousy day, even when it's Crystal Billy and I'm mortified, I'd rather present these acts than scoop ice cream. Performers are out there putting it on the line. I love that. I've always loved that."

"So get back into show business."

"Can't. Or can't yet. Sam and I still owe way too much for our partnership. I've been trying to save from these bookings, but it's going to take me years to pay my way out. And that's just me, not Sam." She almost went on to make a crack about Sam's goo-goo eyes around Cecilia, but she felt the ground grow marshy under her feet, and drew back.

"How much do you need?"

"Oh, come on, David. Zillions."

"How much?"

"This wasn't what I was after. I was just talking. I'm not going to extract your savings."

He stared at her with bloodshot eyes. Vivy shrugged. "For me, something like thirty-six thousand. For Sam, the whole forty. Unless he's been socking spare change away, which would be a surprise."

"My father left me some money. It's just coming clear of probate. And I have savings. Look." His voice, still rough with emotion, was strangely animated. He hardly sounded like himself at all. "Listen, I can buy you and Sam out. I'll buy your partnership. This is a good idea."

Vivy coughed. "David, you—" She loosened her jaw. "Thanks, but no. No way. That's your and Cecilia's baby money. You'll need every penny."

"You helped me get the job I wanted," he said. "I'll help you get the job you want. You and Sam can both go. Everybody wins."

Vivy kept squinting at the road and veering. David's fight with Cecilia, whatever it was, had roared right into the car with them, a presence David could see but Vivy could not. She felt scripted to be stupid, like the dim servant in a murder mystery. "I can't take your money. Jesus."

"Think about it," he said. "Just think."

"Look, there's something I need to tell you."

"This is the day for it."

"The last time I came up here for supplies? The blackberries? You didn't give me an invoice. But I took the money from the store just the same." David was silent. "So you may not want to offer me your savings, seeing as how I've already helped myself." He exhaled, but his expression didn't waver. She said, "Shit. David, I'm sorry. I was mad at the store, mad at Paul, mad at Sam. It didn't have anything to do with you. I can give it back tomorrow. What a stupid thing to do. I'm *sorry.*"

When she managed to shut up, the silence in the car pulsed, and Vivy couldn't decide which had been her stupider error—taking the money or admitting that she'd taken it. She studied the highway before her, the foothills shimmering in the heat.

David waited only about half a minute to speak. "I know you're sorry. You have a lot of impulses, but you try to put things right."

Vivy frowned. A Tercel whipped past, the little boy in the passenger seat sticking his tongue out. She was having trouble keeping up to the speed limit, not her usual problem.

"People get the wrong idea about you," David was saying. "They think you don't pay any attention, just because you like to get things done. They think you're self-centered. But I've worked with you, and I tell them. I've never known a more generous person, a more considerate one."

"Who?" Vivy asked. "Who's saying self-centered?" She saw the chain very clearly: Nancy talking to Cecilia, Cecilia talking to David. Then, worse and more likely: Sam talking to Cecilia. She pressed on the accelerator again.

"No one in particular. Life Tie-ers. You know how people talk after the meetings."

"People will crawl up from their deathbeds to catch the post-meeting postmortem," Vivy said. "Everybody gets to have an opinion about everybody else. Everybody gets to share it."

"'Our collective strength outweighs our individual desires,'" David said. His tone was difficult to decipher. If he'd been Sam, Vivy would have laughed.

"The smartest motto we've got. Every time I have a desire I ram into the collective strength."

"Keep ramming. Plenty of individual desires have gotten through. Yours might as well."

Caught by his tone, Vivy glanced over. What she could see of his face, mostly turned away, was twisted. Misery smeared itself over the quivering mouth, the clouded eyes. "I can't do anything but blunder today, can I?" she said. "I didn't mean to step on your toes. It's just that you and Cecilia always seem so united about these things." A spasm passed over David's plump lips. Helplessly, Vivy asked, "Are you okay?"

"Cecilia might be pregnant. We're not sure. Don't tell anybody yet."

"I can keep a secret. But you sound like you just found out your arms are going to fall off. This is happy news, remember?"

"Oh, you might not think so. She and Sam had sex."

Vivy swallowed. She inhaled so hard her lungs pinched. Her foot drifted up from the accelerator and David said, "Don't stop." But everything in her system—heart, brain, the tidal pool-like rippling and swelling of organs—seemed to have arrested in mid-function. She had no desire and hardly any capacity to speak. "This. Is a surprise."

"Isn't it. So you can see why I'm not turning cartwheels to hear that there's a baby on the way. Samantha, I guess, if it's a girl. Would you please keep driving? You're making me nervous."

She bore down: fifty-five miles an hour, sixty-five, eighty. The engine's rattle filled the air, and outside the car, fields of sugar beets tore past. Vivy watched the turnoff for Mineville approach, and then appear, and then recede.

Northeast, into the foothills. Already the valley farmland, so flat that grandmothers rode bicycles to the market, had begun to falter and climb. Cultivated fields roughened into pastures and grazing land, and mild, broad-faced cattle gazed moodily toward the road. Seeing the cattle reminded Vivy of Court Hellerman, Marteeny's rancher, and his admiration for Life Ties' high principles and the wisdom of the group. She was glad he was missing this chapter in the saga.

"Watch it," David said as she roared up behind a fifty-five-mile-an-hour van loaded with car seats and a golden retriever, a YOU CAN'T HUG A CHILD WITH NUCLEAR ARMS sticker disintegrating on the bumper. She yanked her Fiesta around the van, then yanked it again to avoid the steel retaining wall that suddenly appeared beside her. Below them threaded the Feather River. The tires sang.

"Do you want me to drive?"

"Do you want to quit telling me how to drive?"

"The woman in that van is probably on the verge of a heart attack. And then you almost had us in the river. Wherever it is that we're going, I'd like to get there in one piece."

"You were the one who told me to drive faster."

"I'm trying to keep us from having an accident."

"You really are an old maid, you know that?"

His mouth tightened. He turned his head again and studied the scruffy fields, making Vivy feel like a bully. She should have remembered that the man was out of shape for a quarrel; he lacked the advantage of regular workouts. Sam wouldn't have even flinched at such an easy jab, but then Sam was busy jabbing in some other rings. Vivy clenched the steering wheel and followed the highway's steep curve, pushing ninety.

"Yes," David said in an odd, high voice. "Yes, I suppose I am an old maid."

"I'm sorry. I was just letting off steam. I shouldn't let it off at you."

He shrugged and faced forward again, one hand braced against the door. Emotions played in order across his face: anger, hurt, self-righteousness. He seemed to be taking up all the emotions in the car, leaving Vivy only the sense that she was spinning violently. Even though she was every bit as injured as David, she couldn't manage to feel injured. She couldn't feel much of anything, except the desire to drive fast.

A roadhouse whipped by, some billboards for spas and lodges further into the mountains. The highway was climbing more purposefully now, and the car groaned and shook, slowing despite Vivy's foot jammed against the floor.

She halfway admired Sam. After so many years of well-controlled flirtations and benign crushes, after a lifetime of staying in the fenced yard, he had finally broken out. Or he had finally gotten caught.

Whichever, for once Vivy was not the one in the doghouse. For once she would get to wear the forgiving expression. She twisted the idea around, trying to get used to it. Later, she supposed, would come the fury, featuring unbidden images of Sam and Cecilia twined around each other under the sign advertising Cherry-Berry Swirl. Later, she would twist at the thought that she herself had challenged him, however drunkenly, to seduce Cecilia Moore.

"How far are you planning to go?" David asked.

Vivy shrugged. "If I turn around right now we still won't get to Mineville before three. Might as well call this day a loss."

"That's what I was thinking. So let's go someplace."

Vivy glanced around, wondering just where they were. The walnut trees and oaks were well behind now, replaced with scrubby, wiry conifers, some of them growing at sharp angles to the rock-studded dirt. If she rolled down her window, the air would be tangy and more complicated than the air in the valley. College students came up here to hike or ride trail bikes, and there were lakes, too, somewhere, and a few restaurants. "You navigate," she said.

"Take the next right, and go right again after that," he said.

She had forgotten that David used to spend weekends tramping up and down these foothills when they were in college, collecting samples, doing plant things. Vivy had brought them onto his turf. She could see his posture ease and his grip on the door loosen. Of course, he might just be relaxing because she had slowed down to sixty.

Right, then right again, then straight ahead. After the first set of turns Vivy was lost, the roads—identical, flimsy strips of asphalt banked by pines—leading only to other roads, like roads in dreams. She had the faint sense that she could drive for days and never achieve a destination. Fine. For a moment she reached toward the radio, then rested her hand back on the steering wheel. No decent reception up here, everybody knew.

"Right turn about a hundred feet ahead," David said. A hard right, too, which he hadn't mentioned; Vivy's tires slewed on gravel, and a funnel of sunlight poured onto them from the sudden clearing in the trees. The gravel parking lot fronted on a broad, heavy-beamed building with long windows and a deep view of all the hills they had just ascended. A wooden sign announced Bearkeep Lodge, the name vaguely familiar.

"Isn't this a little rich for our blood?" she said.

"My treat."

"I still don't think you can afford it."

"Business lunch," he said. "We'll celebrate our new status—you a free woman, me a cuckold."

"Try whipping up on yourself, David. It's possible you can make yourself feel worse." Vivy had thought that she and David were allies here, and she hated to see him snatching all the righteous sorrow for himself. Nevertheless, she waited beside the car for him, making sure they could walk into the beautiful building together.

Bearkeep Lodge was rustic within an inch of its life—dark beams and low ceilings and wood-burned plaques on the walls. Vivy thought, "Know Your Vision. Embrace Your Vision. Make Your Vision." The people who ran this place knew their vision right down to the ground. In the window of the gift shop hung not only beaded silk blouses, but also centerpiece-sized replicas of the lodge, exact down to the hanging baskets of flowers and the tiny mat at the door. While she watched, a woman walked out of the shop with two of them.

A sign at the reception desk listed a full slate of leisure options: Swedish massage and herbal wrap, sensory-deprivation tanks, aromatherapy, yoga classes at 6:00, 10:00, 1:30, and 4:00. Vivy could hear kids laughing and splashing, and she automatically glanced around.

"Hot tub," David said.

Clicking on high heels, a hostess materialized from the dining room to their right, her blonde hair upswept and her smile outlined in dewy, expensive pink. "Two for a late lunch?" she asked in a slightly accented voice—French? Swedish? She was certainly someone's vision, Vivy thought, watching David's wordless nod. The hostess led them to a table with a view of a lake so purely, deeply blue, so closely ringed with trees, that a small cry escaped Vivy. "It's lovely," she said, not wanting to explain that the beauty was actually hurting her. It seemed a long time since she'd seen anything beautiful, and that image had been a roly-poly contortionist folding her legs behind her head. Vivy moved her chair so that her back faced the window.

David moved his so that he could gaze over her shoulder. She watched him track something, his eyes scanning left to right. "Hawk," he said. "Good place to watch them."

"Been here before?" Vivy asked. He nodded. "Not me," she said. "Quite a little retreat."

"It's written up in guidebooks."

Vivy traced a line with her finger across the lustrous tablecloth. After all his time in these parts, of course he would know about Bear-keep Lodge. He would have hiked past it time after time and watched the birthday parties, retirement parties, wedding parties. The place was built for occasions. Even as a twenty-year-old, he would have seen that it was just the place to bring a bride. "Look, David, was it really all that smart to come here?"

"I wanted a change of scene. You should look at the view. It's the whole point."

Vivy gave up trying then. She opened the menu and let the hurt silence between them curl like a dry sponge. The menu went on for pages. Even the bottled waters, eight dollars per, were given a paragraph of appreciative description. She buried her face between the tall, vellum-look pages, gesturing David to go ahead and order when the waitress, another blonde, came to the table. Vivy expected him to choose some morose, whole grain sandwich for fifteen dollars. But he smiled at the waitress, who smiled warmly back.

"I'll start with the oyster salad. Then the ratatouille, and a cheese tray. I like sauvignon blanc. What do you recommend?"

Vivy swiftly rearranged her order, chucking the Greek salad for scallops *en croute* and suggesting that she and David split a bottle of wine—so much nicer than ordering by the glass. If David lived anything like the way she did, this meal would blow his budget for two months, but she was catching on to his rebellious mood, and pondered

what it meant to sit with a man who could mount a rebellion by ordering a plate of oysters.

"Bring the wine right away," he said.

The waitress dimpled. "I guessed," she said.

Startled by the knowing lilt in the woman's voice, Vivy glanced
around the dining room, noticing for the first time that only couples
were seated—no families, no singles. One man dreamily fed forkfuls
of cake to a woman who leaned across the table, close enough to kiss.
Other couples whispered huskily, leaned toward each other, found excuses to brush each other's hands. Ordinary people with children and
jobs had eaten two hours ago; only those who had somehow slipped
their tethers could lunch in this swoony way, filling the room with an
ardent hum that rose like a scent. Vivy dipped her fingers in the wine
when it came and dabbed it on her hot cheeks.

"Cheers," said David.

"Back atcha."

They were on their second silent glass before Vivy, alerted by a dis-
ruption in the honeyed atmosphere, looked up. She had felt no more
than a small shudder in the air, but when she saw Nancy and Paul
standing at the doorway to the dining room, Nancy's hand on Paul's
shoulder, the shudder turned into a shock wave. "Heads up," she said
to David. He turned just in time to see Nancy's hand clutch Paul's arm.
Without waiting for the hostess they crossed the room toward Vivy
and David.

Nancy spoke first, two tables away. "Paul and I came here to celebrate our anniversary. We hiked to the lake and swam. We toweled
each other off, then found a ridge nearby where we could be intimate. I
could hear the echo of my voice across the canyon, and the sound was
strong. This is what we came here for—to reclaim and redefine and
revive ourselves."

"What are you two doing here?" Paul asked.

"Drinking wine," Vivy said sourly at the same time David said,
"This is a business lunch."

"Where are Cecilia and Sam?" Paul asked, and Nancy asked, more urgently, "Are they on shift together?"

Vivy said, "Why Nancy, you old scoundrel. Arranging the schedule so that you and Paul could sneak up here for a little splendor in the grass. I don't remember you calling a meeting to share that plan."

"We discussed it two weeks ago," Paul said. "After the report on the new lease. Check the minutes."

"Never mind. I'm sure it's there."

"I'm not one to change the rules," he said, a pure Paul line, all needle and hook.

"Vivy and I," David said doggedly, "are sharing a lunch. Discussing business."

"So let us in," Paul said. "What business are you discussing? Assuming it isn't a hostile takeover." He and Nancy seated themselves on either side of David. Vivy tried to imagine them engaging in noisy mountaintop sex, but her imagination, which had enough today, balked.

David took a long pull from his water glass. "We're discussing what we would do if we didn't have Natural High, and what those ideas tell us about how we should expand. The company saved us both, right when we needed to be saved. But what would we have done if that life raft hadn't come along?" He picked up his water glass again and gestured at Nancy. "What would you have done?"

"Our goal unites us," she said.

"So join me in this. It's an exercise to help us appreciate all that we've worked to create."

He was talking Nancy's language now. The lines around her mouth softened, and she pressed her finger to her lip. "Paul and I didn't move straight from college into entrepreneurship, you know. For four years we belonged to a radical organization. The real thing, not just liberals putting up school levies. Everybody we knew liked to sit around after dinner and talk about inequities, but we wanted to go beyond talk. We wanted to touch people's lives."

Vivy glanced at Paul, who wore his customary remote expression. The Paul sitting at the table looked like he wouldn't touch anything without first pulling on latex gloves.

"The group was very strict. We lived together in a house outside of Sacramento—women on one side, men on the other. We got up every morning at five. I went door to door with a partner, registering people to vote. Paul worked in the legal services office. At night we heard lectures about ownership of the means of production."

Vivy exhaled noisily and reached for her wineglass. Nancy said, "Paul and I weren't interested in ideology. We were interested in making a difference. In one month I registered twenty new voters, which was good work. During the lectures I'd think about the faces of those people."

"You're right. It was good work," David said.

"When the cadre leader talked about the powerlessness of the poor, you told him how many people you had registered," Paul said. "He asked you how it felt to co-opt the ignorant into a fascist system."

"It was a while before we found out about the arms stockpiles," Nancy said. "Not that they had much. Two boxes of rifles and some handguns. I'd never seen a gun before."

"Jesus," Vivy said.

"They were beautiful. I was surprised."

"It was hard to get out," Paul said. "They tailed us. They found my parents' phone number and threatened them."

"We knew we wanted to come back to El Campo, but we stalled," Nancy said. "We didn't want the organization following us here and harassing our friends. We went up to Redding and waited tables for a year, until the calls stopped. We studied the food service industry. After what we'd already been through, working out cost projections and thinking about inventory was easy."

David shook his head. "What a story."

"Back from the gulag," Vivy said. She smiled to make sure they knew she was joking. She was impressed by the part about the stockpiles, and twice as impressed with David for getting Nancy sidetracked this way.

"The gulag of Redding, California," Paul said. He and Nancy exchanged a look, part smile, a private expression. Vivy imagined whispering to Sam the news that Nancy and Paul still had secrets. But Sam might at this moment be whispering secrets to Cecilia. She reached for her wine again.

"My life is whole now, and satisfying," Nancy said. "I don't think about those old days very often. But I still remember how hard it was for the poor people we visited to keep clean. Some of them didn't have hot water. Lots of them didn't have a scouring pad. Even living with the group in that bungalow and eating black beans every night, I still had a scouring pad." She shuddered. "Bugs."

"Real revolutionaries are not squeamish," Paul said, a grin lifting the corners of his hard mouth. Vivy wondered whether she was drunk.

Nancy said, "If I was going to start all over again? Without Natural High? I'd start a cleaning service for the poor. Washing machines, Ajax, elbow grease. Something that would be a real help to people. It would be work we could be proud of."

"How do you feel about the work you do now?" Paul asked silkily.

"It's not so serious, is it? Nobody gets sick from a lack of ice cream. Nobody dies."

"Your life commitment. Not so serious."

In the pause before Nancy responded, Vivy watched a shadow fall across the other woman's face. She hadn't imagined she could feel sorry for Nancy. "We're not going to change people's lives with ice cream," Nancy said.

"No?" Paul's soft voice made Vivy close her eyes and wrap her hands around the base of her glass. "Then what have we been doing? What have we been building every day? And what have you been thinking while the rest of us have discussed better food for a better world?"

"Is this a test, Paul?" Nancy's voice was soft, too—round and strangely sweet. "We've gone without sleep. We've groveled for a lease. Are you truly asking whether you can depend on me?"

Vivy glanced at David to see whether he heard the pleading in Nancy's voice, but David was shut tight. Vivy was left as witness. She would rather have been handed a burning stick to hold.

Paul said, "'Marriage creates a single unit, without boundaries or divisions.'"

Nancy pressed her hands against her cheeks; for an instant she resembled a Renaissance cherub. "I deserve better than this, Paul. I deserve a little credit."

The room swam before Vivy. She gazed at the deep blue tablecloth and bit her lip, letting the conversation course along without her. Why couldn't she work with people who liked to talk about movies? Nancy said something stalwart about challenges, David said that he had plenty of those, and the waitress, who had been hovering behind Paul, took advantage of the moment's pause to set David's and Vivy's plates before them. Yes, Nancy said, she'd like a menu. Paul stared at the oysters on David's plate until David started saying something about trust.

Vivy poured herself more wine. She would have liked to help David, but he couldn't be helped. Had she been with Sam, she could have tossed in a comment about anything, extraterrestrials or roller derbies, just for the glee of watching him work her material in. He had never let her down. Until now. She closed her eyes and let out a cry.

David stopped in mid-sentence. "Are you all right?" Nancy asked.

"Too much wine?" said Paul.

Vivy shook her head. "I'm worried," she said. She didn't think she slurred too much. "Where will Natural High be in ten years? Where will we all be?"

"Why, Vivy," Nancy said, her voice so gentle that Vivy's tears, poorly dammed, spilled down her face. "Shit," she mumbled.

"Shh. It's all right," Nancy said.

Vivy shook her head. "It's the only thing that holds us together. And it's coming apart."

"Nothing is coming apart." David's voice was firm, reassuring, a little bit severe. What a perfect father he would be. The thought made her cry harder. "Stop it, now," David said. "This is enough. All we were doing was talking."

"I hate talk."

"As you often tell us," Paul said. His voice sounded a little more comfortable than usual, as if a laugh were tucked deep inside of it. Vivy risked a look at him, and he met her eyes.

"Why are you here without Sam?"

"He's with Cecilia." Catching David's expression, she added, "On shift. Where he's supposed to be."

"Are you guys all right?"

"No."

"Vivy." Paul's voice was coaxing. Everybody at the table, Vivy thought, was coming on like a good parent. And then she understood: she was the child. "Vivy, will you bring your problems to Life Ties? Will you let the group help you?"

"Paul, she's in no condition—" Nancy said.

Paul tapped his bony finger beside Vivy's hand. "You're in a good condition. And you're exactly right. Things are coming apart. But you can bring them back together. This is your chance. You've been waiting. And we've been waiting for you."

"What am I, the Messiah?" Vivy said, trying to keep herself from thinking of Sam's laughter at such a word applied to her.

"Will you?" Paul asked.

Vivy twirled her wineglass. David's face was studiously blank. Surely he knew she had no choice as long as Paul's finger steadily tapped the tablecloth. Longing for Sam's shelter, she had been hurled first into David's mild harbor, then into Paul's rocky one. "Hell with it," she said. "Sure. Like you say, what is the group for? And I've sat through all those meetings without talking." She picked up her mostly empty glass and drained it. "It's time for people to listen to me."

ELEVEN

Sam

UNABLE TO TAKE ANOTHER minute of Cecilia's icy courtesy, Sam slipped out of the store two hours before their shift was over. His wordless escape would anger her, he knew, and she would disguise her anger the next time she saw him with more chilly politeness. A few more shifts with Sam and she'd be the only person in California's Central Valley in danger of death by freezing.

Five blocks west of Natural High, between a residential hotel and an empty lot, squatted The Blue Spot, a peeling-paint dive regularly singled out at public meetings for its stink, its fights, the motorcycles parked out front. Sam hadn't been there in years, but now he took the most direct route. No other bar in town could do him better than a tiny, sour-smelling shitbox, dark as a bat's asshole, just the place for a guy whose wife was off riding with another man and whose woman would sweep the same section of floor four times in a row to keep from looking at him.

In college, when he thought seediness meant authenticity, Sam had been a Blue Spot regular. He'd liked the blue lightbulb over the door that was burned out half the time and the window in the bathroom that held a piece of cardboard where somebody had broken the glass. The floor was gummy, the bartenders surly, the waitresses famously raunchy. Sam had proposed to Vivy here. Now he picked a table in the unlit back and hunched over the house special draft. It tasted, as Vivy had always claimed, like moose piss.

"Party's never gonna get going if you don't do better than that." The waitress, low-slung breasts and an orange mouth, pointed at his glass.

Sam shrugged. "Some days it just doesn't taste good."

"Honey, it never tastes good. You want me to bring you something else? I like to start the day with Jim Beam. Gets the scum off my teeth."

"I'll bet it does. Sure, bring me a shot."

But he couldn't finish that either. Maybe because the waitress had put the thought in his head, the bourbon tasted like mouthwash. Everything about this place hammered on him—the bad drinks, the music he didn't know thudding from the jukebox, the three guys wearing greasy denim jackets and wallet chains—give it a *rest*—playing pool. He pushed the glass around on the table for a while, then left a walloping tip and scowled back into the hot afternoon.

Soaked joggers lumbered beside their panting dogs. A girl in a tank top, thin as a whippet, shrieked "That's what I'm *telling* you" into her cell phone. By the curb a professor-faced man, his beard striped with gray, settled a sweaty baby into a bicycle baby seat. A kid shot past on a skateboard and Sam, dodging him, jumped into a young woman with an extremely short skirt. "Are you all right?" she asked, her tone not cordial.

"No," Sam said. "Sorry." He backed into the narrow shade of the roof overhang and watched her hurry home to more than a rented house, a saggy couch, a used-up low-end TV that turned newscasters' skin green. He knew he was swimming into the deep waters of self-pity. He would like to see anyone who had a better right to be there.

On his own street, air-conditioning units buzzed in window after window, making the street as loud as a factory floor. Sam picked up his listless pace. At least his house should be quiet—the kids still at the pool, Vivy still investigating some distant corner of the cosmos. Sam could lie on the couch and listen to dust fall. After that Laszlo and Annie could scream or Vivy could pick at him and he would go ahead and perform all the loud, expected actions: yelling, swearing, breaking things, every inch the loser.

But because he was a loser, the house was like a prison riot. Home early, Laszlo and Annie slammed in and out the back door along with two neighbor girls, a boy from Laszlo's school, and somebody's wet, wagging, footstool-sized dog whose nails scrabbled on the linoleum and whose hind end kept slamming into walls. Sam positioned himself in front of the door and caught Laszlo's shoulder as the boy tried for his second lap. "Where's your mother?"

"Dunno. Can Justin spend the night?"

"Dunno. Depends on your mom. What direction was she headed when you saw her last?"

"She went out this morning before you. She told me to come to the store and see her clown, or else clean up the kitchen. Good one, Mom."

"She hasn't gotten home yet?"

"So now can Justin spend the night?"

"If you ask me, no. So you'd better not ask me again."

Sam loosened his grip and Laszlo dashed away, leaving Sam with the mess. In the sink and over all the counters sat crusty dishes and glasses with hardened milk rings. Both Sam and Vivy had been on KP strike, a little game of domestic chicken they played from time to time. Already the kids were eating cereal out of mixing bowls, now stacked haphazardly in the drainer. Across the top of the stove stretched a film of grease flecked with tomato sauce, bits of broccoli, and something brown. An abandoned piece of toast, hard as a shingle, stood in the toaster. Hard Pavements Make Good Roads. Sam wished his life hadn't arrived at a point where every thought came accompanied with its own Life Ties motto.

He pulled out a chair to sit down, but someone had left a saucepan filled with scummy water on the seat; the water sloshed all over Sam's feet, and he uttered, "God *damn* it" through clenched teeth. When a twenty-year-old left the kitchen uncleaned for a week at a time, the gesture indicated an age-appropriate challenge to middle-class mores. When two thirty-seven-year-olds left it filthy, they were living in the kind of squalor that appeared on the nightly news, Child Protective Services people hoisting hollow-eyed kids on their shoulders and tenderly carrying them away.

Giggling Annie and the girls raced in again, Laszlo and Justin howling behind them. The dog, missing its timing, caught the screen door on its nose and barked. Sam waited until they had all thundered back into the kitchen, then stood in their way and held the door. "Out," he said. "Outside, and stay there."

"But we have to come in," Annie yelled. "That's the game!"

"You know what? I have a pretty good idea that you haven't practiced your violin today. The next time you come in, you're going right to the living room. I'm going to be working in there, so I'll keep an eye on you."

"No fair," she said, but the other girls tugged her onto the porch, where the dog was still barking. Sam lingered near the door and watched the game dissolve. The children stood in a loose knot, the dog wandering between them and nosing their hands.

"What work does your dad do?" Justin asked Laszlo, who shrugged. "Dunno."

Vivy would have loved that. Once upon a time, Sam would have reminded himself to share it with her.

He let his hand drop. His fingers brushed the countertop and caught in a ring of something sticky. If he waited for Vivy to lift a hand to any of this, he could be waiting another week, until she was giving the kids dinner on pot lids. If he cleaned it himself, she would smile like a cat. "All spick-and-span! How very nice." And then leave her unwashed coffee mug on the table, signaling round two.

He pulled out another chair, this one holding only a telephone book, a T-shirt, and a spelling quiz of Laszlo's. He was worn out from playing against Vivy, tired of strategizing. What had once been a marriage had turned into an endless rehearsal of tactical espionage, drill for a war that never quite broke out. No wonder he had fallen in love with Cecilia, who merely wanted to know how he was when she asked him how he was. If love was what he had fallen into. He didn't want to run away with her. He just wanted to talk to her.

Dimly, without heat, he wondered where Vivy was. It was easier, God knew, to sit in the kitchen without her than to worry about what all of her hints and jokes might mean, about money, about Cecilia, about who knew what. Did that mean that their marriage was in crisis? He cracked a smile whose ugliness he could feel. Gosh, maybe they should get counseling. *Marriage is our first strength, our full humanity, our unique creation.* Sam pondered, gazing at his filthy kitchen. He may have come to hate his marriage. He may have come to hate Vivy. He knew beyond question that he had come to hate his life.

When visioning, Life Ties instructed, always stay with your insights. Allow them a chance to take root; don't rush on. Take at least ten minutes by the clock. Sam gave himself five minutes before he stood, cleared the sink, and turned on the tap until the water ran hot.

He cleaned selectively, making sure the line between shine and grime was obvious. Half of the kitchen table, half of the stove, including two of the encrusted drip pans under the cooktop. Half of the floor— lengthwise, following the turn in front of the back door. Getting into the spirit of his own gesture, he cleaned the left half of the refrigerator shelves, including a haze of grape jam that had been smeared across the second shelf for months. Half the counter, half the cupboards. The air tightened with the smell of Ajax and Formula 409, and he regretted that he couldn't divide the smell in half, too. One curtain from each of the sets of café curtains, which got him into the laundry room. There were enough clothes heaped there to make division easy.

He stopped short of vacuuming. The big purple rug Vivy had picked out was her responsibility, although Sam happened to know that Annie had spilled orange drink on it someplace, the stain lodged safely in the mulberry-colored expanse. Ignoring Annie's socks and a stuffed anteater under the window, he straightened up the two weeks' worth of *Valley-Heralds* that should have been set out for recycling pickup. He was reading about a proposed new water desalination plant when Vivy swung open the front door, rustling a shopping bag.

"If it isn't Sure Shot Jilet," she said.

"Not funny," he said. Vivy had come up with the nickname for him years ago, when she got pregnant with Laszlo even though she was on the pill. The name was enshrined when Annie was conceived despite an

IUD. Since then Vivy had gotten her tubes tied, but she still brought out "Sure Shot" when she was feeling especially amorous. "Kids are out back."

"Anybody bleeding?"

"Not yet. Where were you?"

"I went up to Bearkeep Lodge with David Moore."

"Good one, Vivy."

"Ask Nancy and Paul. They showed up glowing after the sex of the century and accused David and me of having a tryst."

"Were you?"

"We were eating oysters and drinking wine." He turned around. Her tiny, pert mouth was pursed like a Kewpie doll's, and her green eyes sparked.

"Still working to seduce David?" he said.

"Shoot. I should have. Missed opportunity."

"Oysters have a reputation."

"I know. I ate one off of David's plate. Sadly, that's all I did." She studied her fingernails, which she had painted red, as she did from time to time. "Still, I'd eat one again."

"I'll remember that," Sam said.

Vivy bumped her purse higher onto her shoulder, picked up the shopping bag, and sauntered down the hallway to the bedroom. Were they fighting? Usually her banshee fury could be heard in the next county. Now she sounded friendly enough, but the hot glitter in her eyes unsettled Sam. He picked up the paper and began from the beginning the article on desalination.

Vivy stayed in the bedroom a long time. His damp hands moistening the edges of the *Herald,* Sam envisioned the scene as it always played in movies: her closet and drawers yanked open, her suitcase yawning on the bed. She furiously half-folding scarves, blouses, changes of clothes for the kids. Pure fantasy. She and Sam kept the suitcases in the garage.

Then, approaching from the bedroom, Vivy's voice: "Look, honey, you're way off here. He's trying to help you. He's giving you choices because he wants you to be happy."

Sam looked up. From the hallway Vivy nodded at him. She was talking into a thin iPhone, which had never existed in their house before.

"Well Jesus, Marteeny, if you don't want to do it, you don't have to. Nobody's twisting your arm. You twist your own arm better than we could do anyway."

She listened again, ignoring Sam's stare, then said, "Fine. Let me go to an expert." Holding the phone away from her ear, a confident half-smile hovering at her mouth, she said, "If a fiancé tells his intended that she should have her own career, should she believe him? How does she know he isn't trying to give her space so he can back away?" A tiny wail rose from the telephone. "What if the fiancé—say, Court—is sure that his intended—say, Marteeny—wants to go back on the stage, and he wants to help her get there. Is he just pushing her away, even though he says he wants to help?"

"Nice phone, Viv."

"Because you know how men are. They'll say they love you and how they're always thinking of you, but they're really keeping an eye on the door."

"You know how women are? They'll throw you curves. They like to change the rules. They'll say they want communication, but what they really want is the upper hand."

"Not Marteeny. She's just been explaining: she wants to get up every morning and make the same bed, go to the same grocery store, cook at night on the same stove. She wants reports on all of the cows. And there's Court talking about getting rid of the ranch. He's ready to see the world."

"Give me the phone," Sam said, ignoring for the moment Vivy's peculiar smile. "Marteeny, sweetheart, is that you? Are you all right?"

"Situation normal," she moaned. "Everything was going fine. I planted a rosebush. Then we came down to see you. Now Court says he has a whole new understanding of who I am, and that means a new understanding of who he can be. He's talking about selling the spread and getting a mobile home so we can travel to shows. 'Gigs.' He thinks El Campo is well located for us to drive to gigs up and downstate. Sam, he wrote an ad for the paper to sell off some of his stock. I had to stop him from dropping it in the mail."

Sam imagined the scene—kitchen windows looking out on grazing land, a heavy pine table comfortably cluttered with mugs and a jar of wildflowers. Marteeny tearing the envelope from Court's hand, wailing, blessing him out, while Court fingered his shirt cuffs and admired her spirit. Sam had seen the cycle before, but he was still amazed. Life Ties hadn't backed the man off from the woman. It had made him fall in love all over again.

"That guy is nuts about you," he said. "He wants to show you off to the whole world. You don't have to go anyplace, but you should pay attention to what he's telling you."

Before he could say more Vivy lifted the phone from his hand. "There you go, Marteeny—you heard it from Brother Sam. Now just calm down. I'll call you soon, and we'll talk about dates. I've found you a couple of jobs that are less than a day's drive away from the ranch. Tell Court you don't need that mobile home yet." After she ended the call, she bobbed her head at Sam. "You get an A."

"I didn't know I was taking a test."

"You were."

"Do I win my own phone?"

"This one's yours. One-sixth yours, one-sixth mine. Natural High bought it, to allow me more efficiency in my work."

"And all the partners okayed this purchase? I don't remember that."

"Not yet." Vivy balanced the phone on her hand, then tilted her head back and balanced it on her nose.

"Go slow."

Straightening, she produced the Kewpie-doll mouth again. "I borrowed some money. It's mine. I'm a partner. I'll pay it back."

"Darling," he said. His mouth suddenly seemed to be jammed with teeth. "Angel. Light of my life. Felon. You have embezzled company money so you could buy an iPhone."

"I am more sick than I can tell you of putting off everything in the world in order to retain the privilege of working for an ice cream company. A telephone, Sam. A business expense."

"What are you going to say when Nancy confronts you? I give her twenty-four hours."

"I don't think she'll have much to say."

"Guess you know some different Nancy than the one I work with."

"I know lots of different people. Of course, so do you," Vivy said, pushing her hair back and moving toward the kitchen. When she got to the doorway she laughed. "A test?"

"I just took care of what I thought was my portion. You can do what you want. If I'd known you were taking money from Natural High, I'd have left you a little more to clean."

"Sam, baby, it isn't that bad. It isn't the worst thing I could have done. I just wanted to get a little of my own back. Don't tell me you don't know how that feels."

Her scalding fingernails tapped, and Sam said, "I won't tell you that. So now that you've got a phone, do you feel like you've got what you need?"

"What do you think? Would you be satisfied?"

"No," Sam said, and Vivy looked at him with teacherly satisfaction. Sorrow ran through him in a thick current. They knew just how to talk to each other, just what to say. They hadn't said anything that needed saying in years. "I love you, Vivy."

"There you go." She shrugged. "That and two hundred bucks will buy you an iPhone."

THE CARS WERE BOTH more than ten years old and had been cheap even when new. Maybe they could bring $500. Most of the furniture Vivy had picked up second hand—underneath her slipcovers and crackle glazes, the pieces were threadbare, split, loose at the joints. Salvation Army, where they'd gotten the stuff in the first place, wouldn't want it back. Somebody might pay $50 for Laszlo's bike. After that, what did they have? A handful of rent receipts.

Sam couldn't stop tallying, sickened at how little he would be able to offer when brought to account. He had been content to live lean. He and Vivy made cracks about their membership in the working poor. But he had liked part ownership, however mortgaged, in an actual company, and he liked the idea that he was working toward a secure stake. Now Vivy had blown that security sky high, and he couldn't bring himself to say one word to her. "Communication Is the Key that Opens All Doors." Not all doors should be opened. Anybody who'd been married more than twenty minutes knew that much.

When Nancy didn't call before Sunday night's Life Ties meeting, Sam's jitters sped up, his pulse thudding in his head like a handball. That afternoon, Vivy had blown out of the house to take the kids for new bathing suits and pizza. She'd meet him at the meeting, she said. Left to himself, Sam wouldn't have even gone, but it was their night to bring cookies. Now he sat in the semicircle with the bag of Safeway cookies beside him, his ass already aching from the hard seat, Vivy nowhere in sight. Two people had asked about her, and Sam had come up with an idiot grin and made a joke. Another minute and he would be breaking into soft-shoe. He felt as obvious as a single tooth in a baby's pink mouth. He could kill Vivy.

The ordinary setting-up sounds for the meeting—the drag and stutter of chairs over linoleum, the sigh of the coffeemaker—washed over him fitfully: loud, then soft. Loud again. He watched Cecilia pour water into the coffeemaker, bring out the tray with sugar and tea bags, and finally settle beside David. Stealing glances, Sam felt like an adolescent or a criminal. He wondered which of those words she would use. He could figure which one David would use.

He had to hand it to them. Wretched as they obviously were, at least they dwelled in their wretchedness together. Their misery sealed them into a single unit, seamless as an egg. When David shifted on his chair, Cecilia looked at him with quick worry. Sam wondered how it would feel to be the object of such concern.

A hand, bony as a claw, clamped on his shoulder. "Where's the lovely life partner? She promised she'd come tonight." Paul displayed his mirthless smile. Years ago Sam had heard that Paul scared kids off his porch at Halloween—not by bellowing or roaring, but by smiling. Sam and Vivy had cherished that story like family silver.

"She must have got caught in traffic. She went up to the mall to get some new clothes for the kids."

"You might want to get her a watch for Christmas. A stopwatch. Ha."

"Look, tell whoever's leading we can start without her. She won't mind."

"I know," Paul said. "But I was hoping to see her." Squeezing Sam's shoulder again, he walked back up to the front of the group, where Nancy stood beside another woman holding the Statement of Beliefs. What was going on? Meetings started all the time without Vivy, and without Sam, too. As she liked to say, they'd seen the movie before; they didn't need to catch the credits. Sam watched Nancy shake her head and felt his throat constrict another fraction of an inch. The goddamn iPhone.

The woman stepped forward. "Welcome," she said, and launched into "We believe that we are put on this earth to improve it." Sluggishly, couples joined in, and the meeting stirred to life.

Still Vivy didn't come. Through the Statement of Beliefs, through the opening comments, the monologue, through the confession of the man who'd spent his second wedding anniversary in bed with a perfume saleswoman who had just sold him a bottle of Chanel for his wife.

"Even after errors—especially after errors—we are here so we can work with our partners," the leader said. Sam twisted on the unyielding chair. Other couples ticked their eyes over at him, each glance a sting. Cecilia and David stared ahead like Easter Island statues.

He checked his watch. Thirty minutes. There was no shame in coming to meetings with a spouse who acknowledged a problem and was committed to solving it. A stark beauty attached to couples determined to stand together, clutching the frayed ends of their hopes and intentions. But no beauty or dignity could be claimed by a chump sitting alone, clueless about where his wife might be. Sam imagined a dizzy kite, cut from its string, swooping over the mall that housed the phone store, over a car dealership, over a bus or train or airline counter. Thirty-two minutes.

The man who had invested in Harmony Orchards had actually made a little money. A couple with three dogs was quarreling over diets and feeding schedules. A woman had instructed her children to tell their teachers their father hit their mom every night, though he'd never lifted a hand to her. The talk was slow and distracted, and Sam could feel everyone's relief when the leader began reciting the Gathering of Hope. He was on his feet as she finished, halfway to the door, before Paul's voice and frightening smile stopped him. "Hey, buddy. It's your turn to man the refreshments tonight, remember?"

"No," Sam said. But when he lifted his head he saw Cecilia standing behind Paul. Her unguarded face, looking out the dark window, was wrenched out of shape, her mouth soft with a sorrow Sam felt like a burn. "Yes," he said.

So Sam poured coffee and replenished cookies while Life Tie-ers nodded at him and pressed his hand and Cecilia kept the width of the room between them. Although he would have very much preferred not to, he heard scraps of every conversation—no one in the whole damn group knew how to whisper. "What did he expect?" "I wouldn't have come. Or stayed." "Where's he going to go?"

"Home, as soon as we're finished here," Sam said pleasantly.

Elena, the wife of the man who invested in Harmony Orchards, held out her cup for a refill. "You don't know where she is, do you?" With her sleek head craned forward and her quivering nostrils flared, she looked like a hunting dog on the scent.

"Nope."

"She could be in Sacramento. She could be in San Francisco."

"If she is, I hope she's picking up a ball game. I have twenty bucks on the Giants."

"You can relax here," she said, clasping his wrist. "You don't need to pretend."

"I am relaxed. I'm Mr. Natural." Another one of Vivy's names for him. He'd shared that with Cecilia, but she'd never seen the R. Crumb drawings, and didn't know what he was talking about. He turned to find David watching him, his blunt features rigid.

"Is she okay?" David asked.

"No. I have her at home stuffed in a trunk."

"She's never run away before. Something must have happened."

Sam pondered the other man's girlish mouth and thin, lank hair, the whites of his eyes the color of old mayonnaise. For fifteen years he had disliked David Moore. Sam said, "The last thing I know is that she drove up into the hills to have lunch with you. You tell me what happened."

"What's this?" Elena said.

"David and Vivy went out to lunch. A cozy little afternoon at Bear-keep Lodge. Vivy showed me the guidebook where it says the view is the most romantic one in California."

David took an audible breath. "Vivy's my best friend. She's gone out of her way to help me. She deserves one nice lunch at a nice restaurant."

"Which you were able to give her," Sam said.

"You're really unbelievable," David said.

The man who bought the perfume said, "The day of my anniversary I looked at that sales clerk and thought, 'She deserves something nice.' I was Galahad. The next thing I know we were in room fifteen at the Riverview and I was giving her something else nice."

"We're not talking about that," David said. "Can't anybody keep their minds out of the trash?"

"Only you, David," said Sam. "You're made of better stuff than the rest of us."

"Better than you, yes."

"This is denial, man," said the perfume man to David.

"Believe us. We've been there," said his wife.

"David's telling the truth. He likes Vivy, and they went to lunch, and he's never laid a hand on her," Cecilia said tonelessly. She was leaning against the wall, a cup of coffee between her hands. She said, "You all can think whatever you want, but he's telling the truth." Then she put down the coffee and bolted to the bathroom in the corner of the room. Sam made a low noise, and David looked at him with loathing.

"What's going on?" asked Elena.

David said, "She's pregnant."

Sam's throat closed entirely. Trying to inhale, he choked and had to pound himself on the chest. When he looked up, he saw Nancy's narrow eyes on him.

"You don't sound happy," Elena was saying to David.

"I'm not."

"Why not?"

"It's between Cecilia and me."

Shock stopped the conversation, and the Life Tie-ers flicked glances at one another. Even though this gathering was social hour, not meeting, and David could refuse to answer if he wanted, Sam couldn't ever remember those words being said in this room.

Setting down her cup, Nancy smiled—an expression that was only a little bit terrible, like the smile of an Amazon queen. "David Moore. I have never told you how much I truly like you."

She crossed the room until she stood only inches away from the end of his dark brown beard. David took a step back. Nancy said, "I've always wondered if Cecilia understood what a jewel you are. You have a real vision of the future. There have been times that you kept me going."

Not a cup was raised, not a foot shifted. Sam would not have traded places with David for all the money in California.

"A long time ago I started to depend on you. You clarified ideas that I couldn't always get across. You had a way of putting things. I looked forward to meetings because I'd see you here."

Sam's wasn't the only head that swiveled to look at Paul, who gazed at Nancy with no expression at all. David had an expression. He looked appalled.

"I admired you," Nancy said. "I respected you. You were my comrade. And it seemed the most natural thing in the world one day to be having sex with Paul and find myself imagining your face, your beard, your arms."

"I don't want to hear this," David said.

"As soon as I realized what I was doing, I made Paul stop right there."

"That's right," Paul said. His face might have been stark, but his voice was drenched with emotion.

"I told him what I was doing. We fought."

"We did," Paul said.

"We decided I needed to recommit to the marriage. I painted the house."

Sam let out a soft laugh. Vivy had always said there was a reason Nancy had spent two weeks one August up on the ladder with scrapers and brushes.

Nancy said, "I spent hours on visioning exercises. I visioned myself and Paul, and I visioned you and Cecilia creating a child. Your desire. I thought it was your desire. Was I wrong?"

She stood before David, her arms outstretched, as theatrical as a teenager. When David spoke, his voice was tremendously irritated. "Dead wrong."

"Then what can I wish for you?"

"A monastery sounds pretty good," he said. "No talking."

On the downbeat, before Nancy could reply, the door squealed and Vivy—blazing, laughing, glittering like a sequin—let herself into the room. Couples practically leaped back to give her room. Her pistachio-colored dress made her hair glow red as a stove coil. She was drunk, Sam thought. Or something like it. She was revved up too high, her eyes brilliant, her movements jagged, and when she finally focused her thousand-watt smile, she focused it on Paul.

He said, "We're on Daylight Savings Time here, Vivy."

"Figured you could get along without me. I found a sale. Jackets for both of the kids, new shirts. Shoes. Annie had to sit on Laszlo's lap on the way home—no room in the back." She didn't glance at Sam.

"I was counting on you," said Paul.

"Here I am. Here you are. Let's dance."

"Didn't you have something you wanted to say to the group?" said Paul.

"The meeting is over," Sam said.

"The meeting's never over," Vivy said.

"David was explaining how much he likes to talk to you," said the perfume man.

"That's true. He likes to talk to me more than Sam does. Pathetic, isn't it?"

"About Sam." Paul looked at no one but Vivy. Sam rubbed his uneasy hands against his thighs.

Vivy said, "He cleaned exactly half of the kitchen. I thought that was pretty funny. Passive aggressive, but it still got half the stove clean. I did the other half the next day."

"It's a danger sign!" Elena's voice was almost a screech. "Your marriage is crumbling right here in front of everyone. Can't you see?"

Vivy cleared her throat. When she spoke, her voice lacked any malice. It was merely loud. "I'm happy to talk with David, who needs a friend right now. It's nice to have a friend. For those of you who are wondering, David and I did not have sex. Sam and Cecilia did, though. In the store. Right before Cecilia got pregnant."

She looked at Sam with her eyebrows raised, as if inviting him to add a further statement of his own. As if he could. A roar went up—insistent, hortatory voices, outrage, satisfaction, some moron offering congratulations. Staring at Vivy's flushed face, her dilated eyes and chapped, excited lips, Sam shook his head, meaning *I'm sorry,* meaning *It isn't what you think,* meaning *You shouldn't have done that.* She shook her head back at him, and he didn't know what she meant. They stared at each other perhaps a full minute, until her familiar face began to look strange to him, and he dropped his eyes. Then, though he would have preferred not to see this, Sam watched Cecilia emerge from the bathroom. She faltered at the noise, put down her head, and moved back to her chair as if she were walking against a current.

Entr'acte (5)

Après Vivy, le déluge.

The women have divided into two groups—the ones who call or visit Cecilia, bringing her coffee and advice and baby things, and the ones who phone Vivy on the home line, where we can get through. We are eager to commiserate, already worked into a fury on her behalf. "You have been *used*," we remind both of them. It's convenient to need only one speech. "Sam should be crawling to you. On his knees."

"That seems a little extreme," Vivy says. On the rare occasions we catch her, she's halfway willing to talk, which Cecilia isn't. Cecilia excuses herself and hangs up. When we talk to Vivy we can hear her washing dishes, walking from room to room. She's a busy woman, and we are not her first priority, but we already knew that.

"This is how abuse begins. If you don't confront the abuser early, the behavior will only accelerate. We don't want to find you in the emergency room."

"I'll call in Fredd to act as my bodyguard."

"The juggler? Vivy, this isn't a joke."

"Oh, yeah it is." When she sees us at meetings she smiles, but several of us have noticed that her smile looks tired. So, of course, does Cecilia's.

The call schedule we tried to set up didn't work. Cecilia won't talk, and Vivy's line just goes to voicemail, three or four hours at a stretch. If she does pick up, she usually has to rush off again, saying she's been scheduling acts all day. Nobody believes a handful of clowns and magicians requires so much time. Some of us call David after an hour or more of frustration, to see if his phone is tied up, too. It never is, those

188

people admit sheepishly. A person only has to look once at David to know he could no more have an affair than grow an extra set of hands. Still, there are lots of ways of straying.

Sam has demonstrated that much. Beware of him who has no needs. For years now Sam's been laughing, joking, going along to get along. None of us can remember a meeting when he voiced an opinion or suggestion; when anybody pressed on him he slid away like water. But the stubbornest, fiercest desires are the ones nobody talks about. The things we crave—security, money, a really good car—are exactly the things we can't bear to voice, even if we secretly move heaven and earth to get them.

Sam did some secret moving, but it's clear he and Vivy still aren't talking about it. He creeps around, furtive as dust. And Vivy skims through her days like a bat, operating on radar. She stays on the phone, but she doesn't talk to anyone—not the talking she needs, anyway. On shift at the store, she chatters like a ticker tape machine. The only person who can make her shut up is David. Sam told us that.

David told us he is committed to Cecilia, and we believe him. No one, not even Paul, makes commitment sound so final as David. In his voice we can hear the echo of doors clanging shut, Cecilia like the princess locked in the tower.

Still, there's something between Vivy and David. They exchange glances, and there's that lunch at Bearkeep none of us has forgotten about. This wouldn't be the first time we've seen people who didn't even like each other tumble into each other, pushed by the need to claim a patch of their lives as theirs alone. Even the most devoted spouse needs a life, we all know, though we don't say it where our spouses can hear us.

TWELVE

Vivy

FOR THE LATE AUGUST Parkersville Peach Festival the weather—consistently wrong this year—cooled off. A low-pressure trough had swung through the valley, bringing mild days edged with a teasing breeze just when summer's fullest, most incapacitating days should have arrived. No one could remember an August so pleasant, and people surged out of their houses, eager to breathe fresh air for the first time in months. The modest festival, which usually brought in no more than five hundred at the gate, swelled to three times that number. Vivy looked at the crowd with frustration; she could have negotiated another two hundred dollars. She would give Marteeny the extra money out of her own pocket.

Glowing Marteeny had shown up a few pounds thinner, encased in vivid red leggings and a tunic—apple red, fire hydrant red, a color so brilliant Vivy felt like shading her eyes. She whistled. "What a tomato."

Marteeny made a face. "Court. He ordered it for me, can you believe it? From a catalog. There's a cape, too. Red lined with white. I'm the world's biggest radish."

"It's good. You want to look like a performer."

"I don't want to look like a stripper. God knows what kinds of mailing lists Court's on now."

"Sweetheart, he did the best he could. They don't make catalogs for gals whose knees bend backwards. Besides, don't knock stripper clothes. You'll have the 800-numbers handy when you want to bring a little extra zing into your marriage."

Making a face, Marteeny plucked at the shimmery fabric at her knee. "I guess that's what you and Sam use to keep the spark alive."

"No, it isn't," Vivy said. "Now, you know that you go on fourth, right? I'll have your music cued up. I've already talked to lighting, and I'll have your water ready. What else will you need?"

"Vivy." Marteeny squeezed Vivy's hand. "Shut up a second. Thanks for doing all this. I couldn't have started again on my own."

"My pleasure. But you're not on your own. Court's here." Somewhere. Marteeny had said he was trolling the parking lot to find room for his RV, which he preferred to park several spaces away from any other vehicles.

"He shouldn't be. There's a cow that could have mastitis at home. The truck threw a rod last week. But all he can think about is new shows for me. He talked for forty-five minutes about exposure. He thinks—oh, I don't know what he thinks."

"Don't you remember what Sam told you?" Vivy said. "Court thinks you're the best thing that ever was, and he wants the whole world to see what you can do. He also thinks you might be a new life for him, excitement and new RVs instead of cows."

"He thinks this is fun." Marteeny tugged at her crimson tunic, the stretchy fabric sponging under her fingers.

"So do you," Vivy said.

"I know. But it wasn't what I was expecting."

"Welcome to marriage." Vivy looked again toward the parking lot. Court must have found a spot miles away. "Don't you need to be warming up?"

"I thought you were my friend," Marteeny grumbled, reaching for her heel and pulling it over her head. Vivy's hamstrings twinged at the sight. Breathless, Marteeny said, "So—how come—Sam isn't here?"

"Had to work."

"Tell him I'm—disappointed. He needs to come next time. It doesn't feel right, only half—the team."

"Team's changed. He's gone uptown on us. He doesn't want to do the old acts anymore. He wants to spend his days at the store and nights listening to Mozart. Or maybe the other way around."

She'd hoped Marteeny would be too busy grunting to hear the ripple in her voice, but Marteeny carefully pulled her foot back to the ground and shook her regimented curls. "What's going on?"

Vivy dug into her purse as if she needed anything that was in there. "Divergent interests. I want to get my old life back. He wants a new one."

"Can't you talk things out? You've got all that training from Life Ties."

"Talking, it turns out, is not actually one of our strengths. Which is good and pretty goddamn ironic." She looked down at Marteeny. "I guess you thought you and Court had a lock on career disputes."

"I'm not that self-centered yet. Still, I thought you and Sam—well, I thought you two were solid. This is pretty upsetting. You and Sam have always been my models. You kept laughing, and you kept liking each other. You had your own world. At parties, meetings, whatever, you were standing together on the same little chunk of land. I would look at you and think, 'That's a marriage.' That's what I wanted."

"Me too," Vivy said. She leaned forward and smoothed a curl back from her friend's damp forehead. "Look, don't worry. Sam and I go up and down. We've made it through low spots before. Whatever happens, we always wind up together." Which wasn't as consoling a statement as she would have liked, but was the best she could manage. Court, finally, was striding toward them, waving wearily. Gray dust coated his boots and jeans like a layer of felt.

"Good to see you," he said, nodding at Vivy. "Where's your partner?"

"Holding down the front. I was just telling Marteeny."

"I thought Life Ties believed in togetherness."

"It does," Vivy said.

"I do, too. If Marteeny's going back on the road, I want to be there with her. Isn't there a slogan about this?"

"No," Vivy said.

Court grinned. "'Marriage creates a single unit, without boundaries or divisions.' I've been studying up. So what do you think of our star?" He swatted dust from his elbows, the seat of his pants. "I picked her outfit myself."

"You did a good job. Nobody'll miss her."

"I remembered what you said about showmanship. If Tina has a fault, it's a lack of showmanship. She hides her light under a bushel."

"Huh," Marteeny said, tipping herself onto her hands and stretching her legs into a horizontal line. Once she had her balance, she lowered her right foot until it touched the ground, then her left, each of her quivering legs straight as a yardstick. A knot of peach-eating tourists strolling past pointed and applauded with their sticky hands. Marteeny clapped her legs together, flexed her arms, and whipped to her feet in a single, showy motion. Court must have had her doing push-ups. The little crowd shouted "Encore!" while Marteeny took a pretty bow. Then she stuck her tongue out at Court. "Explain to me again about that light and that bushel."

He beamed back at her, twisting a few strands of his measly beard. "I told you it would work."

Vivy turned away from them, surveying the Peach Festival's good, deep stage flanked by booths with pickled peaches, peach cake, peach pit dolls, quilts and aprons and jackets and tablecloths bordered with dancing peaches. She didn't resent her friend's confident, affectionate exchange with her fiancé. She didn't even envy it. She simply couldn't bear it.

"Look, I've got to go follow up on some things," she said, staring at a pyramid of peach preserves. "Court, you make sure she's warmed up. We're on before students from Sunshine's School of Twirl, which will work for us. All those moms and aunts will be staking out their seats, so we'll win audience share. I'm going to make sure our check is ready."

Head down, already walking, Vivy was two stalls away before Marteeny or Court could answer her. She needled into the crowd, reminding herself to scan the stage for nails or glass or tape before Marteeny went on, and to test the CD player too. Once, just before a Strikes and Spares performance, somebody else's CD got slipped into the machine.

An arthritic piano version of "Singin' in the Rain" blared out instead of the icy, atonal nocturne the dancers used. Sam had leaped onto the stage and turned cartwheels for the thirty seconds it took for Vivy to find the right CD. He got a standing ovation. Vivy groaned. Memory was as treacherous as knives.

Imagination was more treacherous still. She hadn't been able to make herself contemplate Sam and Cecilia, but she hadn't been able to shut thoughts of them out, either. Like floaters in her vision, dim shapes trickled before her all day: Sam's dark head bent to Cecilia's stemlike throat, his hand pressed against the knobs of her spine. Vivy felt like World War I soldiers she had read about in college, men who marched for hours before they felt their own wounds—fingers blown off, wet gaps in the flesh of their arms, chest, face. She skirted a pie booth and a ring toss. *Hut*, two, three, four.

"Vivy! Vivy Jilet!"

She jerked up her head. "What." Two couples from Life Ties, waving, *skipping* for Christ's sake, bore down on her.

"I should have known I'd see everybody I knew if I got out of town. It was such a nice day that when we got up we said, 'Let's do something.' So we come to Parkersville and run into half of Life Ties. Where's Sam?"

Vivy didn't have any notion of the woman's name. Her round face was set in a fringe of bright blonde hair like the eye in the center of a daisy, and she clutched the hand of a man with soft brown hair, soft brown eyes, a soft brown beard, the basic attributes of half the men in El Campo. Vivy supposed the woman held his hand to make sure she didn't mix him up in the crowd. Behind them stood another couple, people Vivy did remember—the man who had invested in David's orchard, and the woman who had sandblasted him for it.

"Work," she said.

"I wondered if you came here because you're angry with Sam," said the woman who had harangued her husband. Elena, Vivy remembered. She'd been insistent about the pronunciation, very European: ELAYna. "But it looks like you're already forgiving him. Bring him a peach pie, if he loves peaches. Or maybe don't."

"Have you seen the bareback riders?" Vivy gestured toward the barns on the far side of the fairgrounds, the most distant point from the stage where Marteeny would, quite soon, be performing. "They're worth going out of your way for."

"This must be where you scout for new acts," Elena said.

"There's a roping demonstration that'll be starting on the half hour." Vivy talked fast, pulling up everything she could remember from the brochure she'd half read. "Kids jumping from horse to horse, lassos, all kinds of fancy stuff. Chance to give your feet a rest."

"Wouldn't that be an act to bring to Natural High," said the laughing blonde. Vivy could see she meant no malice. But Elena did. The woman was taking careful note of Vivy's face, itching to call her on something.

"I don't think anyone would want to be inside a small room with ten horses." Vivy produced a meager laugh. "Nancy put the kibosh on me when I wanted to bring in dogs."

"Sam defended you on that," Elena said.

"Sam puts in a lot of time defending me." Catching Elena's arched eyebrows, she added, "I put in time defending him, too."

"Must be hard, to think about defending Sam now," Elena said.

"'Hard Pavements Make Good Roads.'" Vivy stretched her mouth in another horrible smile, hoping to hasten them away. She had to beat it back to Marteeny; already she could hear music that might be the intro for the first act, twelve-year-old twins singing "Memories."

"What are you going to do if David orders Sam out of the company?"

Vivy tried to decide whether the woman's thrilled, scavenging expression was ghoulish or merely unseemly. At least her husband, standing a loyal step behind her, had the decency to look embarrassed. "We're partners. David can't issue orders to Sam or me. You'd better get moving, if you want to catch that horse show."

Three of the four turned, but Elena leaned closer, every plane of her face rough, like a crude mask. "Maybe you can keep working together. I couldn't. But you should know there's discussion of barring Sam from

Life Ties. People think he needs some kind of punishment. If Sam is misguided enough to make a mistake that big, he needs the group to give him a correction."

Later Vivy would have the clear impression that she heard a crack like the snapping of a board. "I guess you think that's going to break his heart. You're Johnny-on-the-spot, aren't you? Keeping an eye on everybody's lives and handing out corrections. Look: we're not in jail, and you're not the warden."

"We trust the group to see what we ourselves are blind to."

"Maybe," Vivy said. "Maybe I'm just getting my vision back. Sam and I have been married for fifteen years. Every single day we get up together, and every night we go to bed together. I've brought him to the hospital twice. He's brought me three times. I can see all of this just fine."

Elena hadn't backed up an inch. Her mouth trembled from all the words boiling behind her tight lips.

Vivy said, "One night years ago he kept wandering around the house, kicking at the furniture, keeping the kids up. 'Just tell me what you want,' I said, and he said, 'Who are you, Santa Claus?' So I took off and found an open-all-night Kmart in Stockton that would sell me a Christmas tree. It was April, but the manager sent some kid up a ladder, and he lugged down a tree in a box for me. Ornaments, too. Then I bought a TV. I was there till two in the morning, pushing the credit card into outer space."

"You—" Elena began.

"—When I drove home Sam was standing at the door. 'Don't look,' I said, and started hauling in boxes. By dawn we had Christmas. '*Mom* did this?' Laszlo kept asking. He was only about five, and couldn't figure a Christmas tree in April. Sam said, 'Your mom is something. She's something.'" Tears splashed over Vivy's cheeks, and her lungs made a grating noise. "So why don't you tell me about my marriage," she said. "Why don't you just explain it to me."

"Would you do it for him now?" Elena asked.

"Drive to Kmart in the middle of the night? That's easy."

"But would you do it?"

The rough tears shuddered up again. "Let me give you some advice from fifteen years in the trenches. Always do the easy things. Conserve your strength. You don't know when you're going to need it."

Elena's husband, his bald head moist in the sun, was looking at Vivy with enormous pity. "I don't mean to make things any worse for you, but Elena and I are here together. You're here by yourself."

"Don't I wish," Vivy said, turning and walking toward the funnel cake stand. Clenching her eyes and teeth, she felt a sharp dot of appreciation for the man, whose pity had given her enough pride to walk away. She smiled with half her mouth when she heard Elena's fading voice insisting, "Strong medicine is good medicine." It wasn't a Life Ties motto, though it should have been.

For perhaps five minutes she stood behind one of the pie booths, taking ragged breaths that kept dissolving under the force of tears that wouldn't stop. She hadn't cried in—how long? She'd forgotten the pain of it. When she forced open her streaming eyes she glimpsed fairgoers carrying peach balloons and wearing soft orange velvet caps veering to the far side of the booth. They shushed their kids and frowned at her, a woman who didn't have the plain pride to conduct her crack-up at home. *Hey. You're seeing something unusual here, a once-in-a-lifetime performance. My husband has never seen what you're seeing. You think I don't know anything about self-control? I know everything about self-control.* She leaned against the booth's rough post and rocked her face against the dirty wood. Over and over she ran her hands down the post, until a thick sliver jabbed into the side of her palm. She straightened then and swore, but her tears slowed.

Across the sweet, peachy air, the first phrases of Marteeny's snazzy music rang out. Court, bless him, must have taken care of the CD player. Vivy wiped her face with the tail of her damp blouse and hurried back to the stage, where Marteeny was already upside down. She tucked her heels behind her shoulders, her body neat as an envelope, and a woman in the audience said, "Ow." People laughed, and a steady, encouraging pulse of applause started up.

Marteeny casually unhinged a shoulder and chattered about her mother, who said a well-reared young woman sat up straight, wore high heels every day, and voted a Republican ticket. "Don't tell my mother: I don't vote," Marteeny said. She rolled across the stage in a smooth split, then bounced up to a handstand. "But anybody my size wears high heels if she doesn't want to get stepped on. And—" she flexed her back, then curled it, then flexed it again, her whole body a precarious shimmer "—nobody can beat me for posture." Vivy joined in the audience's applause. Why resist? Marteeny's regal smile lifted all of them from their wretched little lives.

Sam could protest about all the other acts: Elphenevel, Laurel, even Fredd. But Marteeny had a gift. She touched people, left them better off. Wasn't that what a gift did—improve whatever surrounded it? Sam had his own gifts, and Vivy had not lost track of them—he had a sailor's rolling gait, an easy way of conducting himself, a wicked, silky capacity for insurrection that had delighted Vivy until it was turned against her. But she had gifts herself. No one knew them better than Sam, even if he needed to be reminded.

"Finale," called Marteeny, upside down and straight as an I beam. She balanced first on one hand, then the other, then carefully lowered herself until her weight was supported by her head alone, her arms and legs rotating in their sockets. No matter how many times Vivy saw it, she couldn't keep from gasping. The audience cheered; kids stood up on their folding chairs and chanted "More! More!" Vivy clapped until her palms stung, right through Marteeny's several bows.

While Court held Marteeny's cape and swept her offstage, Vivy groped through her purse for the car keys. She needed only five minutes to shoulder backstage, kiss Marteeny, and remind her that Forty-Niner Follies were coming up in Nevada City. Court, beaming, said, "They loved the headstand, didn't they? It's a showstopper. Maybe she should hold a sparkler."

"Where are you headed off to?" Marteeny asked, and Vivy smiled against the quick tears that kept coming back.

"I want to find Sam," she said.

"Give him my love," Marteeny said.

"Our love," Court said, wrapping Vivy in a hug that smelled like dusty hay. She sniffed her blouse several times on the drive back to El Campo, which she took fast.

Sam's car was not in the carport when she pulled up. Instead, Cecilia sat on the porch playing with Annie, and Vivy froze long enough to hear Annie say, "The *blue* hat goes with the *blue* bear. So where does the *red* hat go?"

Cecilia set down the soft, hand-sized bear when Vivy got out of the car, but neither of them spoke. Cecilia's features looked sharper than ever, the bladelike bones ready to slice through her tight skin. The shadows ringing her eyes and curving around her mouth were tinged green, and Vivy supposed the other woman was going through all the drama of morning sickness, an inconvenience that Vivy had never felt in the least. She looked old, David's child bride. Vivy wondered whether Sam had noticed that.

"Gosh," she said. "Company."

"Mom's here," Annie announced, and Cecilia pulled herself to her feet, brushing off her long skirt.

"I hoped I could catch you," she said.

"Mom always gets the hats wrong," Annie said.

"I'm sure they look fine."

"They don't," Vivy said. She didn't like standing beside the car, a pose that seemed indecisive, but she was in no hurry to join Cecilia on the porch. "Annie knows how they're supposed to go."

"I see," Cecilia said, further raising the nap of Vivy's irritation. If the woman felt all that meek, she wouldn't be shanghaiing them this way, assuming Vivy had nothing better to do than chat with her husband's lover.

"So where does the red hat go?" Annie said, swatting at Cecilia's skirt.

"Honey—" Cecilia began, at the same time Vivy said, more sharply, "Annie!" Both women stopped. Vivy nodded at Cecilia. Let her finish what she started.

"Your mother and I need to talk."

"We're not done!" Annie scowled and clenched her fists. She was too old for a tantrum, but Vivy could see her eye Cecilia and calculate: no telling what this lady might let her get away with.

"Don't nag, honey. I'll finish playing later, okay?" Cecilia said. Annie tossed her head and stamped off the porch, but Vivy knew she would be watching Cecilia from the yard, ready to pounce if she tried to get away without another round of bears.

Vivy made Cecilia wait a long, awkward stretch before she crossed the driveway to the porch. From the step Cecilia said, "I'm here to apologize. It's over. I hope that's what Sam told you. I don't let him talk to me anymore."

Vivy shrugged and seated herself on the porch swing. "I never cared about whether you talked to him."

"I've never been so ashamed. If I could undo it, no matter what it cost, I would. I've hurt everybody I love. I hate myself. But I wish you hadn't brought it up at Life Ties. I'd already told David. We would have been happy to meet with you and Sam."

"Happy," Vivy said.

"It would have been better," Cecilia insisted, a patchy blush spreading across her cheeks. "Bringing it to the meeting was humiliating. I deserve to be humiliated, but David didn't. He wouldn't have hurt you that way."

"'Secrets Are Toxic,'" Vivy said.

"You don't really believe that."

Vivy shrugged and pushed the porch swing higher. "I do and I don't. You really want to know why I brought it up? I watched my husband stare at you like you're his sun and moon."

"I'm not in love with him," Cecilia said.

"You're not making things any better."

"I'm not trying to defend myself. But Sam and I—we came together at a low point. Isn't that the same thing that sent you and David up to Bearkeep?"

"Yeah," Vivy said. "A low point created by you and my husband."

Cecilia bit her lip and looked at her shoes. Let it out, Vivy thought. Anger could clarify the mind, if Cecilia would just let it.

"So you've apologized," Vivy said. "Is there anything else?"

"Yes. A lot." Cecilia straightened her slumped shoulders. Now, apparently, they were coming to the scripted portion of the conversation. "Things with David and me are pretty tight right now. Yesterday, when he came home from Mineville, I asked him how the new tree grafts were going. 'Bad,' he said. I asked why. He said, 'Do you know how long it takes to know you've achieved a single successful graft? And do you know how much time I have to spend at the nursery?'" Cecilia looked levelly at Vivy, shame already miles behind her. "Has he talked to you about this?"

"No," Vivy said. David told Vivy one set of facts, Cecilia another. Sam likewise. The four of them were parallel planes, never intersecting.

"He stood looking out the window. He doesn't look at me anymore. He said, 'It's the one thing I want to do in my life, and I can't do it enough.' You know he doesn't usually talk like he's in a movie."

"No," Vivy said.

"So I told him, 'Listen to yourself. Get out of Natural High. You're killing yourself trying to juggle Harmony Orchards and the store and meetings. It's time to get out. Why are you hanging back?'"

"He believes in the cause."

"Some weeks, bad weeks, he doesn't bring home a hundred-fifty dollars from the orchard. Even if he went full-time, it wouldn't be enough. I told him I'd work extra shifts and take on more students, whatever it took. We had enough in savings now to get us started, go a couple of years if we were careful."

"Ah," Vivy said.

"I guess you know where I'm going," Cecilia said.

"Not necessarily."

"He told me the whole thing, Vivy, that he offered you the savings. I said he'd given away our future, and he asked me what I thought I had done. We yelled. We never yell."

"Why are you telling me this?"

"There are still secrets. You can do what you want with your secrets, but I'm trying not to have any." She pushed the fine, clingy hair away from her mouth. "So I'll tell you what I secretly suspect. I suspect that all those acts, all your old friends, have been coming in a little cheaper than you've said. And the debits you've drawn from Natural High haven't entirely been going to the acts, but to feathering Vivy Jilet's nest. Sam said you were showing up with clothes he'd never seen before."

"Son of a gun. Did he tell you that?"

"He told me a lot of things. I didn't ask him."

"No, you wouldn't ask. You never ask for anything. Just take."

Cecilia kept talking, looking over Vivy's shoulder. "The way he talked—he's scared about what's going on with your money. I got to thinking of all the times I've heard you talk about things you wished you had—cars, a house. You want things. Things cost money." Cecilia leaned toward Vivy. "I won't say anything to the others. I'll help you at the store, schedule any acts you want. I know a few performers myself, you know. Just give David back the money."

Vivy let the porch swing slow to nothing. David hadn't mentioned his savings again since their drive to Bearkeep. She had supposed he'd come to his senses. Good grief, did he really think she would take his inheritance and life savings? The very thought was insulting. Surely, he knew her better than that, and he was only misleading Cecilia in order to punish her. Their conversation sounded considerably more vicious than Vivy would have predicted, like a fight she and Sam might have had. The hot tears were back, faster than she could brush them away.

"Sorry," Vivy said. "David knows where his money goes. Ask him. I've got to say, though, you've got more balls than I thought. Telling the woman whose husband you just slept with that she should give *you* money. I didn't think you had it in you."

Cecilia flushed again and pressed one hand against her stomach. If she were trying to impress Vivy, she should have picked another gesture.

Cecilia said, "I'm not asking you to help me. I'm asking you to help David. He's got to get out of all this. It's killing him. Look, Vivy—please."

"Who do you think told David about the job in Mineville?"

Cecilia frowned. "He went up by himself to check it out."

"How do you think he found out about it?"

"Well, he was an obvious choice," Cecilia said. "He'd written papers."

"Obvious," Vivy said. "You think? It took me half an hour just to get him to say he'd go up and look. Here was this job doing exactly what he wants to do, that he'd written papers about, and he was going to let it float right by. I about twisted his arm off."

"Why are you telling me this?" Cecilia said.

"You're not the only one who can see things."

"Then you should see what he needs now. He needed that job, you were right. Now he needs to give it more time."

"Go away," Vivy said. "Please. Now."

"Will you think about this?"

"I don't know what I'll think about."

Cecilia backed slowly off the porch, plucking her long skirt away from her legs. Vigilant Annie watched from the yard, but she had inherited her father's discretion, and contented herself with setting the bears on top of the fence and making them wave goodbye. After Cecilia's car had turned the corner, Annie said, "Mom?"

"Later."

Vivy pushed the swing and studied the basket of drooping impatiens. The plants had a will to live. They should never have withstood the long waterless lapses when Vivy forgot about them, or Laszlo's habit of kicking the basket when he roared out of the house. She knew a symbol when she saw one, and wondered now what would happen if she started fertilizing the plants, watering every other day, tenderly shuttling them out of direct sun. She couldn't imagine them thriving.

The point that Cecilia had overlooked was that David wanted to give Vivy the money, even if Vivy had no intention of taking it. Saintly David, always thinking of other people. Vivy gave the swing such a shove that the heavy eyebolts groaned. If David just gave Vivy enough money she would go away, and she would take Sam with her. Pretty crass, no matter how noble he tried to make it look.

It was David's unfortunate luck that money, so long Vivy's problem, was no longer the problem. The boys in Elphenevel were restless, calling every other day to nag. They wanted to play more dates—they were ready for out of state, they said. They had enough songs for a CD. When she asked them what about school, Fredd's nephew said, "We need a manager, not a mom." A debatable point, but he went on to say that if she got them just six gigs a month she'd still be bringing home close to $3,000 after taxes, proving he'd been paying attention in his accounting class anyway.

What was the other option? Staying here while Nancy agonized over new ice cream flavors and Cecilia grew great with child? Vivy pressed her fist as hard as she could against the swing's wooden slats. She needed to talk, but the only person she wanted to talk to was Sam, and his head was already filled with his memories of Cecilia, which he would refresh in a heartbeat, given the chance. If Vivy thought she could break through to him with a Kmart Christmas tree, she'd start driving right now. The next move was his, though, not hers.

She stared at the washed-out blue impatiens, then the rest of the clutter on the porch: the lid to the rusted-out Smokey Joe tossed on top of Annie's bike, one of Laszlo's rollerblades nosed into a sack of potting soil, Annie's paper dolls of Princess Kate scattered on the welcome mat. Vivy supposed she could clean up half the porch, sweep off one side of it, give the plants half a drink. It might not be a bad gesture. But she closed her eyes instead and listened to the crisp afternoon—distant yelling, thumping car radios. The slight breeze made her skin prickle.

When Laszlo came home he stomped into the house, avoiding the impatiens that Vivy had moved into the shade. After a while, Annie followed him in. Vivy stayed on the swing, her eyes closed, alone until nightfall.

THIRTEEN

Cecilia

EVEN WHEN SHE PUT her back into it, a musician could only find so much work in a town the size of El Campo, and Cecilia had already found most of it. After she drew a flyer showing a toothy boy and his violin, made a thousand copies, and stuffed them in mailboxes and under windshield wipers all over town, she got four new students. She called her clients, asked if they could recommend her to others, and got a handful of vague promises—forgotten, she knew, as soon as they hung up. She wrote to the schools in the area, K-12, public and private, but even the Montessoris wanted a more impressive résumé than Cecilia's BA in music and six college recitals.

Next, unavoidably, she would have to widen her net, traveling beyond El Campo to Sutton or Sanosta, no less than forty-five minutes round trip for a lesson that would gross Cecilia $20. She spent half an hour making calculations—subtracting the mileage, wear and tear on the tires, her fee if she stopped for a cup of coffee versus her fee if she didn't. Money, to which she'd never given much thought, now sat squarely at the center of her brain—just one more way, Cecilia thought, that she'd come to resemble Vivy.

Cecilia's overwhelming mistake had been in underestimating the woman. For years she had laughed at Vivy's distracting jokes without pondering why Vivy wanted to keep people laughing all the time. Too late now, Cecilia thought about magicians' patter, designed to misdirect the viewer's attention. And with a grinding resentment that bordered on admiration, she thought about a woman who would work with such single-mindedness to grab hold of contentment and not let go. Cecilia wondered if her own hands had that much strength.

Her talk with Vivy had refined Cecilia's goals to a single point, and that point was David. Vivy may have been the one to open the door to his happiness, prodding him into Harmony Orchards. But Cecilia was going to make sure the door stayed open—partly as atonement, partly as gift, but mostly because he, no less than Vivy, no less than Cecilia herself, should get to do what he wanted to do.

When she told him as much, he smiled flatly. "Good luck." Most of his sentences lately were tiny and guarded, separated by wide moats of silence. When he came home he greeted Cecilia and waited for her to greet him back. Then he slid open the door to the narrow balcony outside their bedroom and checked on his tomato plants.

Despite the onset of cool weather, he was harvesting two dozen tomatoes a day, and in the evenings he sat out on the balcony with a notebook, taking notes and sketching blossoms he found interesting. To Cecilia the hairy, lumpy vines looked arthritic, but David saw growth patterns and blossom set. He talked, if he talked, about hybridizing and test varieties. At night Cecilia pushed the fresh tomatoes around her plate.

Even now, into her third month, the only food she could keep down was ice cream, and she'd been packing that away as if she were storing for winter. After the daily bout of morning sickness, which often lingered to become afternoon sickness, her mouth craved Mocha Crunch or Triple Vanilla, Very BlueBerry, Carob Chip, flavors she usually disliked. She ate until her teeth ached, half a carton at a sitting, and she sat a lot. The daily intake should have been padding her in rosy flesh, but the calories rushed away every morning, and the figure that confronted her in mirrors looked like a crone's.

"You need to eat balanced meals," David had said, staring at her full plate of beans à la Mediterranean, made by him with fresh pole beans and basil. "You need vitamins."

"I know. But my stomach has its own appetites."

"Appetites you feel are best fed at Natural High."

After a pause to indicate she'd heard and understood and accepted the slap, she said, "The books say in another month I'll start craving nutrients. Once I'm over this early part, I'll want every tomato you can give me." Which was why she was standing out on their balcony this morning, deep in the tomato plants, a light sweater over her shoulders and a watering can in her hand. David had handed her the sweater before he got an early start to Mineville. She was trying. He was trying.

She was working the long neck of the watering can over the second row of plants when the phone rang and she hurried inside, wiping her damp hand against her slacks. Just yesterday she had stapled a new set of flyers all over town, advertising her piano for sale. She had nearly reconciled herself to the loss of the piano.

"Cecilia? This is Walter Scurwicz-Hays." He had to say the name twice. "Elena's husband," he said. "From Life Ties."

"Of course," she said, more disappointed than she should have been. Women from Life Ties had been calling for two weeks now, offering Cecilia blankets and cribs and their great willingness to listen. They described this willingness again and again in the silence Cecilia provided. Now here was Walter, who probably wanted to talk to David and offer manly support. All of them should get merit badges. She poured herself some coffee, still fresh enough.

"How are you doing?" he asked.

"Oh, busy, you know. I was just taking care of some chores. I have to get back to them."

"In your condition?"

"Somebody needs to water the tomatoes."

"Put your feet up and watch *The Price Is Right* while you can," he said. Cecilia smiled politely at the phone. She was having a hard time relating this chipper voice to the dismal creature who showed up for Life Ties next to his Valkyrie wife. "But how are you doing?" he was saying. "You and David. Are you feeling okay? You haven't been looking great, to tell you the truth. Is David helping you?"

"Oh, yes."

"There are a lot of things a husband can do while his wife is pregnant. A lot of chores around the house. It's a good time to learn all the things he's been taking for granted."

"I didn't know you had children."

"We don't. But Elena is fond of telling me everything I don't know." He laughed warmly and Cecilia laughed too, a little.

He said, "The chores aren't the important part. I know you two have been knocked for a loop. Can you talk to each other?"

"Oh, yes," Cecilia said.

"Not a word, eh?"

She shrugged. "A word." The same one, over and over: Sam, Sam, Sam.

"Do you mind if I tell you something? I'll shut up if you ask me to."

"If it isn't much. I don't mean to be rude, but I can't take much."

"It isn't much. Just remember the group is all around, and we'll help you. You're in the middle of the ocean, and Life Ties is a raft. I know what I'm talking about."

"Thanks," Cecilia said. She listened to the light tick of her coffee-maker, something in the mechanism contracting.

Walter said, "What do you most want to tell David right now?"

"Oh—you know. It changes."

"If you could say anything, right now. What do you really want him to hear?"

I'm sorry, she thought automatically, but she had said those words so many times. "I'm tired of saying I'm sorry," she said.

"What would he say? If you told him that."

"'We can only build from where we are standing.' And he thinks he's standing in rubble. He thinks I've destroyed his life." Now it was Walter who kept silent. Cecilia stared at her ragged cuticles. "The thing is, we started building years ago. I think of our marriage as a solid house, a big one. One mistake doesn't knock down the whole house. But one mistake followed by scraping, scraping, scraping—" She broke off, her lips rubbery.

"Tell him."

"He isn't interested in my opinions right now."

"Communication is the ground of commitment," Walter said, managing to make the slogan sound new, like conversation. "And that doesn't mean he gets to keep kicking you. Communication doesn't mean saying the same thing over and over."

"I guess you've given this speech yourself," Cecilia said, feeling a rueful surge of near-affection. She didn't know Walter's middle name or whether he had any brothers, but she knew that he had spent $20,000 on a used Alfa Romeo, and that during sex he liked to use so many oils and lotions that not only the sheets but the mattress pad had to be washed afterward.

"Daily," he said cheerfully.

"Don't you get worn out?"

"Sure. And I get resentful and so fed up with her I want to go out and hit something. I saw an ad for a never-used punching bag."

"So why stay?" Cecilia said. She stopped, a fist at her mouth. She hadn't even articulated the words to herself and now here they were, falling into the ear of a man she hardly knew. Suddenly, she was full of words. "At first you think the misery's going to end and the two of you will start being a couple again. But the ugliness goes on and on, both of you trying to be noble, both of you dying. It doesn't get better. Why stay?"

"You tell me. What did you used to like about David?"

"He was good. He had the right answer." She smiled grimly at her coffee mug. "He still does."

After a tactful pause, Walter said, "I've always thought a good marriage would be exactly like an adventure movie. I wrote a script for one once, even though I knew it would be too expensive to film—it had wild animals and an avalanche. The way I wrote it, the hero and heroine got to the end together." He paused. "Of course, in real life we might not. But I'd rather we did. I'd hate to start at the beginning again."

Cecilia closed her eyes briefly and swallowed. "That's a good answer. Did Elena understand what you were doing?"

"She said it was a good metaphor, but it would still be too expensive to make."

"Did you want to kill her?"

Walter laughed. "Just say your piece to David. Give him a chance."

Give *him* a chance. Walter hadn't heard David's angular voice, hadn't seen his little eyes gleaming as he asked her Sam's opinion on mutual fund investing or the weather. Even across the dinner table his eyes, resting on her, were tight as pins. When he and Cecilia had first dated, the tenderness of his eyes made her feel shy. Now the memory made her breath catch and tear, pain cracking through her like voltage. She would do anything to see his eyes look that way again. She said, "You know the right things to say."

"I'm just reminding you of what you already know."

"Thank you," she said. "Thank you for calling."

"Hang on. I didn't actually call to talk about Life Ties business; I called to talk about business business." In the faint pause she heard his voice drop to a different register, and he sounded more like the uneasy, browbeaten man she remembered. "I need some help. I work at CAA, the big office out on the way to Marysville."

"I know where CAA is." The biggest corporation for miles, the Creative Agricultural Applications industrial park was the size of a small airport. It squatted on four hundred acres of fertile valley land. David mentioned it frequently.

"We're planning a seminar next month. 'Fields and Dreams.' It will last three days, and we'd like to have music in the evenings and between sessions. Maybe a little trio—something for people to look forward to after discussing fertilizers. I know this isn't the kind of thing you usually do, but could you make an exception for us? The company will pay professional rates."

In the space of a breath—a long breath—Cecilia's heart rose and dropped again. "Well, this comes out of the blue. It's very considerate of you. But I haven't performed in years. And I don't know other musicians around here. I don't have the connections you want."

"You could round other musicians up. Go to the music school.

You'd know all the procedures. Look, if I can delegate the music to you I'll give you a bonus for being the go-between. What is it called? The promoter, like Vivy."

"Impresario," Cecilia said. "Or manager. But you haven't heard me play. Most people don't hire without an audition."

"I've heard what people say, and you're what we want—someone skilled who knows how to reach an audience. Not too highbrow, but not junk, either."

"You're very flattering." Staring at a "Boat of Commitment" napkin on the table, Cecilia air-fingered the opening of "Summertime." "This is all on the up-and-up, right? You're not offering me a job just because of Life Ties?"

"I like to help more than one person at a time. It happens that I have to hire somebody, and the seminar's a month away. It also happens that you play the violin and need work for a whole bunch of good reasons. So you win, and I win."

"What are you going to tell Elena?"

"This was Elena's idea. 'We have to help one another,'" he said, capturing his wife's faint accent and Slavic cadence.

"She told you to call?"

"We decided I would call," he corrected her.

Cecilia imagined Walter and Elena murmuring together in a kitchen she imagined in granite and fancy maple, planning out Cecilia's life. Walter talking and Elena shaking her head, cutting him off, presenting a plan of her own. The two of them together. Walter's voice, buoyant as it never was at Life Ties. Never, no matter how long she lived, would Cecilia understand anyone else's marriage.

Walter said, "What are you going to do now?"

"Head out to the music school. Find a pianist and a cellist. Get practicing light classics."

"I meant about David," he said.

"I'll tell him about your call, and I will invite him to congratulate me."

"You're not in this by yourself," Walter said.

"I know," she said, and added, "thank you." She was already turning back toward the balcony as she hung up. Although her hands rattled with impatience, she finished watering the tomatoes, more careful now than before. She reached deep into the tangle of leaves to get to the farthest pots.

It took her only half an hour to shower and zip up one of the black skirts jammed into the back of her closet. Swiftly she buttoned a white blouse and skinned her hair back from her face in an uncompromising ponytail, then eyed her reflection: humorless, driven. Anyone would take her for a musician, or at least a music student.

She hadn't driven to the school, or the university that housed it, in years, and now she was shocked at the changes. The broad, lovely expanses of soybeans and sugar beets had been hammered into corporate centers and little housing developments that nosed up against little malls anchored by Tractor Supply Company on one end and Walmart on the other. She'd seen the developments before, but usually when she drove out this way David was with her, bitterly reciting every crop that had been buried. With him beside her, she didn't need to notice or grieve. Now she drove with dismay drumming through her. Something terrible had happened, and she hadn't even noticed. She couldn't have stopped it, but it would have been good to notice.

In the music school office, real students—pale, slender, all of them carrying their flutes or violins or a trombone in its ungainly case—glided past Cecilia, their heads almost visibly bursting with music. From the practice rooms one floor up, she heard a pianist struggle with a Brahms intermezzo while someone else whipped through scales and a trumpeter played the same fanfare again and again and again. On the floor where she was four students stood at the end of the corridor and sang a string quartet. "Bum ba-da-dum *bum*," sang the cellist, and the first violin actually clutched her hair and corrected him: "Bum ba-da *dum* bum. How many *times*?"

Cecilia watched them with hungry, covert fascination. Five years had passed since she herself had drifted through these halls thinking Allegro-Adagio-Rondo, thinking tempo, key signature, fingering, phrasing. Thinking of those things fiercely, and without cease, if she could call such obsession thinking. "Does music make you happy?" David had asked her in those days, and she had said, "No." He had brightened, misunderstanding her. What she had when she played was perfect concentration, a coherence that she felt at no other time. Now, she thought, watching the string quartet try again, she would call such concentration joy.

"Can I help you?" The frail-looking secretary's voice was a small notch above a whisper, and she blinked as if Cecilia had awakened her. Resting on the computer keyboard, the woman's fingers were twig thin, spatulate at the tips. Flautist's fingers, Cecilia thought. Too easily she could envision the BA in music framed and hanging primly over the music stand at home.

"The jobs board?" Cecilia said.

"Next to the door. It hasn't moved. And there's nothing new."

"Typical," Cecilia said. The bulletin board's beige surface was leafy with announcements for upcoming recitals, concerts, and—no surprise, they were everywhere—an old handbill for Natural High. She had to lift an acid yellow flyer for a flute recital and a poster of the Guarneri Quartet to find the few three-by-five cards. Two mothers were looking for piano teachers for their children. A Sacramento department store wanted a trio to play show tunes on Saturdays. The Holiday Inn in Yuba City was holding auditions for a lounge act.

Cecilia ripped down the Natural High ad and in its place tacked up the announcement she had brought: JOB in letters three inches high. Underneath, she had written the rest—the date, the place, her phone number and email. She straightened the Guarneri Quartet, thanked the secretary, then paused by the door, gazing down the hall where the string quartet had stood. They were gone now, the muddled cellist probably still getting his line wrong, and the hall was just a hall where she had come to do a little business. Before Cecilia could leave, a girl all but lost in a baggy shirt and painter's pants drifted in. She glanced hazily at the board, then snapped her head up and fished in her purse for a pen.

Driving home, Cecilia calculated. Auditions would have to be set up quickly, and rehearsals even more quickly. Work at the store would go on, of course, but she could cancel some of her lessons until after the seminar. She brightened, remembering that Annie and Laszlo Jilet were scheduled at the end of the week. Perhaps a little vacation would prompt Annie to move her violin case from one side of the room to the other. At least she'd lay a hand on it. Laszlo was something different, but even he could stand to go a few weeks without a lesson. The boy wasn't Mozart.

She got to work as soon as she returned home, leaving messages for two parents and speaking with one harassed mother who wasn't sure how much good her boy was getting from his lessons anyway. Then Cecilia reached Sandy McGee. "I'm preparing for a performance," Cecilia told her. "We'll just put a hold on your lessons for a month. I know you're good about practicing, and we'll pick up where we left off."

"So I'm on my own because you have something more important to do," Sandy said.

"We're taking a small vacation. Even Isaac Stern took vacations."

"Not when he was my age, he didn't. What about my recital?"

"Sandy, we haven't scheduled a recital."

"You *told* me. By the time I learned the étude, you said. You were going to give me a sonata."

"But you haven't learned the étude," Cecilia said.

"How am I supposed to learn it if you're canceling my classes for a month?" Cecilia held the phone an inch away from her ear and waited. Nothing was easy. Nothing. Sandy said, "It's easy for you. You've forgotten what it's like to need a teacher."

"I haven't—" Cecilia said.

"I can't do it by myself. And I think it's selfish of you to cancel my lessons. I could come at some other time. You could fit me in. You just don't want to bother."

"I'm going to be busy. I'm not going to be a good teacher," Cecilia said.

"Better than no teacher," Sandy said. Then, "You're not busy yet, are you? You could give me a class now."

"Today?"

"I can be there in half an hour."

"Sandy—"

"You can show me things to work on for a month. You can show me what to do to get ready for a recital. Please, Cecilia. You can't just walk off and leave me."

The child's voice was uneven, the whine broken up by an unnervingly mature note of longing. "It's the only thing I want," Sandy said, softly now, in control of her dynamics. "Please. I just want to play."

"Half an hour," Cecilia said. She knew Sandy wasn't quite telling the truth. The girl didn't just want to play; she wanted to play well. But her desire was too fierce for Cecilia's puny defenses of logic and experience to beat it back.

No sooner had Cecilia hung up than the phone rang—a pianist with a reedy, unpleasant voice calling about the job. After him, a wistful percussionist. Cecilia was scheduling her third audition, listening to her computer chime as one email after another arrived, when Sandy banged on the door, ten minutes early, red-faced, wisps of hair sticking to her hot face and neck. "I ran," Sandy said when Cecilia waved her in.

"I can see that," said Cecilia, one hand over the phone. "Go into the bathroom to wash your hands."

"It was hard, with the violin, but I didn't want to waste a minute."

"I get your point, Sandy. Go wash your hands."

When the girl returned, hands damp, she watched from the doorway until Cecilia ended the call. "Maybe you should turn it off."

Cecilia swallowed her remaining half cup of bitter coffee, her annoyance and her amusement exactly balanced. Showily, she powered the phone off. "Shall we begin?"

Sandy waited for her to sit down in the hard chair before taking her violin from the case and setting her music on the stand. Instead of launching herself into the notes as she usually did, she stood as if rooted. She took enormous breaths and twice pushed her hair back from her face. The girl was doing just what Cecilia told all of her students to do: waiting and thinking about the music before she began to play it. Never before had Cecilia seen any of her students take this advice. Sandy gave herself a full minute of concentration, perhaps more waiting than she truly required, then lifted her violin.

Her first note quavered, but it was one note, not three, as was the next. Sandy frowned at the music, she bit her lip, and she kept letting the sound dangle like a loose thread while she reworked her fingering. But she held her bow with her fingertips, only smashing it over the bridge twice. Cecilia could hear a melody struggling to emerge—if not music, exactly, at least an orderly succession of notes. When Sandy finished, Cecilia leaned forward and said, "That's better. That's much better. Can you hear the difference?"

Sandy pointed to the third measure, one of the places she'd paused. "Right here," she said. "Tell me what I should do."

"Use your fourth finger on the A. Good," said Cecilia, though the sound was less confident and the girl's wobbly fingers, unused to the new configuration, hesitated.

"It isn't good," Sandy snapped. "Don't baby me."

"What do you want me to do, yell at you?"

"I want you to have some standards. God."

"A," Cecilia said, struggling to keep down her grin. "D. F sharp. F *sharp*. You're the only student I have who thinks I'm not hard enough."

"Well, that should tell you something," Sandy said, playing the measure six times in a row, until her fingering was not quite so halting. Then she pointed at the next difficult measure, only half a line further along, and said, "What about this one?" Measure by measure, note by note, she force-marched Cecilia through the simple piece, and although Cecilia stole yearning glances at her watch after thirty-five, then forty-five, then fifty minutes, she let the lesson go on until Sandy reached the final measure, put down her violin, and, bending at the waist, bowed to Cecilia, a habit she'd picked up from some article about European music schools.

Wincing, Cecilia eased up from the cane-bottom side chair. If she'd known Sandy was going to play for so long, she would have sat on the couch. "That should give you plenty to practice. What kind of ice cream do you want?"

"I don't want ice cream. Could I have something to drink?"

"All I have is coffee and water," Cecilia said.

"Water'd be okay. I just want—look, we need to talk."

Cecilia, leading the way to the kitchen, glanced back. The girl was frowning, her green eyes glassy, her mouth a quivering line. "Sandy, what's wrong? You played well."

"Well for what? Well for Sandy McGee, considering? Not well for Anne-Sophie Mutter. Thank you," she said when Cecilia handed her a glass of water.

"Nobody plays as well as Anne-Sophie Mutter. She was a prodigy," Cecilia said.

"She played Mozart's D major violin concerto with Herbert Karajan when she was thirteen. I'm twelve."

"Kara-*yawn*. You can't use Anne-Sophie Mutter as a yardstick. Talent like hers comes up once in a generation."

"So I should just stop? Because I'm not a prodigy?" Sandy rubbed her hands along the cool glass of water.

"It depends," Cecilia said. She resisted the urge to smooth Sandy's frizzing, almost colorless hair. The girl sat with her arms crossed and her shoulders hunched, a picture of defensiveness. "If you're hating every note because it isn't as good as Anne-Sophie Mutter's note, then you should just stop. It isn't ever going to be as good as Anne-Sophie Mutter's note. Mine isn't either."

"Then what's the point?" Sandy's voice, like the water in her glass, trembled, and Cecilia paused before she answered, searching for the right words, which didn't exist.

Cecilia said, "I try to bring some life to the music. I try to find something I've never found before. When I can do it, I feel like I've discovered a new part of myself. That's my goal. You tell me what your goal is."

Sandy studied the wood grain tabletop, damp now from the damp glass. Cecilia had never before made any of her students cry, although she herself had cried regularly when she had been a twelve-year-old taking lessons, frustrated at her clumsy fingers—too short!—and the implacable music. Sandy was a tidier crier than Cecilia had been, and a swifter one, too. She stood up, quietly walked to the bathroom, blew her nose, and rejoined Cecilia. "What do you think of Cho-Liang Lin's Mozart recordings?" the girl said. "He has a crisp attack, but is there any warmth?"

"Technique," Cecilia said carefully, "can sometimes lead to expressiveness. Better that than the other way around." Encouraged by Sandy's thoughtful frown, she made a pot of coffee and put Itzhak Perlman on the CD player. And so when David came home from Mineville he found his wife and her student sitting in the kitchen, dirty ice cream bowls in the sink, snorting as they took turns imitating bad violinists playing Liszt.

"Oops," said Sandy when she saw David.

"You're early," said Cecilia.

"Don't let me interrupt," said David, standing in the middle of the room.

"Zing-zing-zing!" Sandy sang, bending over an imaginary violin and tossing an imaginary mane back from her brow. Cecilia laughed, which wasn't easy with David holding his place smack under the ceiling light. Sandy zinged again, less confidently.

"And then with the handkerchief," Cecilia said, picking up a napkin and extravagantly dabbing at her face.

Sandy, glancing at David, let her arms fall. "Anyway," she said. "That's how it sounded on the radio. I guess I'd better go."

"Do you want more ice cream?" Cecilia said.

"I've got work to do," the girl said, already on her feet. "So do you. Don't forget to turn your phone back on."

"Goodbye," David said. Sandy nodded and left the room at a trot. Once the front door closed, he said, "You could have introduced us."

"I'm sorry. That was Sandy. The Squealer. I didn't realize you hadn't met."

"I haven't met any of your students. You make sure they're not here when I am."

"That's a favor to you. Trust me—you don't want to hear Sandy play the violin."

"Trust."

"Oh, David. Not even a little comment about one of my students?"

"Interesting word for you to use, that's all."

He held his place in the middle of the kitchen, big and solid as an appliance. Cecilia looked at the napkin Sandy had left crumpled on the table: "The Boat of Commitment Can Sail Over the Waters of Uncertainty."

"David, I'm sorry. I've said it until I'm hoarse."

"So now you're going to stop saying it?"

"I don't know. I'll be sorry until I die. But I'm not sure I'm doing either one of us any good by padding around after you saying I'm sorry, I'm sorry, I'm sorry." Unbidden, a new thought bloomed: her baby, growing, napping, coming to consciousness by hearing its mother apologize twenty times a day.

"Maybe not. But I can't just pick up as if everything's fine. Every day I—can't." He clenched and flexed his big hands, still lined with soil from the orchard. Never had Cecilia been in such a hurry to come home that she left a place without washing dirt from her hands. She wondered what he had thought, hurrying home to her.

She said, "Do you want to leave? Do you want me to?"

"Do you want to go?"

"No," she said. "But I asked you."

"No," he whispered.

"We're stuck."

"But good."

"We could call somebody from Life Ties. I got a call today from Walter Scurwicz-Hays. He'd be right over. He'd facilitate our passage."

For the first time, David's eyes—sharp, and bright with moisture—met hers. "I really don't want that," he said.

"Me neither. But they're closing in. So we'd better figure out what they would say, and say it first." She pointed to Sandy's napkin. "How about that? These qualify as uncertain waters."

"Where's our boat of commitment?"

"Something carries you home every day. If you had a different kind of boat, it would carry you away."

He was silent for a long stretch, his jaw working under his beard. When he spoke his voice was blank, and while she could hear some emotion surging underneath the rigid tone, she couldn't tell what that emotion was. "You sound very knowledgeable," he said.

"'Marriage is our first strength, our full humanity, our unique creation.'"

"Do you believe that?"

"Yes." Watching David's haggard face, she could feel in her own chest the colliding waves of fury and misery. She didn't feel love for him—or hate, or resentment, or fear. She simply felt her body rock in time with his. When he left the room, she was not surprised. She would have done the same.

He went back out the front door, stepping quietly down the metal stairs to the parking lot. This surprised her. She remained motionless as she heard him open the car door, then slam it shut. But he didn't turn on the ignition. Instead, he reascended the stairs. When he came back into the kitchen, he carried a long wooden produce flat.

"Blackberries," he said. "Since you can't eat tomatoes. These are sweet. I thought you might be able to keep them down."

"That's considerate," Cecilia said. "Thank you."

"I think they'll help you," he said.

"Yes, they will." The glossy, purple-black globes blurred as she looked at them, but she blinked and made out David's fingers holding out a berry to her. Brushing his steady fingertips, she took the fruit from him and ate it. And then another.

Entr'acte (6)

STAY IN LIFE TIES long enough, and there aren't many surprises left. People drag their hungers behind them like tin cans on a string—for a mother who loved enough, for a sister who came home, for a boyfriend who didn't shoot himself, for a dog that didn't die. Nothing goes away. After a while we get tired of all that wanting.

So we're heartened by David and Cecilia. They have traded in all the hungers they couldn't fill for the one they could. After plunging into the stormy waters they've emerged more united than ever. Watching them, some of the old-timers dab at their eyes. We can feel the new commitment that has risen between them, solid as a house, bankable. Seeing how they look at each other, as if each provides the one food the other needs, justifies a lot.

Lately, they hold hands wherever they go—the Safeway meat counter, the gas pump. They hold hands at Life Ties too, although that in itself would not make them special. One man spent a whole meeting holding the hand of the wife who had just given him gonorrhea. Later, somebody said the man wanted to make sure he knew where those hands had been. If Vivy had been there, she would have pointed out that hands weren't the problem. Her absence made no difference. We all thought the same thing, and in her voice.

Now that David's holding Cecilia's hand night and day, he can't reach out to Vivy. He doesn't murmur with her after meetings. Unless he's on shift, he doesn't come to the store for act nights. It doesn't take a genius to work out that he's avoiding Vivy, and we all have our own ideas about why.

He is, he tells us often, happy. So is Cecilia. She nods. Yes, she is happy.

Growth Begins at Ground Level. A newbie caught up with Vivy after a meeting and, ignoring our coughs, said Vivy and Sam could rebuild their marriage as the Moores have done if they would only acknowledge their pain and disappointment.

"Shucks," Vivy said. "Why didn't somebody tell me?"

The newbie—so young she made your eyes smart, much too tiny for the walloping wedding ring she wore—looked around and dropped back a step.

"Sam! Sam—c'mere, darlin'. This sweet child says the gates of heaven will open to us if we just tell each other how pissed off we are."

"Shoot. Who knew?"

"You don't have to be sarcastic," the young woman said.

"Oh, yes we do," Vivy told her.

"You're in the group. You should play by the rules."

"There are lots of rules," Vivy said.

"Vivy knows all of them," Sam said.

Later we argued for half an hour about whether he meant to distance himself or pull up close to her with that remark. Then we argued about whether they were approaching a real crisis, one that might make them finally confront their rickety marriage. "They come to make fun of us!" the newbie cried. "They don't try at all. They could never come to another meeting and they wouldn't notice the difference."

There she's wrong. Sam and Vivy need us, all right. They need our nods and whispers, and they need our applause when they pull off something daring. Sam and Vivy are show people, and show people need an audience. Those of us who understand that stay in our seats. It's the performers who decide when an act is over, not the audience. But it's the audience who gets to applaud or not, which is the best part.

FOURTEEN

Sam

HOLDING HIS VIOLIN BY the neck, Laszlo pointed the instrument at Sam. *"En garde!"*

"If you break that, you're going to be in trouble like you've never seen."

Laszlo stabbed at him. "Long live freedom! Long live free choice! Soldiers of liberty will fight to throw off the Deathmaster's cruel—"

"—oppression," Sam filled in, grabbing the violin by the chin rest and placing it safely on the coffee table. "You've got exactly two minutes to go wash your hands and comb your hair. Where's your sister?"

"Like I would know."

"I'll find her. You—get moving." Sam hurried down the hallway toward Annie's room, aware that Laszlo was sneaking behind him and making monster faces. On another day Sam would have whirled, roared, grabbed his son and tickled him to the ground, but the violin lessons he'd wheedled Cecilia into giving the kids was supposed to start in ten minutes. "Wash your hands *clean*," he said without glancing back.

After checking the girl's bedroom, the kitchen, even the low branches of the walnut tree out front, Sam finally found Annie behind the garage, arranging a fussy garden with a blue hydrangea head and a lapful of grass. "I was right here," she said when Sam hauled her up. "You don't have to be mean."

"Have you practiced your violin?"

"You always ask me that."

"Annie, you can't learn if you don't practice. Oh, for Pete's sake," he said, catching sight of her shorts. "What did you do, look for mud to sit in?"

So they were five minutes late getting to the lesson, the kids poking each other and squirming on the steps up to Cecilia's apartment as if they might make a run for it. "Sorry we're late," Sam said when Cecilia came to the door.

"They'll be finished in forty-five minutes. You can pick them up then."

"Actually, I was thinking about staying. If that's all right." Sam could feel his children writhing behind him, taking in Cecilia's startled expression. "I'm not convinced they've been practicing right. I thought if I could sit in on the lesson, I could reinforce what you tell them."

"Learning an instrument is surprisingly personal," Cecilia said. Her mouth looked as if she'd been sucking lemons. "An awful lot has to do with learning to hear. They have to hear what I say, and what the violin is saying, and what the music might want to say. I'm afraid you can't do anything to help there."

"I'd like to learn to hear too. And I'd like Laszlo and Annie to see how much I care about this. I could benefit from their lessons myself."

"Jeez, Dad. Tell us something we don't know," Laszlo said. Cecilia frowned, but Sam knew he had her. She had griped too often about parents who dropped their undisciplined kids off and then came back half an hour later with coffee breath, grinning like they should get an award.

"I don't think you're apt to get much from osmosis, but come in if you want to," she said. "Let's get this show on the road."

Three months had passed since Sam had last seen Cecilia's apartment. The walls were still the color of vanilla ice cream; the shoebox-sized windows, set so high they drew attention to the flat, low ceiling, still glared curtainless into the room; the brown couch where Sam perched was still hard as a bench. Nevertheless, he felt a change in the room, and he tried to sort it out while Cecilia set Annie's music—just scales, drawn as fat, happy faces—on the stand at the end of the room and corrected the girl's posture. Laszlo slipped through a doorway leading to the hall. Sam assumed he was going to the bathroom until he heard the faint sound of a television.

Annie picked up her bow. "Think before you play," Cecilia said. She sat with her stiff back to him, and Sam felt his own back stiffen in response. To hell with her. He had come to help his children, and if Cecilia was too much in love with her own suffering to see that, it was her loss. Too bad, though, that she turned her back on the one parent in El Campo who really cared about his children's music.

Lightly, Annie pushed her bow over the strings. The noise she made resembled a wheeze. "Again," Cecilia said.

On her second try, Annie produced a note. Then, biting her lip and grinning, she produced several notes mashed into one another, ending with a squeal. "Pay attention," Cecilia said, and Sam bridled at her weary tone. Music might not be his business, but he knew his daughter, a girl who ached to please, and he saw her helpless eyes. She would do better if Cecilia encouraged her, made some jokes, showed her the right way to hold her fingers. The child was only seven.

Annie embarked on a scale while Cecilia clapped out the tempo, or rather, Cecilia clapped out a tempo while Annie's notes crawled and wandered. "Stop," Cecilia said, and Annie did. "Play a D. Now stop. Now E. Now stop. Now F sharp. Thank you. That's what a scale should sound like. Do you think you can remember that?"

Annie dropped her head. Sam could see tears wanted to break through her angry stare, but Annie, like her mother, wouldn't cry in front of people. Good, he thought. Hang tough.

"Start again," Cecilia said.

The bow trembled as Annie set it against the strings, and three strangled notes wobbled forth again. Annie might have made the exact same noise on purpose. Vivy would have.

Her eyebrows raised, Cecilia turned to Sam. "Hear the difference?"

"No."

"She should practice until you can hear a difference." Then, to

Annie: "Don't stop." Cecilia started to clap time again, as relentless as a metronome.

"What happened to your piano?" Sam blurted. Or, for that matter, to her metronome. The corner of the room that used to be reserved for music—he'd finally figured out the change—held only a floor lamp and some cardboard boxes.

"I sold it."

"Why?"

"We need the money. Go on, Annie."

While Annie struggled up the rungs of her scale, Sam sat back against the horrible couch. He guessed he shouldn't be surprised. Life Tie-ers had been talking about David and Cecilia's strapped circumstances, and Elena was chairing a committee to collect lightly used baby things for them. "Why buy?" she said. "Babies grow so fast. Many people have crib sets they can pass along."

"Can I contribute?" Sam had asked.

"You already did," Elena said. His expression must have been a beaut. She patted his arm and said Vivy dropped off a portable crib, a changing pad, Annie's old high chair. Vivy hadn't mentioned the donations to Sam. She also let him discover for himself the rumor, wild around the edges of Life Ties, that Cecilia had gone into Sacramento for a DNA test. Some members were convinced David was the father. Others insisted she hadn't gotten results yet. "Those tests aren't cheap, you know," Elena had said, looking at Sam meaningfully over her spearmint tea.

Annie lifted her bow. She was actually panting, and she pressed her hand against the small of her back. "This is hard."

"Practice until you're out of breath, every day. Then practice for two minutes more. You need to build up stamina. Do you know what stamina is?" Annie nodded, then looked at Sam and shrugged.

Cecilia picked up her own violin from the bookcase. "What do you want to hear?"

"The elephant song," Annie said.

"Don't put your violin down. You've got a part in this, too. Play a

G." After a minute of frowning, Annie drew her bow across the top string. Cecilia matched the note, raised it a notch, then launched into a sprightly version of "The Baby Elephant Walk." Sam was surprised Annie knew the old tune; Cecilia must have played it for her before. After going through the melody once she said, "Do you want to march?" but Annie glanced at Sam and shook her head.

"Then you have to clap," Cecilia said, and played another round while Annie clapped along, more or less in time. This was more like it, Sam thought, bobbing his head to the beat. This would teach a child to love music. Still, he couldn't help wishing Annie were clapping out the rhythm to Chopin, not Henry Mancini. Music—real music, true art—could mold the heart. It could change a whole life. This was Sam's revelation, his vast realization that no one, so far, cared about except Sam.

When Cecilia told Annie she could go get her brother, the girl darted out like a rabbit, and a damp silence hung in the room. "I hope this is doing you some good," Cecilia said.

"I'm trying to be a good parent," he said. "Do they have any hope at all?"

"What are you hoping for? Annie can learn to keep time. She can learn to read music."

"What about Laszlo?"

She smiled briefly, an expression so complicated he couldn't decipher it before it was gone. "If they were going to be prodigies, you would have known by now."

"When did you know?"

"That I wasn't a prodigy? Not early enough." She strode to the hallway. "Laszlo!"

The boy slunk in and glared at Sam. "Does he have to be here?"

"Apparently," said Cecilia.

"But I can't—you know."

"Scales first," she said. She kept her back to Sam and began to clap, setting a moderate tempo. Laszlo lifted the bow and began to play real notes, distinguishable, not the smear of sound his sister had created.

"Good," Cecilia said, still clapping. "Again. *Con brio.*"

Sitting up straighter, Sam studied his son's profile. The boy frowned, a handful of curls tumbling over his high forehead. That he had been practicing was clear. But Sam hadn't heard any practicing. He certainly never heard Laszlo working to produce these careful, unsteady, but nevertheless clear notes.

"Now in E," Cecilia said. Although she kept her back turned, Sam could hear the smile, and could feel it broaden when Laszlo finished the scale on two firm tones.

"I've been thinking about my wrist," Laszlo said.

"I can hear it," Cecilia said. "Keep thinking: light, light, light. Now it's time to play your piece."

Laszlo glanced at Sam. "It's not ready."

"But your audience is here. I'll help you," Cecilia said. Laszlo started to raise the violin again, but she said, "How do you start?"

Laszlo's shoulders drooped, but he turned to face his father. "Death-master VI. By Nintendo." Then he pulled a piece of paper, a sheet of handwritten music, from his violin case, placed it on the music stand, and sighed.

He started by tapping his foot, rocking back and forth, establishing his rhythm before he started to play. When he put the bow to the strings, odd, disjointed notes zigzagged from his instrument—peculiar pauses, strange intervals. Smiling, Cecilia stood close to the boy, pointing at the notes, singing some of them. The ploinky-ploink of a video game soundtrack bounced from the violin while Laszlo tossed his head and bent at the waist like a concertmaster. It was a brilliantly Laszlo joke: if Sam demanded the boy play violin, the boy would play his own music. But it was *music.* Sam could only guess the amount of time Laszlo and Cecilia had spent side by side transcribing the soundtrack. His breath rasped a little at the thought.

The entire piece took less than two minutes. When Laszlo lowered the violin Sam rocketed to his feet, his hands banging together. "Bravo!" Cecilia raised her eyebrows, then nudged the slumping Laszlo to take a bow. She brushed back the boy's hair and kissed his forehead, and Sam's smile drained away although he kept applauding.

"Surprise," Cecilia said.

"I was going to wait until the recital," Laszlo was saying. "I missed the A. You weren't supposed to hear it yet."

"I couldn't be more surprised. Or impressed."

"I wasn't sure you'd like it," Laszlo said. "It isn't Mote-sart."

"Mozart liked to goof around. He would have liked this. Besides, you've got lots of time to learn concertos," Sam said.

Laszlo looked at Cecilia. "I told you."

"You know," Cecilia said, speaking to the air, "the violin is a versatile instrument. I'm going to show Laszlo a jig I think he'll like."

"You love classical music," Sam said. He thought his voice sounded reasonable. "It's what you trained for."

"It's not the only music I love. And a person's life doesn't stop just because she's trained for something. In two weeks I'm going to play at a seminar for CAA. I've been practicing night and day to play greatest hits from *Oklahoma!* They aren't easy. I'm going to be paid three thousand dollars, which is two thousand, nine hundred dollars more than I've ever been paid to play Mozart."

"Wow," Laszlo said.

"No kidding," Cecilia said.

"I wish you had let me buy your piano," Sam burst out, hoping she wouldn't say, *With what?*—able to call on all the afternoons he'd blabbed his and Vivy's financial woes to her. "With the way Laszlo's going, maybe he should start piano, too. You could teach him."

Ignoring Laszlo's scowl, Cecilia handed the sheet music back to the boy. "I want this CAA job. You don't have to offer me options."

"I guess David was very supportive when you told him you'd be playing Rodgers and Hart?"

"Rodgers and Hammerstein. Laszlo, what do you want me to play before you go?"

"'Whole Lotta Love.'" He plopped onto the sofa, but Sam noticed that he nested the violin gently on his lap. Here, in front of Cecilia, he wouldn't dream of clowning around with it.

Her face tight, she turned away from the couch and faced the fireplace as if an important audience waited there. Even then she paused a moment before lifting her violin, which shone like amber, and starting in: *bum*, ba-dum-*bum*. Somehow, staring at the fireplace, she managed a credible approximation of the tune's insistent rhythm guitar, then plunged into the high, sharp melody. Sam found himself absently singing along, the words as familiar as breath, on the radio every summer since Sam had been a teenager. *You need coolin', baby I'm not foolin'.* Laszlo could have picked better. Still, even on this idiot song, Cecilia was amazing. How closely she must have listened to the thumping, crashing notes to imitate them so well.

Annie drifted into the room, and she and Laszlo both threw back their heads and yowled, "You need *love*!" when Cecilia slid down the final, raucous chords. "Does Vivy know you can do this?" Sam said over their noise. "She'll book you in a heartbeat."

"You haven't talked to her much lately, have you?" Cecilia said.

Sam glanced at Annie to see if she'd heard the glint in Cecilia's voice. She had, of course.

On the drive home the kids were broody, hardly bothering with their squabble about seat belts. Sam hummed tunelessly along with the string quartet on the radio, then cleared his throat. "You've both learned a lot. Cecilia's a good teacher, isn't she?"

From the backseat, Annie elaborately shrugged. Beside her, Laszlo stared holes into the rearview mirror.

"You're getting a lot out of these lessons, I can tell. And music will open new doors to you."

"Three thousand bucks," Laszlo said.

"Light's green, Dad," Annie said. Sam turned up the radio when the announcer noted smoothly that the quartet, from Denver, would be performing that night in the auditorium at Sacramento State University. "Bo-ring," Annie said.

When they got home, the kids sheered out of the car before Sam had pulled all the way into the garage. Vivy was in the kitchen. Astoundingly, she was not on the phone. "Hey," she said.

"Hey. I just went with the kids to their lesson. Our son is a prodigy, you'll be interested to know."

"That's handy. We've already given him a good stage name."

"I mean it, Vivy. He's something."

"Tell me some news. I'm the one who hears him practicing every day. He's got quite a vocabulary when he's frustrated."

"I never heard him practice," Sam said.

"He wanted to surprise you. He knew the way to your heart."

Vivy's green eyes gleamed at him, more catlike than usual. He glanced around the kitchen. The room, since their two-part cleaning spree, had slid back into its everyday disarray—cereal dishes on the stove, open orange juice carton in front of the toaster. "Can we start at the top?"

She shrugged.

"I'm not in love with Cecilia."

"What do you know. She came over here two weeks ago and told me that she's not in love with you, either. Guess that makes everything all better."

"It was a mistake. A whopper, but only that. It won't happen again. Do you believe me?"

"Sure," Vivy said, her voice flat. "Like I said, she came over here. You'll forgive me for saying so, but she doesn't light up when she says your name."

"It's over. I'd like to move ahead. I'd like us to move ahead."

"Well, that's nice. But I can't help wondering where I stand in your galaxy of love interests. Are you sitting here because Cecilia kicked you out? Or did your night of passion prove what you wanted was here at home all along?" She paused. Her voice was thinning to a single, high note. "Everything hit the skids after that night at Chanticleer's. I was drunk, Sam. Did you think what I gave you was permission? Please don't tell me that."

"I won't," Sam said gently. "I liked her, sure, but I wasn't looking for permission. I was just mad at you."

"You know what I do when I'm mad at you?" she said.

"Spend." The word was out before Sam could call it back, and Vivy's expression sharpened as if he'd turned a dial.

"Let me make sure I get this. I'm the one who drove you into Cecilia Moore's arms because of my terrible, spendthrift ways."

Sam said, "I know who you are. I know how you act. Vivy, I *know* you."

"You say. You want to see my latest expenditure?" She crossed the kitchen to the desk, unlocked the drawer, and pulled out a navy blue bankbook that Sam hadn't seen before.

"Take a gander. See what I've been out buying."

Sam stared at the figures—$500, $175, $450, $600, $600. A long column, and onto page two. "This is savings."

"Christ, you're quick."

"Shit, Vivy. What have you done?" He started to shake, and rested one hand on the sink.

She had been craning to watch him, but now she turned away. He barely glimpsed how the laugh crumpled and fell from her mouth. Her slim, pretty shoulders quivered, and Sam shook his head. She hadn't cried in childbirth, and she hadn't cried when she fell from a ladder behind a festival stage and gashed her elbow to the bone. He shook his head harder. What had she expected him to say? Hooray?

"I—cannot—believe you," she said.

"That makes two of us."

"This is worse than Cecilia, for the record."

"I agree." Sam knew better than to try to touch her. But he didn't pull away, and he waited.

Vivy needed only a moment to stop shaking and turn to him, her shining eyes enormous. "What does it take, Sam? I *earned* this money. Haven't you heard me telling you how much Elphenevel brings in a night? Fredd's up to seven-fifty. And other acts, including Marteeny. Straight fifteen percent." She was yelling, her voice raw. "Why do you think I've been doing this?"

"You want to buy your way out of Natural High."

"Half right. I was going to buy us both out. Buy us the hell out of here. It was going to be a *present*. I was going to *give* this to you." The tears were back, running down her face, falling onto her cotton blouse until it stuck to the freckled skin underneath. Sam felt an enormous tenderness, large enough to crush him, although he could find no words to tell Vivy.

She said, "At first when I found out about Cecilia I thought, 'Good, we can go, it's time.' And then I watched you. I watched you watching her. And I thought, 'Sam doesn't want to go. He wants to stay here. I can't make him do what he doesn't want to do.' So what do you want? You tell me."

He held out his hand, and she suffered him to touch her arm. Even crying she held her chin up like a warrior princess. When he opened his mouth, the sound that came out was gentle. "There isn't enough here. Not even for one. It isn't an escape, no matter how much you want it to be."

"There's going to be more."

"How can there be? Even at fifteen percent. Unless you've been booking the Beatles."

"You're still not listening. It isn't just the old acts anymore. This band—call them headbangers, call them whatever you want, but they're ready to break big. They're already breaking big. We could make more money in a year than we've seen in five years with Natural High."

"Bands fall apart. It happens every day. We're not twenty years old anymore. What about Laszlo and Annie? We can't exactly tell them we don't have money to eat this week because Mommy's act got locked up for wrecking the dressing room."

"We—diversify." The choked words halted, one at a time, in her mouth. "We book Fredd for fairs, Norma's Big Band to play dinner dances. We do everything—old acts, new acts. The ones we love, and the ones that pay the bills. But 'we,' Sam. Not 'me.' It's more than one person can do. I can't scout, and negotiate, and go through the auditorium bathrooms after Elphenevel's finished at midnight to get rid of the kids hiding in there."

"Are you asking me to join you?" he said. "Start again? Do the whole thing from the ground up?"

Vivy lifted her chin. Her moist cheeks sparkled. He had never in his life known better company. He shouldn't have lost track of that. "Don't let me force you into doing something you don't want," she said.

"I can only think of one thing I want," he said, studying the Formica countertop, hundreds of tiny gray starbursts against the dull, creamy background. "There's going to be a string quartet concert tonight at Sac State. Will you go with me?"

"You're asking me on a date?" Vivy laughed, a bark, a hiccup. "You're asking me to sit next to you for two hours and listen to violins? If this is atonement, it's a humdinger."

"Not exactly. It's a gift to you."

"If I go will we be good as new?"

"No. If you go I'll buy you a glass of wine after."

In the pause that followed he lifted his eyes. She wore the patient expression she usually put on when she talked to other people's babies. With her index finger she traced a line from his nose to the corner of his mouth. "It's funny, Sam. I keep feeling sorry for you. That doesn't make sense, does it? I'm not the one who strayed. But I look at you and think, 'Poor Sam.'"

"I'm not surprised."

"I'm not sure this concert is going to help."

"You don't have to go."

"I'm clear on that. But I think we should go." She wiped her face. Her eyes, he saw with relief, were finally dry. "No telling what a night out might do for us. And when it's over you can explain to me why what we just heard was better than wallpaper."

"It's not something you can explain."

"Try, Sam," she said, her words both order and plea.

THE PROGRAM, WHICH THE radio announcer hadn't mentioned, was part Mozart, the String Quartet in D Minor, plus Schubert's Quartet in G Major. The performers were adequate; their faces narrow with concentration, they ran through their notes crisply. Sam nodded and tapped out time on the armrest, following the ribbon of melody as it unfurled. Twice tears rushed to his eyes for no reason he could define, except that something beautiful was releasing itself and he was grateful. How late he had come to this. The rest of his life would not be long enough for him to hear all the music he now craved.

During the final Allegro he closed his eyes. Inexplicably, he remembered his best friend when he was Laszlo's age, Keith Rogers, a boy who had two holsters and four cap guns. Once they'd been playing stakeout and Sam's mother wandered into the yard, reminding Sam he still hadn't cleaned his room. Both boys opened fire. Sam was grounded for a week.

The applause came too soon, and Sam kept his eyes closed for another moment before he joined in. Beside him, Vivy put her hands together politely, then took Sam's arm as they joined the meager crowd dribbling up the aisles. She smiled and squeezed his arm. "You didn't hear any of that, did you?"

"I heard all of it," he said. He could almost smell the smoke from the caps.

"Did you hear the cello player lose his place?"

"Never happened."

"You looked like you were asleep." She pulled her hand from his arm. "Where's my wine?"

"Wait." Sam put his hand against Vivy's shoulder. Outside the concert hall, on the other side of a small patio, a young, skinny man was playing the clarinet. Before him stood five concertgoers and an open clarinet case. "Wait," Sam said, though Vivy had already stopped.

The unaccompanied instrument sounded thin in the night air, its tone almost unendurably sweet, and the steady, circling, minor notes called out to Sam like a receding memory. The melody was not quite familiar, and each note seemed to slide into him, the feeling so intimate he wanted to hide his face. His heart shimmered, pain and pleasure twined. Balancing himself with one hand against a concrete pillar, Sam willed Vivy not to move or speak, and she didn't, until the last note eddied and the man took the instrument from his mouth.

She waited a decent moment before she crossed the patio. The others applauded lightly, tossed dollar bills into the case, and moved toward the dark parking lot. Heart banging, still leaning against the pillar, Sam watched. "You are some kind of good," he heard Vivy say, and the man said something he couldn't catch.

"No. You're better than that. You've got something special. If you don't know that, you should. You shouldn't be playing on a sidewalk."

Another murmur, and Vivy said, "Actually, it is my business. I'm a promoter; so is my husband, the guy you left slayed there by the building." Weakly, Sam lifted a hand. "He's the one who would get you bookings. He takes care of the music end of things." She opened her purse and quickly scrawled something, then pressed the paper on the man. "Listen, please call us. People don't get to hear music like yours. You're the real thing. You can bring something wonderful to people." She looked back at Sam. "Right?"

"Right," he said loudly.

When she returned to him they began walking without a word. The area around the campus was unfamiliar to both of them, the businesses and few restaurants mostly closed even though it wasn't ten o'clock yet, and the fat half-moon barely clear of the horizon. "Sacramento," Vivy sighed. "Roll up the sidewalks."

"It's a nice night to walk," Sam said.

"Sure. Take in the sight."

"We'll stumble on something."

They did, too: two blocks from campus, a single neon Heineken sign glowed modestly in the corner of a bar window. "There we go. Just what we were looking for," Sam said.

"We've got to start raising our standards," Vivy said, but she picked up her pace.

At the door—heavy wood and iron, faux tavern style—Sam paused. "Can this clarinetist be my atonement?"

"Depends. Do you feel like you're suffering to work off injury?"

"No," he said. "That guy is one in a thousand. A million. Couldn't you hear it?"

"Sounded like a horn to me. But while you were listening, you looked like he was killing you."

"The real thing makes a person feel something. It's not exactly suffering, but it hurts."

"So long as it hurts," she said, and went on ahead of him into the bar.

FIFTEEN

Vivy

VIVY WAS BLAZING. VIVY was roaring. Excitement sparked in her hands and neck and jerked her awake at night. Her breaths tripped over one another. At the base of her throat her pulse quickened, and then quickened again.

Sheeted with dim gray moonlight in the bedroom, she turned over and studied Sam. He seemed to sleep dreamlessly, his arms and legs flung across the mattress, his broad mouth faintly turned up as if someone might soon tell a joke. Her heart stretched open and slammed shut, her ribcage rattling like a loose window in its frame. She didn't know why this hectic new energy rampaged through her. Yes, she did. No, she didn't. Superstitious, she flopped onto her back, stared at the ceiling, and did not think.

During the day she sashayed from room to room, the iPhone propped against her shoulder. Her nervous hands wanted to touch things, so she twiddled pencils or juggled plums. She booked Fredd on TV—not public access, but a network affiliate morning program, real exposure—plus a daylong juggling clinic at a grade school. She found a county fair and a girls' club convention for Marteeny. An amateur comedians' association phoned, specifically asking for Laurel, whose ungainly stand-up was gaining rabid audiences. Vivy arranged for El-phenevel to play in Redding and in Chico—when she agreed to the Chico date, the house manager put his hand over the phone to yell, "*Got* 'em!"

Laszlo and Annie called her Phone Mom. While she was on hold for a house manager in Stockton, Sam said, "Just out of curiosity, do you ever hang up?"

"Every call is going to be the last one. Then one more call comes in."

"You sound like a magnate."

"What do you think? Will success spoil Vivy Jilet?"

"Vivy's not spoiled," Sam said. "Vivy's just getting ripe." He gave her butt a squeeze at the same time the manager came back on the line saying he thought they could put something together.

She had been working nonstop since her night with Sam in Sacramento, when they had closed the listless bar. That night, their first real drunk since the night at Chanticleer's, had been the turning point. Instead of nipping at each other like roused dogs, in Sacramento they had started inching toward each other, and by the third round Vivy felt a bleary affection for the place's single neon sign and jukebox that featured Elvis Presley singing "Blue Christmas" on three different numbers. "Your heart really isn't in this, is it?" Vivy had said to the bartender, who glanced up from her magazine and said, "No."

Ignoring the bartender's sighs, Vivy and Sam kept ordering drinks, rocking into the old rhythm. They found "New York, New York" on the jukebox. Into the second refrain, the one with the chorus-line horns, Sam started crooning "Is That All There Is?"—the song he and Vivy used to sing to each other in college when they were feeling world-weary. He must have reached into deep memory to come up with it. "Then let's keep dancing," Sam sang, tilting his head like Peggy Lee while Frank Sinatra bellowed about making it anywhere.

"You're killing me," Vivy said. "All you need is the headband."

"Never underestimate your old man." Taking the damp napkin from under her wineglass, he folded the paper into a tiny square, bunched the corners together, then held it over the squat candle guttering in its red glass teardrop. The paper puffed and bloomed, its corners softening like petals before it caught fire, and Sam dropped it onto the struggling flame. "A fire flower. For you."

"Kind of short-lived, isn't it?" she said.

"Sophisticated pleasure is fleeting. You have to love it while it's burning there in front of you."

"Huh. What's the outside limit?"

"Three hours. After that it's not sophisticated or it's not pleasure."

"Day at the beach," she said.

"Not sophisticated."

"Picnic."

"Ants. Not pleasure."

"Opera."

"Sopranos? Are you kidding?"

She smiled. "Life Ties."

"Public service. After an evening with Life Ties, anything seems like pleasure." Sam leaned across the table. She could smell his gin like cologne. "You want to know a genuine, textbook, sophisticated pleasure? Telling the assembled forces of Life Ties to kiss my sweet ass."

Vivy swirled her cabernet and admired her husband. She had been so wrong. He hadn't lost any of his old moves. She hadn't, either. "Marriage," she said.

"One long string of pleasures." His blurred gaze fixed on her. "The sophisticated among us know this. Sometimes you go a while before the next pleasure comes in, but it's always coming."

"Do you feel it coming in now?"

"All we have to do is stay out of the way." He reached across the table and touched her jaw, a new gesture. She started to wonder who had taught it to him, then shoved the thought, which wouldn't help anything, out of her brain.

"I have something to share with you," he was saying. "I know two people who have been modeling a good marriage for Life Ties. They've been carrying on a good marriage for fifteen years."

"I know them too. So does Marteeny. She said she wants a marriage just like theirs."

Sam nodded. "There you go. Marteeny has—" he squeezed his eyes, hunting for the phrase, "—historical memory." Vivy rested her chin on her fists and thought, as she did from time to time, that the long folds of Sam's face gave him the expression of a friendly hound. Also, he could use a haircut.

He said, "She could send a testimonial to Life Ties. Better yet, she and—whozit—Court could come down and study with us. We could hold seminars. Anti-Life Ties."

"Life Unties," Vivy offered. "Although Court and Marteeny have become very big on the group, you know. Court goes around saying the slogans. He can't wait till he and Marteeny come back down and they can go to another meeting."

"Loose Strands," Sam said.

"Fringe."

"We'll create a viable alternative—" he had to try the phrase twice to get it out straight, "—to Life Ties. We'll gain a percentage of market share. And that will be a very sophisticated pleasure."

"'Market share.' Listen at you. You're talking like a promoter."

"It's important to have a dream," he said.

"Tell me about it," she said, signaling the bartender and feeling the seed of a fresh happiness curl its first root through her heart.

By the time they snorted and bumped their way home, the seed was growing like a beanstalk. Even though she hardly slept—she dropped into a winy haze for an hour or two, then woke up parched, in plenty of time to watch the dawn—when she got up the idea had spread through her: stem, blossom, tendril. She could hardly wait for Sam to clear out of the house so she could get moving.

She called Court first thing, letting the phone ring sixteen times before she gave up waiting for an answering machine. She kept trying all day, between the other calls, amiably swearing at him for being a rancher and off on the range somewhere. That would be the first thing to change.

At three, when he finally picked up, he told her he was on the barn extension. "Hope you don't mind I'm eating lunch," he said. "Ham."

"Pretty late for lunch. Marteeny would scold you." Locking eyes with Laszlo and Annie lurking beside the refrigerator, Vivy swatted them toward the backyard, mouthing *or else violin* to hurry them up.

"It doesn't quit," Court was saying. "You know when I last rode out to check the fences? A week ago. You know what I found just now? Two sections of fence down. You might not have even caught me, but I was so disgusted I came back for chow."

"Man's gotta eat sometime."

"People love to think about the open range. They see movies and think it's all horses and sunsets and big sky. But nobody loves to do the work."

"If you don't do it, it doesn't get done."

"A person signs on for this life. He knows it isn't going to be a party."

"Still. You can get tired of it. Or just tired."

"You're a good heart, to listen to my grumbling," Court said. "No wonder Tina thinks you're her best friend. What brings you to call an old ranch hand?"

"I'm being your best friend," Vivy said. It took her fifteen minutes to outline the plan, a speech she'd ironed out around four that morning. She pointed out how he and Marteeny would both benefit, and how Marteeny's career would have a chance to flourish. He wouldn't even have to sell the ranch; he could lease it. Values being what they were, he'd get enough. Vivy hadn't actually checked land prices, but she was pretty sure she was right.

"Haw," Court said. "Values being what they are, I could lease half of the acreage here and let the rest go straight to burdock and still have enough."

"There you go," Vivy said. He and Marteeny could take a shot at a new life, see some new things, give her career a real chance while still having a safety net underneath them and their marriage. "This is a big idea, I know," she said. "A lot of money. A real decision. But an opportunity for both of you. The answer to a lot of unhappiness."

"Let me think," he said.

"It's benefits every side. I know it's a change, but sometimes change is just what you crave."

"You're not letting me think."

"I'm helping you think."

"I can't drop this on Tina as a done deal. Even if it's what I want, I can't drag her south by the hair. She has ideas. She thinks she wants to be a rancher's wife."

"I've known Marteeny for a long time," Vivy said. "I love her to bits, but sometimes she's her own worst enemy. She'll walk away from paradise just because it's within reach. Sometimes you need to present the done deal to her. I know what I'm talking about here, Court. Sam's the same way."

"You have to go behind his back?"

"You have to point him toward happiness and give him a good shove."

A pause followed, and then the scratch of a match. Vivy smiled. She'd never seen Court with cigarettes, but there he was, alone in the barn, sneaking a smoke. After he exhaled he said, "You never did seem right for ice cream." Vivy wouldn't let him hang up until he swore to call her the next day, after he'd tried out the idea on Marteeny.

Since then she'd talked with him practically daily, sometimes calling from the store. Nancy frowned but didn't say anything, which was about typical for the way things had been going lately.

In the five, then seven, now ten weeks since Vivy had detonated her bomb at Life Ties, the partners had been working together almost mutely, passing clean scoops and ringing up sales like cordial strangers. Vivy wondered if it was possible they'd finally used up all the words in the world.

Even Nancy had quit asking questions, just when Vivy was ready for her. She had withdrawn $500 from savings and kept the cash at the bottom of her purse, ready to be handed over on demand. But Nancy didn't demand. She looked distracted, and her undauntable, practical air was replaced with an oddly sweet distractedness. When the store phone rang she raced for it like a teenager, and sometimes Paul visited during her shift, the two of them whispering while Nancy washed the same scoop over and over and over.

Polishing a table, Vivy shook her head. She knew how much her acts were bringing in, checks and percentages and withholding, to the penny. If Nancy was too busy canoodling with Paul to keep track of her store's finances, Vivy wasn't going to help her, although now she regretted that she hadn't taken more. She rubbed harder at the table, trying to scrape up a fleck of carob that was ground into the veneer. The floor had gotten all flecked, too.

She was still working on the table when Nancy drifted over to join her—two o'clock, the store quiet before the regular after school riot. "Hey," Vivy said.

"Hey. Thanks for taking on these tables. They need muscle."

"They need sandblasting."

"That's what Paul said just now when I told him what you were doing."

"You guys need something better to talk about," Vivy said.

Nancy laughed and shrugged. "We've been talking a lot lately. Ever since that day at Bearkeep, with you and David. I thought I'd never get over it when Paul started accusing me and going on about commitment, but then we talked all night. Now we're talking better than ever. Sex is better than ever. I didn't know—"

"Stop right there," Vivy said. "Don't tell me." She dredged up a smile. "I'm telling you as a friend. When things turn good, get out of the way."

"Good advice. I guess." Nancy bent toward the table next to Vivy's, getting her whole broad back into the scrubbing. "But there is something I need to ask you. I've needed to ask for a while."

"Stop there, too." Vivy put down her cloth and went to get her purse. She made a production of it, holding the bag wide open, slapping the ten fifties on the damp table. "I wondered when you'd ask."

"Oh, Vivy."

"Jesus, Nancy, what took you so long? I could have been taking thousands. I could be in Brazil right now, paying gigolos to suck my toes. Did you not even bother to look at the books for two months?"

"I go over them every night. Paul, too."

"So what did you do, overlook a missing five hundred bucks?"

"Four hundred eighty. We figured you had your reasons and you'd pay the company back. And you did."

"Come again?"

Nancy rested her hand, surprisingly cool, on Vivy's. "We trusted you."

"*Now?*"

"When did you have in mind?"

"Five years ago, or never. I can't believe you." Vivy looked at the fresh, dull-green bills fanned on top of the glistening table. "What did you want to ask?"

Nancy sighed. "Paul has a cousin. He's been taking singing lessons. Could he—could you find him a night to perform here?"

A long, rich moment passed. "Paul says he's good," Nancy said. "He won't embarrass you."

"Tell Paul," Vivy said, "that I think we can work him in. Not till the end of the month, though. We're booked pretty solid."

When Sam asked her that night how much pleasure this line had given her, she said, "Two years' wages, easy." The calendar had become a solid block: acts returning, new acts appearing, acts called back by audience demand. Following the request of several customers, Vivy had printed calendars with Fredd's performances highlighted in red.

She was pondering the October schedule—with School Days, a hot pepper jump-rope team, and the Hula King already scheduled—when Sam came back into the kitchen, his hand over the telephone. "The guy with the clarinet is named Arthur. When's our next open night?"

"Two weeks from Thursday. Do you need a contract?"

"I already filled one out." He lifted his hand from the phone and strode back out to the living room. "End of the month," she heard him say. "And if you've got the CDs ready, we can set up a table. I'll take care of taxes and cash box." Vivy pulled up the calendar and typed "Arthur" in the Thursday block. Then "!"

Events were gathering together around her, a soft bag gently drawing closed. She was even getting bookings for Laurel LaRue, who, in response to her new popularity, had put together a new, high-concept act—a woman imitating a man in drag. Wearing spongy falsies that kept popping out of her bodice and dark makeup on her jaw to suggest five o'clock shadow, she cinched herself into a gold sequined cocktail dress, teetered on size ten high heels, and sang a medley of Broadway hits. When Sam admitted that her version of "I'm Gonna Wash That Man Right Out of My Hair" was worth seeing, Vivy's pleasure was so great she could hardly breathe.

On a night shortly after booking Arthur, she was loading the dishwasher, leaving Sam to play rowdy tickling games with the kids. The doorbell rang, and she carried a dripping plate to the door. "Did we come at a bad time?" David and Cecilia said in almost one voice. From the den, Annie's bubbling squeals of laughter, and the sound of somebody hitting the floor." Only good times around here," Vivy said. "Come in."

David entered first, holding Cecilia's hand. They wore matching, resolute expressions. "Sam?" Vivy called. "Could you come here a minute?" She gestured at the Moores to sit, and they bent at the knees like paper dolls, hands still clamped together. Cecilia looked like she was finally putting on a little weight. David had perhaps lost a pound or two—rising from the white T-shirt collar, his neck didn't look quite so doughy. His face and Cecilia's were exactly alike, though, in their crimp of weariness and strained hope. The Moores wore the faces Vivy saw every night on the news, survivors draped in blankets while behind them their house blazed or washed away, saying, "We lost everything we owned. But at least we're still alive."

"You guys want some coffee?" she said, and Cecilia said, "Please," just as Sam, unshaven, rumpled, barefoot, perfect, came in from the hallway."Whoops," he said, while Vivy gestured at the Moores and said, "Company."

"Hardly that," David protested.

"Okay," she said. "Not company."

"You guys want some coffee?" Sam asked, and Vivy said, "I'm all over this one." But she lingered a moment at the door to the kitchen. Sam took one of the chairs opposite the couch and made some quiet remark about coffee. The Moores laughed duty laughs. Sam laughed too,

ha-ha-ha at his own dull joke, something he never did unless he was
nervous. It was his nervousness that Vivy scrutinized, looking to see
where his eyes flew—to the dark TV, to the coffee table, over to Laszlo's
soft beanbags, a gift from Fredd, which lay there. To the heat register,
the windowsill, the half-burned candle on the mantel. Anywhere but to
the Moores and their intertwined hands, a big fist sitting between them
on the couch. As far as Vivy was concerned, they could sit there all
night. She'd make brownies and pull out the foldaway, encourage them
to tell cute childhood stories, let them stay for a week or two, so long
as Sam crossed and recrossed his legs and stared at the chipped baseboards. Vivy felt a hospitable smile lift the corners of her mouth. She
slipped into the kitchen and poured coffee for her guests, remembering
David took sugar and Cecilia milk. When she came back out with the
mugs, her voice didn't shake a bit. "What's cooking?"

"A little bit of business," David said. "It's about time for Cecilia's
students to hold a recital, and we were wondering if we could use the
store."

"You're kidding. That's it?"

"We know how busy things are now. You have so many people coming in," David said. "We thought we'd better ask ahead."

"Come on, you guys. Of course we can have a recital. This didn't
require a state visit."

"We hardly see you anymore," said David. "We haven't been on
shift together, and it's not easy to talk at Life Ties."

"That's for sure," Vivy said. At Life Ties the members craned to see
the four of them. Vivy told Sam she knew now how the pope felt. If she
so much as wet her lips everybody in the room sat forward.

"We don't know what's been on your minds," David said.

"We've been pondering Natural Peppermint. Annie thinks we
should dye it pink," said Vivy.

"You don't have to be thinking about ice cream anymore, if you
don't want to," David said. "You have options."

"After a while, you can't stop. I look at a sunset and I think: Cherry-
Berry Swirl."

"Sunrise, too," said Cecilia, surprising Vivy. She expected David would do all the talking. "In the morning I get hungry just by looking outside."

"But you don't have to think about ice cream," David said doggedly to Vivy. "You can think about anything. I'm just—we're wondering how much longer you're going to stay with the store."

"Is there a rush?" Vivy asked. Silent Sam twisted in his chair. Presently, he was analyzing the kids' backpacks, crashed and spilling open beside a potted fake palm, $5 at a garage sale.

David said, "I thought we had an agreement. You were going to start up your old business. Move, and start it up again. It was what you wanted."

"That's not quite how I understood it," Vivy said carefully. "I understood that you made me a generous offer. I didn't take you up on it, but it was more than good of you."

"You never told me anything," David said, his jaw assuming its familiar clamp.

"I didn't really think I had to. And then after Cecilia came to see me, I understood you two weren't in perfect accord. So I thought I'd better wait to say anything."

"I thought you already had plans for it," Cecilia said.

"I would not do that." Vivy was watching very hard. Even so, she almost missed the look that flicked from David to Cecilia, and Cecilia's curved, acknowledging mouth.

"We are going to have a baby," David said.

"I know," Vivy said.

"It would be best—we would like the baby to have a clear start."

"No unwanted presences," Sam said. "No bad influences." His voice was soft. He was still staring away from the Moores, frowning lightly, as if contemplating a small problem in a formula he'd been working on.

"Look," David said, pulling at the end of his beard and pointing it toward Vivy. "I thought everything was settled. Frankly, you would benefit. But if you've changed your mind, you need to tell me. I have to make plans."

"I just told you. But if you don't mind me saying so, you sound pretty bossy. What does Cecilia want?"

"Not to be having this conversation," the other woman said promptly. Her face had flushed an uneven red, giving her light brown hair a pink cast. She'd finished her coffee and was reaching for David's. "I want to be able to make plans. I'd really like to make plans that involve Paris, but that seems remote."

"Make any plans you want," Vivy said. "The money is yours. Do you want me to put it in writing?"

"And Sam is content with that?" David said, loathing folded into his face.

She turned. "Is Sam content with that?"

"We were never going to take David's money." His voice was like ice. Whenever the kids heard this tone in his voice, they sidled out of the room. "What do you think we are?"

"Partners," Cecilia said. "United. That's why we wanted to talk to both of you."

The last time Vivy spoke with Cecilia, on the front porch, Cecilia's teeth had practically chattered with defensive frenzy. Now she sat quietly beside her husband. Her hand, resting inside David's, was calm. Her face and posture held the patient dignity of someone who has been through trials, and noting this, Vivy felt her anger at the woman crack apart. For the rest of her life Cecilia would remember what she had been through. She didn't need Vivy to remind her. She had David for that.

"One more thing you should know," Vivy said. "Court Hellerman and Marteeny are going to buy us out. Court's selling off some of his acreage, and he's got a lessee for the rest. Cash in hand. He's ready to become part of the Natural High team."

"You're kidding," David said.

"No, she's not," said Cecilia, and Sam shook his head, agreeing with Cecilia, looking as if he'd known all along.

David passed his meaty hand over his face. "Just like that. Out on your own, like a cowboy."

"I checked the bylaws," Vivy said. "There's nothing about getting permission before selling a partnership."

"There's nothing in the bylaws because it never occurred to us that a partner would secretly sell out." David shifted his big rump on the couch, making Cecilia list a little. "You can be the most frustrating person in the world."

"You call her frustrating? I call her challenging," Sam said. "She keeps us all awake. Next thing you know, she'll show up with a whip and a chair."

"I thought the lions were supposed to be wild, not sleepy," Vivy said.

"I'm defending you," he said. "Stay out of the way."

"Vivy doesn't need defending," said David.

"Yes, she does," Vivy said.

David frowned, then glanced at Cecilia. With a tender, practiced gesture, he dragged a long strand of hair from her face. "I guess you two have worked out your own interpretation."

After a pause, Cecilia asked, "When are you going to give Nancy and Paul the news?"

"Soon. I don't know."

"We'll bring a first aid kit," Sam said.

"We'll bring a fire hose," Cecilia said.

Vivy grinned. "More coffee?" She watched Cecilia's hand move to her cup, but David overrode her: "We should be getting home."

"Wait," Sam said.

"What," Vivy said at the same time David was saying, "What else can there be?"

Sam looked at Cecilia. "You need a piano. You can't be a musician without a piano."

"So I'm not a musician."

"Will you let me help you? Maybe I can get you yours back."

Vivy watched, her breaths easy now. Sam was singing the final measures in his and Cecilia's operetta. Still, Vivy watched, to make sure they were the final measures.

"No," Cecilia said. After a beat, "Nice of you to offer. But no. We can afford to buy our own piano now." David's face, Vivy noted, was bone tired, but the rage of the last three months was gone. He'd ridden out his wave. She wondered if he knew there would be another, bigger one, and another after that, and that longtime spouses came to love the waves. "Will you give us the name of another violin teacher?" Sam was asking. "Laszlo will need one."

"Annie too," Cecilia said. "Don't let her give up yet. Talent sometimes runs in families."

Sam looked at Vivy. "Must be your side."

"I had an uncle who sang 'My Funny Valentine' when he was in his cups. Usually started about nine in the morning."

"My singing uncle didn't start till noon."

She shook her head. "He was never going to get ahead with a work ethic like that." Sam smiled. She smiled.

When the door closed behind the Moores he said, "Is that true, about Court and Marteeny?"

"Yup."

"So just like that I'm out of the ice cream biz."

"Do you mind?"

"I don't know."

She watched him prowl his side of the room, feet noiseless on the heavy purple rug. He didn't usually need time to get used to a change in plans. He wasn't like David, who hated to be shaken out of his established routine, his death-in-life. Sam was happy to embrace the stray breeze. But this time Vivy had produced a breeze that was a hurricane, blowing away everything he thought he had, until only she was left. Her hands trembled as she held them at her sides and waited for him to look at her.

Passing the coffee table, he picked up Laszlo's beanbags and started a three-ball toss. Vivy wasn't the only one who had spent dull hours backstage. "Is this the last time you plan to present me with a life change that you've already signed off on?"

"Doubt it."

"Me too. Is this the last one I have to agree to?" He frowned at the soft leather beanbags—purple, yellow, and orange, bright as one of Fredd's shirts.

"You don't have to agree to this one. Tell me if you don't like it. I'll work out something new." She flattened most of the tremor out of her voice, but still Sam didn't look up. Maybe this time she really had gone too far, utterly changing the ground underneath them, although he had changed it first. Or maybe he was reminding her he was still capable of surprising her, as if she could forget. The beanbags made small plops as they hit his hands. He said, "I'm worried about Arthur. He needs to be brought along carefully. Too much exposure too soon could really hurt him. And he needs to think about repertoire."

"Not my field," Vivy said softly.

"He knows other musicians. I've already heard one guitarist who's pretty good. And there's a duo, singer and guitar. All of them are bookable, but not at the same venues. Someone needs to make decisions."

"Someone does."

"If you're going to do this right, you need me."

"I've said so all along," Vivy said. "Haven't I?"

Still frowning at his hands, Sam kept the beanbags moving, purple, yellow, orange, the colors flickering like firelight. Very quietly he said, "You go, girl," looked up fast, and fired the yellow beanbag at Vivy. She had to jump to catch it.

Turning her back on Sam, she tossed the beanbag in one hand, her movement easy. Sam lobbed the next one off to her right and she scooped it up, juggling it with the first beanbag, keeping the beat. Sam waited for her to relax before he tossed the last one, a high, slow blooper off the ceiling, easy to catch. Vivy had all three beanbags going in a smooth arc before she wheeled back to face him. "Good trick," he said.

"You think that's good? Watch this." The first beanbag she threw to him was low and inside, hard to catch, but not impossible. The next one, too.

About the Author

Erin McGraw is the author of five earlier books, the novels *The Seamstress of Hollywood Boulevard* and *The Baby Tree*, and the story collections *The Good Life*, *Lies of the Saints*, and *Bodies at Sea*. Her stories and essays have appeared in *The Atlantic*, *Good Housekeeping*, *The Kenyon Review*, *Allure*, *Image*, *The Southern Review*, *STORY*, *The Georgia Review*, and many other journals and magazines. She has taught at DePauw University and the University of Cincinnati, and currently teaches at the Ohio State University with her husband, the poet Andrew Hudgins. They divide their time between Ohio and Sewanee, Tennessee.